PRAISE FOR *SHOOT THE HORSES FIRST*

"I'm astonished by the historical breadth in this collection of stories and by the sensibility that unites them. It's a thrill to be dropped, so vividly, into such a wide variety of settings and periods—and even more of a thrill to discover the strong new voice of Leah Angstman. Read it!"

—**Ethan Rutherford**, author of *Farthest South* and *The Peripatetic Coffin*

"*Shoot the Horses First* is so flush with palpable historical detail and emotion that it wouldn't surprise me to learn Leah Angstman was a time-traveling scribe writing from firsthand knowledge. Every story here is richly embodied and deeply felt, letting Angstman's exuberant curiosity drive the reader onward to ever more surprising and revelatory places."

—**Matt Bell**, author of *Appleseed* and *In the House upon the Dirt between the Lake and the Woods*

"Historical fiction but make it short stories? (Or histories, in Angstman's words?) Yes, please! I devoured these, a rich meal for any lover of short fictions—dialogue that felt real and immediate, settings that felt immersive and lived in, characters of real flesh and blood leaping out of the past (and present) to share their stories. I felt very lucky to read this book, and I'm now instantly jealous of anyone who gets to read it for the first time."

—**Amber Sparks**, author of *And I Do Not Forgive You* and *The Unfinished World and Other Stories*

"In [these] sixteen sumptuous historical stories, outsiders and pioneers face disabilities and prejudice with poise. ... The flash entries crystallize moments of realization [and the] book's longer pieces shine; their out-of-the-ordinary romances are given space to develop. ... Set in the past among lives complicated by ill health and discrimination, the stories of *Shoot the Horses First* feature epiphanies and triumphs."

—*Foreword Reviews* (starred review)

"In *Shoot the Horses First*, Leah Angstman blasts readers from the Twitterfied nowscape into the manifest past—to an America connected by the burgeoning railroad and shattered by civil war. As inventive and complex as the era itself, these sixteen fictions of nineteenth-century friction contain surprises on every page. Whether it's an impromptu snowball fight on a battlefield during a ceasefire or a wayward orphan finding hope at the end of the line, Angstman astonishes us with complicated characters and crystal-clear prose. She is the literary heir to Shelby Foote, Willa Cather, and E. L. Doctorow. Get off the internet and read this book!"

—**Ryan Ridge**, author of *New Bad News*, *Hunters & Gamblers*, *American Homes*, *Second Acts in American Lives*, *Weird Weeks*, and *Ox*

"Rudyard Kipling said, 'If history were taught in the form of stories, it would never be forgotten.' Nothing demonstrates the wisdom of that better than *Shoot the Horses First* by Leah Angstman. This is an immersive, expansive, and unforgettable collection of fictional histories. Drawn from various points in America's past and clearly well researched, these stories are harrowing and hopeful by turns. All through, there are unexpected kindnesses and betrayals and acts of heroism and transformation. Characters so deeply wrought they seem to leap off the page. Soaring and vast and lyrical, this book is a must-read."

—**Kathy Fish**, author of *Together We Can Bury It*, *Rift*, and *Wild Life*

"Angstman's work is a joy to read. These characters see their worlds in the way that we see ours: naturally, and independent of the vastness of time in which life eventually situates itself in memory. Each one of these stories breathes troubling, beautiful life into the history that inspires it. The exhaustive research that must have gone into this collection lives in an easy harmony with the stories it undergirds, and it's Angstman's chief achievement here to strike that balance with poise and grace. Fear, love, heartache, and wonderment: it's all right here, between both worlds."

—**Schuler Benson**, author of *The Poor Man's Guide to an Affordable, Painless Suicide*

"*Shoot the Horses First* puts the 'story' in history. With scholarly rigor and the soul of a bard, Leah Angstman weaves tales of defiance and resilience that bring the past to life and show us what endures."

—**Jennifer Wortman**, author of *This. This. This. Is. Love. Love. Love.*

"Every now and then, you come across a book that is so good that any words you are able to string together are never going to do the book justice. *Shoot the Horses First* is one of those books, a collection of historical short stories that are impeccably researched ... and are a massive joy to read. They do have one fault, though ... [Each] story is over way too soon, dammit! 'The Light Ages; or, Holes in the Heart' was so moving I almost cried[;] the writing was stunning here. ... As you can probably guess, Angstman is one of my favorite authors, and this is the perfect book [to] become hooked on her work."

—*Gnome Appreciation Society*

"Reading Leah Angstman's work is like going back in time, a time when I knew that I am in good hands and the book will guide me through anything. I wish I could have ten more books from her. Or let's just be greedy for a second and imagine that every time I finish a book, another one appears, and I would have a never-ending supply of gold letters and heartfelt stories worth enough to be alive for. It might sound like I am overreacting [...] but I was so thirsty for these kinds of stories, and the way she writes just resonates with something deep inside my soul that I thought I lost a long time ago. ... I have fallen in love with her work. ... If I look at the stories as a whole, I just have to admit that I loved all of them. ... [An] excellent book from an amazing author who has definitely become one of my favorite authors of all time."

—*No Lite Thoughts*

"[I] learned a lot from Angstman's short story collection. You can tell she's passionate about history and the stories she's telling. [She] is also willing to write the cold, hard truths about what life was like for these people. She doesn't romanticize things, doesn't turn people into caricatures or make life for these characters look more beautiful than it was. It's real, and sometimes it hurts, but it's necessary to know the truth. ... It's rare to read about disabled characters in fiction[;] it's even rarer for these stories to be told with respect and care, and Angstman handles these stories wonderfully. ... It's a truly remarkable collection that any history lover would love to have on their shelves!"

—*Not Sarah Connor Writes*

SHOOT
THE
horses
FIRST

Also by Leah Angstman:

Out Front the Following Sea

SHOOT
THE
horses
FIRST

histories

LEAH ANGSTMAN

KERNPUNKT ● PRESS

Hamilton, New York

Published by Kernpunkt Press
Hamilton, New York 13346
kernpunktpress.com

Library of Congress Control Number: 2022913525
ISBN-13 (paperback): 978-1-7343065-9-0
ISBN-10 (paperback): 1-7343065-9-9
ISBN-13 (hardcover): 979-8-9865233-0-9
ISBN-13 (ebook): 979-8-9865233-1-6

Interior and cover design: Kernpunkt Press
Vintage horse images: public domain, digitized by Gordon Johnson
Author photo: Jena McShane of McShane Photography

The following is a work of fiction created by the author. All names, individuals, characters, places, items, brands, events, &c., are the product of the author's imagination, are used fictitiously, or are entirely coincidental.

Printed in the United States of America

10 9 8 7 6 5 4 3 2 1

This volume contains
notes and glossaries
in the back pages.

For Dad and Jean Moulin.

This is not a dedication;
it's blame for my entire life.

TABLE OF CONTENTS

HISTORY NEVER REALLY SAYS GOODBYE.
HISTORY SAYS, "SEE YOU LATER."
—EDUARDO GALEANO

CORNER TO CORNER, END TO END

I walk across this street exactly thirty-four times a day, dodging a dozen brougham carriages, curricles, and runabouts, carrying exactly twenty-two duffels of linens, thirteen wooden slat-crates of pewter dinnerware, and well over a hundred odd articles in need of cleaning or repair. Tad Bellingham's iron-gilt rocking horse is the heaviest item in recent memory, and Mary Drader's brass lapel pin with the New Orleans Greys flag is the smallest. Her grandpappy died in the Alamo, and the pin came from his coonskin cap. Or so she always says through a haze of tears. But then, heck, everyone's grandpappy died in the Alamo these days, and it doesn't seem like there were that many soldiers in the siege, so there's that niggling feeling when Mrs. Drader cries that maybe, just maybe, it's simply a plain, old pin from nowhere and nothing at all. But who am I to tell Mary Drader, daughter of an English earl and founder of the Ladies Sewing Circle of Baltimore, that her grandpappy never saw day one of the Alamo? No one. I am no one to say that to her. My only job is to make that brass sparkle, and sparkle I make it.

I will never live among the richest families in Baltimore, but I know what it is to be among them, to see their fine pine balustrade staircases and their handcarved mahogany hutches, buffets that span the width of a wall, to watch them wind their expensive music boxes and pick at the ruffles of their fancy dresses like they're embarrassed that I've seen them wearing such frippery. I will wash that frippery clean uncountable times, in all its stages of embellishment, as it receives new sashes and fabric-covered buttons and lowered, raised, lowered, raised, lowered, lowered, lowered necklines that go in and out of fashion—anything to let society think each iteration is an entirely new frock. I'll show up without shame at the rear door in the same clothes I wore yesterday and each day before that, and I'll collect those frocks and scrub them spotless in all their reincarnations.

Mary Drader particularly likes me to take her linens. She has an endless supply of them, that woman. Just as all the fine ladies of Baltimore, she prefers the linens scrubbed until they're soft, never starched, as white as new snow, and folded very meticulously from corner to corner, then end to end, then corner to corner again. Unlike some laundresses and seamstresses, I've learned that the sun at noon will bleach gone the darkest stains in wet fabric—that baking soda and borax dry too stiffly, vinegar leaves a potent stench, but hydrogen peroxide is virtually undetectable.

Jefferson Mooring particularly likes me to take his copper. He says I make it shine as no one else can. Lately, I've gotten his pewter, too, beating out Elizabeth Ward to take on the entire dinnerware collection of one of the most prominent families in Baltimore. I've learned, unlike some of the girls, that a mere kiss of lemon can scour the dullest copper pot to a brilliant luster worthy of kings, and that a strange paste of flour, vinegar, and salt dried onto polished pewter will make it at least worthy of a king's guests. Ma taught me all she learned from her aunts before they lost their home and belongings in the Reconstruction. What I do, I do well.

Today, I have to knock on a new door. I've heard from Baltimore's gossipy laundresses that it is a hard door to knock upon, for the man behind it has a scowl that would curdle milk. I think I know what this means, but since I have only ever drunk curdled milk for the entirety of my life, this does not sink in as perhaps it should. When Mr. Bateman—the Mr. Enoch Bateman—opens his door, I am instantly scrutinized. My black hair is too out of place here. Buoyant, yellow curls and fair, unblemished skin is the fashion. I am leathered from the sun, and I imagine he would not like that my high cheekbones and dark eyes descend from the blood of the Mohegan and not from the breeding of a Yankee gentleman. He thinks me too unkempt, too scrawny. But there are things I have come to learn, and though his scowl is undoubtedly received by all the young maids who approach his elegant silver door-knocker, I know his scrutiny stems not from my scrawniness or my pockmarks, but rather ... from the fact that I am a boy. A *boy* laboring at what Mr. Bateman considers woman's work.

The disgust he shows me is surely the disgust he shows all creatures, but there is new derision reserved for a boy resigned to what this man has decided a station for women. Not even women: *girls*. Mr. Bateman thrusts a duffel of linens at me, certain I cannot possibly fold them corner to corner with any expertise. Next follows jangling oversized pewter spoons crashing into my arms and a spavined copper cuspidor requiring polish to a shine. His smirk says he expects the thing never to shine again and gives me a cold good-luck. Then there are coins, very few of them. Far too few of them. I'll give the coins to Ma and abide the silent appraisal she'll comb over the pitiful lot and then over her cheated son, just as I'll abide Mr. Bateman's silent glower that states plainly that a woman's station is for a woman to learn; and it is for a man to learn a different place.

But he will not be so haughty when his linen is folded corner to corner, end to end, bleached with the wrath of the sun at high noon, when his pewter gleams for kings' guests, when his copper shines with the kiss of lemons.

THE ORPHAN TRAIN

*T*he train rattled through the dusk, interior filled with black smoke that clung to Arthur's lungs. No discernible shapes shown anymore along the horizon when he peered through the car slats. All he could imagine was that he was somewhere called Indiana, and that this Indiana was a foreign world of flat, endless nothingness. A slop bucket passed along his outstretched feet, but his hunger hadn't persuaded his stomach to eat the wretched-smelling leavings that were offered. He stretched out his cramped legs, flexed his toes, and focused on the holes in the secondhand leather that so plainly showed what kind of boy he was. An orphan. He was one of the luckier ones simply to own shoes. *Who would want him? And why?*

Illinois was the end of the line. Somewhere near the farms of the Mississippi, Arthur would be handed to some family who didn't know him, someone who was supposed to claim him—perhaps some woman who couldn't have her own children or some old farmer or fisherman who needed a youthful laborer to do the job. Arthur had heard the stories: the boys who stepped onto the Orphan Train stepped off into slavery. But there was little choice for a scrapper of eleven who slept on

Brooklyn's streets, who in the cold of winter sold matches and rags to survive. They'd rounded up the boys—big men in fine wool jackets and tweed trousers, bowlers upon their heads, adoption papers in their hands. Arthur fingered the paper in his pocket that had been thrust against his chest by a fat, well-fed fist. The choice had been thus: *take the train or take the chain.*

Even when the train skirted into Illinois, with its clanking and screeching and deafening yell, Arthur's pride wouldn't let him touch the slop, despite his gnawing hunger. The whistle bellowed like a degüello when the metal beast jolted to a stop outside its destination. A buzz of murmurs immediately followed—Pittsfield, this place was called. The boy hung his head and scowled. The town sounded aptly named.

The door swung open, and children piled out. There must have been fifty of them in his car alone, and Arthur was prodded in among them like a head of wayward cattle driven where the master commanded.

"Clean 'em up good in the teeth and behind the ears," he heard one of those masters—*agents*, as he'd been taught to address them—call out, and with that, the boys were filed into a large wooden box-crate, stripped of their clothes, and splashed in the faces and chests with buckets of cold, soapy water.

The chill froze Arthur to the marrow, but he forced his hands to scrub soap mechanically into his skin as he awaited the rush of clean water that would plash the soap from him and down through the crate cracks. Loose-fitting, but thankfully clean, clothes were handed to him, as were his paper, his pa's timepiece, and the cardboard suitcase that the agents had given him. Not that there was anything in it. He'd never again see the oversized linen shirt that had once been his pa's, but Arthur supposed that was just as well.

The boys in their new plain clothes were paraded out onto wooden platforms that had been constructed behind the depot for only this purpose. The sweepings of New York's streets would become rural America's problem now. Farmers approached—some grubby and dirty, needing cold water thrown on them, too—and Arthur shied from their poking fingers and inquisitive eyes. Above the din of confusion and the children crying hopelessly for the worlds they'd once known, there arose the bickering words of haggling farmers.

"This one's too skimpy. Got no meat on his bones," one said, clenching his fingers around Arthur's upper arms.

Another felt the boy's skinny legs and commented the same. Two men came by and made Arthur open his mouth to show his teeth, and another made the boy lift his shirt and turn circles in place. Arthur felt tears threatening behind his eyes. He'd never been much of a crier, not even when his pa hit the bottle and then hit his ma. He'd give anything to go back to that night she died and beg the police to let his pa stay, no matter what the bastard had done. But it hadn't happened that way, and now Arthur was here. As another farmer came by, rounding up hardy orphans like he might run out of choices, Arthur slinked back, concaving his stomach until he looked emaciated, slumping his arms until they fair dragged on the platform.

And then a voice caught his ear. It was the lull of a woman, and he could at once hear his mother singing him to sleep again. He could picture her so clearly, where he hadn't been able to conjure her unfragmented image for years. This time, he thought for sure that tears would fall, but the young woman's voice caught his ear again. She was drawing closer. His eyes roamed the crowds to seek the voice. He knew the exact minute he'd found her, with her arm looped through a much-older man's, talking to him sweetly, the voice floating like wispy clouds above other useless noise.

"I just want one that looks kind, Jim," she said, "one with sweetness in his eyes."

Arthur immediately stood upright, puffing forth his chest and projecting as much sweetness into his eyes as he could muster. He didn't want an old farmer looking at his teeth. He wanted this woman to think he had kindness in him and sweetness in his eyes.

"I'm sure you'll know when you've found the one, dear," the man replied, eying the line of remaining boys with the same look of any of the farmers, disinterest, seeking one hale enough to do some farmwork, despite the sentiment to his wife.

Suddenly, Arthur didn't mind doing farmwork for the man if it meant a woman would see kindness in a street urchin. No one had ever said there was anything of merit in Arthur, except his ma. He wanted that back—that feeling of being cherished. He was asking a lot, he knew, *yet maybe just this once* … But the woman passed by. He couldn't have stood any taller—he gave it all he had. Two more dingy farmers stepped in front of Arthur and blocked the boy's view.

"What about this one?" one farmer said to the other, going through what had become the routine.

"Nah," came the reply. "Too soft."

But with that word, that fate-filled word—*soft*—the farmers stepped away, and the woman's head turned back to Arthur, just as the light left his eyes. He hung his head and didn't notice when she'd stepped toward him, until she lifted his chin from his chest. Soft eyes looked back into his. *Soft.*

"This one, Jim," she said. "This is the one."

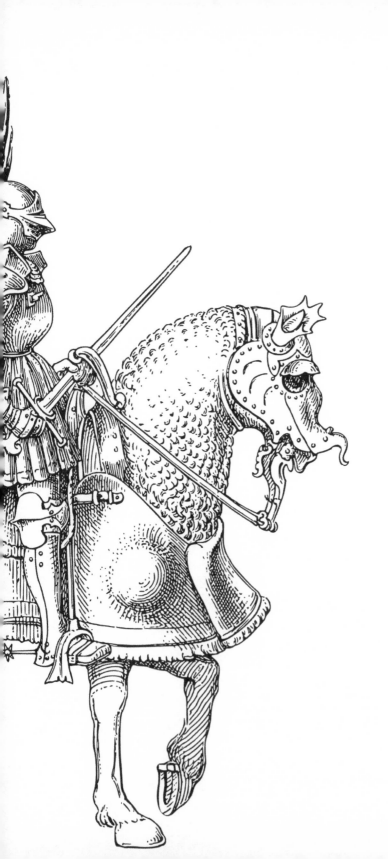

EVERY TIME IT SNOWS

*H*annah dug the chalk-paste dentifrice out of the bottom of the jar with her finger, hovering over her husband's head. "I need you to open up for me, Francis," she said, and he complied, opening his mouth habitually as she ran her finger over his teeth.

"It's snowing, honey," Frank said, some of the paste dripping from his mouth.

"I know it is. You don't have to look at it if it bothers you." Hannah slipped her hand over his eyes before his stare could turn trancelike. "Stay here with me this time." But it was too late. His mind had gone to the snow, and she wouldn't reach him now. She leaned forward and pressed a kiss to his temple, her mouth lingering over the warmth of his skin longer than usual. "I wish you would have stayed with me this time. There're no good memories in that snow, my love." But she might as well have been talking to herself.

"It'll be just this time, Elizabeth," he responded with indifference. "This one time. Please, don't tell my wife I'm here with you. She won't understand. She's too good to understand, and it will break her heart to think her letters aren't enough."

Hannah's lip quivered as she reached out to touch her husband's cheek. "I promise I won't tell your wife," she whispered, and her eyes glassed with unshed tears. They'd fall a hundred times before the day was over, she knew, but for now she held them back.

She'd never know who Elizabeth was. Some woman among the many who had followed the Rebel camp, she presumed, giving the soldiers what they couldn't get so far from home. One thing she knew for damn sure was that this Elizabeth woman had never rubbed dentifrice on Frank's teeth as he nodded off, or fed him from a wooden spoon because he might bite down too hard on a pewter one, or witnessed him struggle to remember his own son's name. She didn't care who this Elizabeth was. Whoever the woman was, Hannah only hoped Elizabeth had given Frank whatever he'd needed while he'd walked through hell—marched, slept, fought, starved, thirsted through hell.

Hannah would also never know what had happened in the winter of 1863 in a place called Fredericksburg. Seventeen inches of snow had fallen over two days when the men were stationed near Rappahannock Academy. All the papers mentioned it at the time. A letter arrived from Frank on that very day, dated weeks earlier, saying how miserable the snow had become, how it slowed them down and soaked through their clothes, clinging to them like a disease. But whatever had occurred between that letter and the Siege of Suffolk had forever taken Frank away from the man he'd been and the wife who still needed him to be that man. His eyes glazed, and she tried not to pity him—this shell of a being, still young at thirty-seven, in the mental state of a decrepit old man.

"Elizabeth, did I ever tell you about the winter war?" Frank said, interrupting Hannah's thought.

"No. But I'll remind you to tell me sometime."

"Remind me to tell you sometime," he said simultaneously.

"All right." She stood and left his side, wandering toward the bookshelf or the kitchen—no real destination. "I'll do that, Francis."

A knock arose at the door. Hannah forced aside the guilt of sudden relief she felt. It was shortlived, however, when her son, Robert, opened the door and handed her the letter they'd all been waiting for.

"They refused you again," he said. "They say there's nothing they can do, that the hospital doesn't handle this kind of care."

"But what about recompense?" she asked. "I can't support him on thirty-four dollars a month, even when I get it on time. They said when he enlisted that there would be recompense for damages, to help out the wives, the—"

"They lied to you, Ma. I don't know what you want me to say. Here it is, right here, writ plain out." Robert opened the letter, searching the lines. "'Your petition declined, with regrets.' They even have the audacity to say that, were he a bluejacket, they might reconsider." He dropped the letter into his mother's hand and peered around her. "How is the old man?"

"I'm fine, Corporal," Frank answered for himself. "Just talking to Elizabeth."

Robert bristled. He hated being called corporal. He'd never served a day in his life, but his own father didn't know him from anyone else who walked in the room. Sometimes there were rare moments of lucidity, and Robert almost hated those more, for when they dispersed, they left his mother in a state of depression that was unbearable. Still, she refused to quit the man, calling on that cold word that hung around the house like a noose: *duty*.

"You weren't talking to Elizabeth, Pa," Robert replied. "Who is Elizabeth?"

Frank's voice dropped to a hush. "Oh, she's just a girl of convenience. Don't tell my wife. My sweet Hannah would never understand."

Robert looked at his mother with a pained expression, and she shrugged. "I think she'd understand, Pa. I think ..." he met her eyes, and he knew, "she understands just fine."

"It was lonely out there, wasn't it, Corporal."

Robert sighed and wrung his hands uncomfortably. "Yes, it was, Sergeant. Our wives would understand." He circled his father, then turned abruptly. "I can't do this, Ma." Without another word, Robert walked through the door and slammed it behind him.

A soft chuckle purred through Frank's throat. "He's touchy."

"A bit touchy, yes," Hannah returned lightly. "He gets it from his father."

"Must be a boorish lout."

A smile touched her lips. "Oh, he's not so bad."

"I have to tell you something, Hannah, honey."

"Francis!" She took the room in strides. "You called me Hannah!"

"Of course. What else would I call you?" Brightness shone in his eyes as he looked back and forth from his wife's face to the snow out the window. Behind the brightness, sorrow still clung, but it appeared more apologetic than lost. "I have to tell you I did some things that wouldn't make you proud, honey. Maybe if I say them outright ... if I hear myself say them ..."

Her mouth fell open, and she took his chin in her hand, dragging those bright, sorrowful eyes toward her. He'd never looked at the snow and spoken. She wanted so desperately to keep him in that moment with her, to know, to understand. "I don't care. It doesn't matter. I'm always proud of you. None of that matters now, don't you see?" Her fingers stroked him—his hair, his hands, his cheeks. "I don't care about what you did out there, who you killed, what you saw, whoever Elizabeth was. It doesn't matter."

"Elizabeth?" he spoke with disdain. "You know about her?" His words hushed to whispers, and he hung his head. "She followed our camp, honey, I never intended … never meant to … I was so …" his pause spoke for his regret, "so … uncomfortable, honey. I needed you there."

"It doesn't matter. None of that matters. Not the women or the soldiers," her words left too swiftly, "or the blood or the snow."

"The snow," he echoed listlessly.

"Oh, no, no, I didn't say that." A trembling hand shot over her mouth. "Please, please, don't leave me again. You said you needed me there; well, I need you here. Please, don't leave me again." She fell to her knees in front of him, but his eyes already seemed far away. She pounded her fists against her forehead and laid her head in his lap. The tears she'd been holding back finally fell, as they always fell.

"I won't leave you, Hannah." He rubbed his fingers through her hair, and her breath caught. "You should've left me, but you never did. I won't leave you, honey. Did I ever tell you about the winter war?"

"No," she whispered, her tears dripping through his trousers, "but I'll remind you to tell me someti—"

"Seventeen inches, Colonel Stiles said," he continued, and she did not dare stop him, even knowing that recounting this memory for the first time could spiral him into a spell that would last for days, weeks. "Ten thousand of us were engaged in battle that day, honey, and we'd been so restless, so cooped up. General Hoke's camp attacked us—my God, Hannah, our own men! Infantry, cavalry—they were all there attacking us as if they'd gone mad. Reinforcements from the commissary came to our aid, but it was too late; we got pelted."

"You don't have to talk about this if it's too hard. I know the snow is so painful for you."

"No, Hannah, don't you see? This was the battle that changed everything. The reinforcements helped us, and Hoke withdrew. Out of selfishness, we planned a counterattack, not to be outdone by our own men.

We formed regular lines and marched our Georgia camp directly into the North Carolina camp with our balls at the ready, but you see, they were waiting for us. They'd outfoxed us. Their haversacks were full of ammunition, and they surprised us and took prisoners."

"Prisoners!"

"The snow was so thick beneath my feet, so wet on my clothes, and I was captured—"

"Captured? I didn't know you were captured. What do you mean 'by your own men'? Your own Rebels captured you?"

"They did, and I was hit repeatedly with—oh, how it stung! I was pelted with ... with ..." Frank unexpectedly laughed.

"With what?" she cried, shaking him. "Tell me!"

"With snowballs," he said simply. "Dozens of snowballs."

"Snowballs?" Her hands dropped from his shoulders. "You mean it was a ... a snowball fight?"

He smiled. A truly genuine smile. "It was the best day of the war, Hannah. You should've seen us, honey, how we laughed, the smiles on the men's faces. I remember that joyous day, that blessed day of reprieve, every time it snows."

CASTING GRAND TITANS

*A*gatha Acton discovered the moss in 42-Lot the day the Know-Nothings started Bloody Monday and stopped the immigrants from voting. It was in all the papers, even the headline of the *Council Bluffs Bugle*, for which same-day news was a novelty. A Monday in 1855 at 6:14 p.m. in the middle of her father's Iowa field, twelve inches from the boundary of 43-Lot where it butts to B-Half. Coordinates 41.67, -91.52, north of Oakland Cemetery and the Goosetown Bohemians, and east of Prospect Hill, off Governor Street. She pulled up her dress and dropped to her knees in the dry prairie soil and came within an inch of it, her eyes wide, one pupil nearly touching it. Her clothbound sketchbook fell open beside her where she'd noted the coordinates, and, with a sharpened stick of paper-wrapped coal, she wrote more tiny letters in the margins of an already-filled page.

Spreading prostrate growth habit, pleurocarpous. Unbranched. Little mounding in the colony. Nonvascular cryptogamic bryophyte. Scraggly appearance. She hypothesized that this appearance would be gone in spring, however, when the production of spore-bearing capsules made the stems leafy green. *Individual stems terete, moderately spaced.* Yet, it wasn't just feather moss. She held her magnifier and studied the lanceolate-ovate, and they were toothed along their entire margins, the leaf surface golden yellow. The ground around it brimmed with flora, despite the dry soil and harsh, sunny conditions. Ferns and dandelions, *Achillea millefolium*, *Agastache foeniculum*, and *Anemone cylindrica*. The nutrients must have been coming from the moss, or somehow being held in by it and spreading to the plants around it.

She'd never seen anything like it. Its vibrant yellow-green had been hidden beneath the shade of a clump-formed Prairie Dropseed that had taken over the whole area. But beneath it was a new moss. Her insides swelled like they were pumped with air, and she dragged her fingers through the crumbly soil. What a beautiful little creature.

༄

A shrill, offtone bell on the Mechanics Academy rang forty whole seconds before the big bell in the cupola of the Capitol. As if the girls weren't restless enough. Their single wooden bench lined the western side of a shack from wall to wall, and the makeshift shop tables came up to the girls' necks when they were seated. Thigh to thigh, they sat. Dorothea picked at her chip of charcoal until it blacked her fingers. Another girl flicked her soil samples at Mary on the end of the row.

Agatha sighed. "Remember Legislature is in session. Mind your voices in the halls."

She wasn't talking about her own classroom. She had been relegated to a twelve-by-twelve room left over from when the contractors built the great Capitol, the first building of the State University of Iowa. Which also happened to be where the Senate and First General Assembly met when they were called to session, so the students had to tiptoe by a chamber of arguing men that spanned the entire second floor between a forest of Corinthian columns, and past the main-floor chamber where the district judicature held court. Agatha's shack had been hastily constructed as a breakroom for the contractors. They'd forgotten windows. It was a black box where she lit candles just to see the bryophytes and cryptogamae that the girls couldn't yet identify. No one could ever see the colors in the dark. No one could count spores or flowers or find her way to the water bucket that hung on the back of the door. The place was meant to be temporary, to have already been demolished. In one corner, a wooden crate spilled over with gardening tools the professors' wives had donated, bent and rusty and half useless. Had there been windows, she would have looked out at the Capitol, the center of the budding campus, in the space above this wooden crate. Instead, she smashed her shins on it repeatedly in the dark. Agatha couldn't blame the girls for being through the door before the official bell sounded. She stared out after them, standing with the door propped to unstuff the room, and hoped they remembered to keep quiet in the halls. The coat-tails of Dr. Yves Jolliet swept around the corner of the Capitol. His office had a window.

"Wait for your chaperone!" Agatha called behind the girls.

Another man, their chaperone, came around the building to greet them, and she closed the door and sank back into the dark, walking to the shop tables and bringing a candle against the twelve halved pota-toes, lying upright, their white centers covered in tiny mosses. Anne's looked probed to death. Coleandra's was oddly black, somehow contam-inated. Dorothea's had been knocked over in her rush for the door, but on its underside was unsanctioned mold. Agatha groaned and sat on the long benchseat and thought about beans. If they were still at $2.25 per bushel, she couldn't buy them, again, for the third week in a row. She needed beans and she needed cornmeal and she needed to see her feathered moss in her field three miles from here. The darkness got to her. The school had hardly started session, and she was already mad-dened by the heightened sense of smell in the unventilated room. Rot-ting potatoes and iodine and hot soil and standing water in glass dishes that would have brought in mosquitoes were it not unseasonably cold for autumn. Frost crunched beneath her feet some mornings.

She lit a candle and leaned over the microscope propped in the cor-ner. Her grandfather's inheritance had gone toward its purchase, and she cherished it as if it were a child. She made the day's notes in her notebook, her moss spores under one plate, and the root system con-taining the residue of some sort of bacterium in its slow-moving last days. *Individual spores 8micm, globoid, papillose. Unchanged.* She'd have to gather a fresher root sample for the other plate.

She took up a copy of the *Bugle* she'd found in the foyer, flipped the pages to the local listings, and ran her finger down the columns of steamboat shipment prices and recent arrests, then the names of fugi-tive slaves who'd been caught and returned. She held the paper close to the light, sighed, then tossed it on the bench, blew out her candle, and stood there, feeling the dark wrap around her.

Walking out of the laboratory shack was meant to be intimidating, she estimated. Men had purposely made it so for her, stranding her out there. When she stepped to the grassy walk where no one had bothered with cobblestones, she stood miniature in the shadow of the west side of the Capitol. Out of view, out of mind, out of earshot. Out of the matter. A slat was already coming off the wood-shingled roof, despite the Capitol being fewer than fifteen years old at the cornerstone. The porous limestone made the exterior look rough as its Greek Revival portico came into view around the side of the building, its Doric pilasters looming over her, Corinthian columns and scrollwork all the way to the lantern on the cupola modeled after an ancient Athenian monument. She walked up the limestone steps toward façade walls and through the double doors, past the inversely-rotated stairway, and down the hall. The door to a spacious office was open. She tapped on it lightly.

"Mr. President?"

University president Amos Dean looked up from a sheaf of papers. "Yes, Miss Arton."

"Acton," Agatha corrected, and she stepped into the room.

A creamy yellow paint ran from the top of the window to the ceiling, and beneath it, light oak wainscoting covered the lower portion of the walls. The office was bright, with a tall picture window facing the circle walk and Clinton Street beyond, and rows of copper wall-mounted lamps with frosted glass globes bearing flower patterns. *Bellis perennis* and a bastardized *Helianthus ciliaris*. They should have asked her to illustrate the pattern; she would have done a better job. A dark wood desk sat along one wall, with a chair on either side—a regal handcarved, high-backed wood for the president, and an insufficient wicker for his guests, the bottom sagging from the large rumps of self-important men. Two cloth-covered armchairs sat beside the window, beneath a hanging chandelier filled with glass light cylinders. Across from the desk, a full-sized fireplace heated the room. Agatha gave a shallow curtsy and tugged at the cane ribs of her dress. The room made her sweat, the sudden warmth after the cold dampness of the shack, and she, standing neck to toe and full-sleeved in black, save for one spruce of white lace lining the high collar of her starched, padded dress.

President Dean waved a hand for her to sit. "What grievances have you brought me?"

Agatha scrunched her nose and did not sit. She wished to remain as tall as she could, as commanding. "I request 73¢ added to the expenditures for more potatoes."

"We're already over budget, Miss Arton."

She grimaced. "I'm asking for 73¢. I'm not asking for glass bottles."

"I can't very well expand budgets for ladies' gardening when we are in want of two more professors." He gestured in the air as if swatting a gnat and went back to his papers.

"It's not gardening. It's botany," Agatha said sharply. "You'd grant it to Dr. Jolliet."

"Dr. Jolliet is a doctor," Dean said without looking up. "With a degree from Heidelberg. The natural history, philosophy, and chemistry departments are endowed and funded entirely upon the honor of having him here." He finally looked up, his feather dripping a spot of ink onto his desk as he held it in the air, then pointed it at her. "*His* family discovered this land. *His* doctorate is useful. You, my dear, have scarce earned a master's."

"I did not *scarce* earn a master's; I did earn one. With scholarship. Direct me toward a university that would grant me more abundance in chemistry, and I'll merrily attend." She stepped toward his desk, and he finally stood from his chair, much taller than she. Her control slipped. "I don't have a proper laboratory. The potatoes are rotting. I need glass experiment bottles that can't rot. *Instructions in Gardening for Ladies* is not an acceptable textbook for the girls. You promised me a lab if I taught women's sewing, and for gracious' sake, I'm teaching *sewing*. In the dark. With degrees in chemistry and botany. And with this early cold coming, what will I do without a stove?"

"There's no ventilation for a stove."

"Yes, I'm well aware," she almost laughed. "And yet I'm only asking for 73¢ for potatoes—"

"Amos!" The voice came from behind her, and she jumped.

Dean's head snapped toward the door, and he smiled. "Yves." He splayed a palm.

"When is our rescheduled chess match, fat man?" Yves said jovially, and waltzed past Agatha, taking the room in swaying strides.

A fitted frock coat hugged him snugly, its lapels wide around his chest then cut away at the beltline, and its pin-buttoned tails down to the backs of his knees. A plaid double-breasted waistcoat came up to a high-collared white shirt that was wrapped around and again with a black ascot that tied in the front of the neck. His muttonchops waged war with the starched collar points. She imagined his hair was parted neatly on one side where it bunched around his ears, but it was lost beneath a shiny felted-beaverskin tophat that he didn't bother to remove indoors. His lips were likewise lost to an oversized mustache that wasn't waxed at the tips, but was pointed trimly. In his hand he held a cane, for no purpose but that it suited him to do so. Agatha cleared her throat, then louder when she still wasn't noticed.

Yves whirled around, his cane following the movement. "Oh, I did not see you there."

"How terribly surprising," she muttered. A gold chain swung between two vest pockets and draped down to his plaid pants, a fob and watch dangling off a custom loophook in the vest, and she stared at it.

Amos Dean grunted and signaled to her. "Dr. Jolliet, Miss Arton."

"Acton," Agatha corrected defiantly.

Yves Jolliet chuckled and tapped his cane on the floor. "Ah! The ladies' gardener!"

"Oh, murder," Agatha snapped.

"Who are we murdering?" Yves said. "Count me in! I love a good murder. Really gets the blood flowing, don't you know!" He held the back of his hand up to his mouth and said to Dean, "I fear someone's already been murdered, by the looks of the funeral raiment." He dropped his hand, winked at Agatha, and turned again to Dean, pulling a piece of paper from the inside of his frock coat, then looking it over. "Amos, old fellow, I need $12 for glass bottles." He laid the paper in front of the president.

Dean nodded. "I'll have them ordered today." A wooden stamper came through the air out of nowhere and landed on the paper with faint black ink. APPROVED.

Agatha made an indignant hmmph.

"And don't cake on that chess rematch," Yves said. "I might let you win this time." He pocketed the stamped paper for the financier's office and turned to Agatha. "I am rather remarkable at chess. Do you play?"

"I'm afraid not," Agatha said.

"Pity." He looked her up and down, not unkindly, but as if he were tucking something away for a memory down the road. "All that talent gone to waste on gardening." Yves tapped his cane again and smiled haughtily and walked out of the room, leaving the door open.

Agatha gently closed it and turned back to Dean.

He was staring straight at her, leaning back in his chair with his hands crossed over his generous stomach. "I'll see if the board will approve your potatoes," he said.

She nodded meekly and turned before she reddened. As she stepped into the hallway, she saw the young ladies being ushered by men down the hall in a group, distrusted to find the correct classroom on their own. Yves Jolliet's figure swayed away from her. She turned back into the president's office. "It's Acton. My name is Agatha Acton. I under-stand your disregard for me, sir, but at least be a gentleman about it to my face." She slammed the door and stepped back into the hall. "Dr. Jolliet!" she called, then remembered the Legislature in session and put a hand over her mouth. "May I speak with you?" she said quieter.

He turned and yelled to her as he walked backward down the hall, "I'm late for testing enzymatic *Solanum lycopersicum* against drought con-ditions, but the party tonight?"

"Party?" she said too loud. "I received no invite to a party."

"The professors party at Nicking House. You don't need an invite. It's an opening gala for all professors. I'll bring cigars and sneak you off to Hotz & Geiger!"

"The brewery? I can't—"

"You must come! Everyone will be there. You'll be the gossip if you don't show."

"But—"

"Tonight, then!"

She sighed. "Tonight."

She couldn't afford to go to a party. The coach alone would be a week's pay. If she were caught anywhere near Hotz & Geiger, she'd be fired, no excuse taken. And supposing everyone knew where the Nick-ing House was? She didn't know where the Nicking House was. If she needed a coach to get there, then she couldn't buy beans. Oh, bother, what did it matter? She already couldn't buy beans. If everyone would be there, then she ought to show. Not because she'd be the subject of their gossip, but because she might be judged poorly if she didn't make the right decisions among the university professors, and then she'd be overlooked for a raise she desperately needed. She had to make the good impression, and it was regrettably more pressing than beans. So, what was one party?

🍎

Agatha arrived on Clinton Street and headed toward the market stores. She didn't want to go all the way up to North Market for the fairest prices, but her slim coin purse held less than a dollar. She was thankful the party wasn't a potluck. She might not be invited again if she showed up with a single stringbean and entreated them to split it twenty ways. She passed the U.S. Land Office and New York Store, the Clothier, Mill-ington & Farwell, and Townsend's Daguerrean Gallery and J. B. Daniel

Hawk-Eye Saddle & Harness Shop. Wood, sandstone, and limestone buildings built three stories high with tall rectangular windows on each floor, roofs slanted sharply against gigantic industrial chimneys. Those who had it in good with Sylvanus Johnson had buildings of brick from his brickyard. She passed a busker playing "Columbia, the Gem of the Ocean" on a mouth harp in front of the door to the grocer—named on the outside only as GROCERY STORE—and she went in.

"Olga," she addressed the pretty young woman whose dress was too proper for the disarrayed shape of the store.

Olga snapped her register drawer shut and launched across the cashmount. "You!" She kissed Agatha upon both cheeks, sprawled prostrate over the counter. White chalk streaked her dress from the limestone. Black charcoal lined both eyes, and a spot of brownish dye shadowed her lids. "You're looking gaunt. There's a sale on onions?" she added hopefully.

Agatha laughed. "Can I afford anything else?"

Olga jumped back behind the counter and came around to her best friend. She pulled a pin out of her blond updo and let the strand bounce in front of her ear. "It's hard. This 'sarned inflation. The banks is printing so much paper money that it's gone worthless now, and what you could afford last week, you can't afford this week." She frowned. "The university making up for the hike?"

"No, ma'am. And now I have to buy my own potatoes. It's doubtful they'll allot me the reimbursement."

"We're plumb out of 'tatoes, actually. Fella in a top and tails came in here earlier this morning and bought us out."

Agatha pulled her face into a moue. "Did he leave his card?"

Olga shook her head. "And I can only lend you credit up to 50¢ this time. Uncle Ira's pulling the strings real tight."

"He's not hiring yet, is he?" She was disappointed at Olga's wince. "Well, tell me when he is."

"You know I will. But it's hard right now, like I say. Things is hard. Money might as well be water from the Iowa River, flowing out of town as it is." She took Agatha by the arm. "I'll show you the sales."

Agatha saw a sign for PATATOS 37½¢, and sure enough, the basket was empty. A pat of butter, 23¢. Kilograms of beef, 7¢. Beans were still at $2.25 per bushel, and now corn was up to $1 per bushel. The ears looked green and unripe, and the yield must have been pitiful; the husks swathed cobs so scrawny they looked like jaundiced twigs. She parceled a chip of pork at 10¢, a hard cheese block at 10¢, one pound of sugar at

9½¢, and a bag of cornmeal at 13¢ on credit. "Would Ira mind if I split a bushel?" Agatha asked, nodding to the beans. She needed those. Those were specifically requested on the homestead. "I can take the wax, since they're cheaper."

Olga winced again, but nodded. "I can't do that counting, though."

"I can." Agatha eyed the bushel basket with 24 pounds of beans, counted the top layer, and multiplied it by the estimated depth of the basket. She figured on 2½ cups of beans per pound. The bushel price divided by the pounds in the bushel gave her 9¢ per pound. She'd round it down for Ira's inconvenience of the matter. "It'll be 2 cups of beans for 9¢. I'll take 4 cups for 18¢, and then I've used up my credit and most of what I came in with."

"I'll never know how you do that," Olga said.

"Come take my botany class. They call it 'Ladies' Gardening,'" she laughed, "Columbia-knows-why." She glanced around a final time. Oats for 45¢ and molasses for 49¢ per gallon. She couldn't afford either one. A barrel of flour sat at $12. She whistled low. Spinach leaves read: 50 CTS PER BU, and she decided she'd better not for now. "And three ounces of Y. H. Tea, please."

"And what is that come to?" Olga asked.

"61¢ per pound. 16 dry ounces in a pound. Makes 3¢ and 8 per ounce. Multiplied by three ounces makes it about 11½¢."

Olga beamed and measured out three ounces of Young Hyson. "They ought to put you on display in a museum."

"I've got my eye on one." She smiled.

"I saw that the lot was still there for it. I suppose it's counting days."

"Can't count like I can," Agatha laughed, but the smile didn't last.

"The university should buy it for you."

"I'll have to invest in tops and tails first." She handed Olga the money over the counter, and her friend put the groceries into a wooden crate.

The city printmaker walked into the store and tipped his hat with his cane to Olga, before remembering to remove it. "Miss Bengstdotter," he said charmingly, but Olga didn't respond.

Agatha said, "How do you do, Mr. Berryhill?"

His attention darted to Agatha, then quickly back to Olga, where it stayed. Agatha looked at Olga, too, pretty thing she was. If Agatha wore a streak of coal around her eyes, she'd be fired from the university on the spot. She imagined she was only hired because she was flat as an ironboard and plain and unremarkable. She wasn't a distraction to the men. But it did suit Olga, her milky Swedish skin and bright blue eyes, and Agatha cleared her throat to prompt Charles Berryhill to move along. He put his hat back on his head and didn't tip it to her as he passed.

"They're all drooling hounds," Olga whispered.

Agatha lifted her wooden crate off the counter, unfazed. "Do you know where the Nicking House is?"

"Across from the Brewers on Market. What's amiss at Nicking's?"

"There's a professors party tonight. I'm taking you with me."

"Oh, I do love parties with stuffy professors' wives! They stick their ribbed bosoms into your face with such pride when they ask if you've *actually read* the latest Dickens or just gleaned the cover in a shopfront."

"Murder, who actually reads Dickens."

"Well, we's not all sophisticated enough to read *Botany for Ladies*."

Agatha snorted. "They won't even let me have that for a text! They said it was too hard for girls to digest. Imagine such palaver."

"You ought to write your own textbook. Get Berryhill to print it for you. Hey, Charles!" Olga yelled across the store. "Charles! Would you print—"

Agatha put a hand over her friend's mouth. "You're a little vermin. You're coming to Nicking, then, yes?"

"What should I wear?"

"Murder, I don't know."

"What are you wearing?"

Agatha laughed on her way out, "What do you think I'm wearing?"

She carried the crate through the door and up Clinton north toward the Presbyterian church at the head of the lane. The shop windows brimmed with fashions and necessaries, and she stopped before one near Market Street, wedged between a slanted sandstone complex and a launderer. The brown façade was painted wood, but beneath it were walls of local limestone from the quarry, and the sign that hung by twine in the vacant window read: FOR SALE / CALL ON BARNES TUESDAYS ONLY. Agatha set down her wooden crate, cupped both her hands around her eyes, and pressed them to the glass, like she did every day. She imagined the botanical museum filling the long, narrow space. Rows of display cases holding lumps of native sod and lichens, charts that explained the difference in vascular tissue between bryophytes and embryophytes. She put aside 50¢ of her paycheck each week, keeping it in a flour jar hidden down in the floor of her prairie lab. She remained hopeful each time she looked at the jar, and tried not to think of it practically, though that was where her mind always went. Her brain was in the field notes. Three hundred twenty-eight paychecks at 50¢ savings each week. It would take her six and a half years to buy the space outright, and then it would have to generate a $4 monthly profit to meet the property tax. She had no idea what the lighting and temperature control would cost. Nevermind 15¢ each for sticks of lumber and 8¢ per brick, if Sylvanus Johnson proved kind enough to spare discounted case mounts with his bricks. She sighed and wiped her finger smudges lovingly off the glass with her sleeve, as if caressing. The strip was developing. The building wouldn't remain empty for six and a half years. Still, she saved for it. And longed, and imagined, and felt it moss over her breastbone with the warmth and promise of an idea.

By the time she made it as far as her arms would carry the heavy wooden crate, she could see the Athenian lantern of the Capitol. She set down the crate and wished she could dispense with enough coin for a carriage, but she'd have to make do. She could catch her breath for a few minutes, and still make it back in time to listen in on the natural philosophy class. She flexed her arms and hands and was about to sit on the crate for a rest, when a swash of coattails went by her, and a cane thunked on the stone walk, and the glint of light reflecting off its surface saturated her eyes. She blinked hard, and when she opened them, he had stopped and turned around to her.

Yves Jolliet clucked his tongue. "If someone doesn't sport that box for you, you'll miss eavesdropping on Philosophy 1."

Agatha drew herself upright. How did he know she eavesdropped on Philosophy 1? He taught Physiological Chemistry 1 at the same hour. She opened her mouth to retort, but he laughed and threw his cane into the air, snapping it at a midsection, then collapsing it in on itself, once and again. Her brows lifted. He stuck the folded cane into his pocket and swooped to her side to lift the crate.

"Light as a paramecium. Are you to subsist on a single pea?"

"There are three individual peas, I believe," she said. "I prefer to call them *Pisum sativum*, of course."

"Three!" he laughed, carrying the box toward the university. "That shall last you a whole month."

"Shall I report back how they fare in this drought?"

He stole a glance at her, and she made sure to be self-satisfied. His eyes remained on her too long. It wasn't something she was accustomed

to, but she felt the look morph into judgment, assessment. That was
more her custom.

"You know a thing or two, don't you," he said, not quite a question,
and not quite as if he believed it.

"Not much, really," she said to appease him. "Not much in accor-
dance with how much there is to know. I notice *you* don't stand outside
the door of Philosophy 1."

He chuckled, "How socratic. I took philosophy at Harvard."

"I took it at Oberlin."

"I took it again at Heidelberg."

"I'd take it again if they'd let me." She eyed his tophat, its perfect
ten-degree tilt. He looked so like a dandy, but distinguished. Not a fop,
but not born into it, either. He had earned what he knew; she could tell
it even if she didn't already know it. "Besides, Mr. Brown is a marvelous
instructor. Such a commanding voice, and he tells it so simply for those
dull-witted boys."

"Brown is a cad."

Agatha looked off toward the trees that surrounded the shack laboratory at the back of the university. "It takes a thief to catch a thief,"
she mumbled, and then came to a halt. "Dr. Jolliet—"

"Yves," he said, turning around to her and walking backward like
she'd seen him do often. "Please."

"That's too personal for me, Dr. Jolliet." She walked toward him
slowly. "I would like to offer you a proposal, if you are willing."

He smirked. "I'm not in the market for a wife."

Just then, a professor of mathematics, whose name Agatha had not
yet learned, came up and smacked Yves on the shoulder. "Checkmate!"
he said as if a punchline to some inside joke, and the men laughed, and
Agatha stopped and watched them walk away with her crate.

She hadn't thought she'd dislike Yves Jolliet. When she first learned
they'd be sharing university space, she'd been thrilled at the knowledge.
But the man thought he was clever. Fields of prairie wildflowers surrounded her, and she studied them, remarking absently on each petal,
the differences in stems. She could come out here and illustrate between
Ladies' Gardening and sewing. And he was, she thought. Clever. He
was. She watched him set the crate down in front of the door to her
little shack, and sink with the mathematics professor into the Capitol,
gregarious all the while.

She remembered when she set foot inside the Capitol that, first, the
Legislature was in session, and second, women were not allowed to be

in the halls unattended. She walked quietly toward Mr. Brown's Philosophy 1, but when she got there, the room was occupied by men of the Assembly, which mucked the arrangement of classrooms. She hurried away from the door and down the hall, listening at each one for which instruction was going on inside. Then she stopped and backed a few steps and stood beside an open door. His voice was softer when he spoke to his class, as if he loved the words, as if they left his mouth with some heartache of attachment. There was romance in the terms, the scraping of his chalk, the way he stroked an idea as if it were animate, and she was immediately enthralled with his affection for a simple root, a simple grain of soil.

"The structure of monocot is one cotyledon, where dicot has the two-seed-leaf structure," Yves said, drawing out a diagram with chalk on a board of painted wood. "Here, xylem and phloem are paired in bundles, which are dispersed throughout the stem." He drew something else.

She desperately wanted to see it, although she already knew it was the vascular system of monocots. How *xylem* and *phloem* sounded on his tongue was a thing of poetry.

"And in dicots, xylem and phloem form rings inside the stem."

She knew without looking that he drew the rings.

"The phloem forms an outer ring, the xylem an inner ring. The floral parts are in groupings of four or five, and the leaves are veined in nets." He urged them to turn to a page in their books, and she wanted to know which book they had. "In studying this vascular tissue at the soil lines of different soil, in instances from very wet clay soils to very, very dry saline, we can see the effect this saturation, or lack thereof, has on the primary roots and the lateral roots, and then in the growth, whether stunted or healthy, of the bud, leaf primordia, and shoot apex."

He pulled a cigarette from a tin in his breast pocket, looked up at her over the top of it as he lit it on his desk candle, and she realized she had stepped from her hidden place beside the door and out into the open to see the diagram. He didn't take his eyes from her as he lit and puffed his cigarette. She met his gaze and didn't break it, a little afraid, a little heated, but determined for something she didn't quite understand.

"We're going to be focusing on the meristematic zone in the root tips," he said to his class, without looking away from her, his expression challenging, daring her, "from root cap to zone of elongation." He finally turned back to his students. His tone gained a sense of urgency, the poetry of the moment lost to the disruption, flustery. "We want to mark the differences in the roots between the overmuddy clays, the lush loams, and the dry salines."

He blew a puff of smoke and looked back at her. Agatha quickly glanced down at the notebook in her hand and sketched, feeling terribly exposed. Her pride would not let her duck for cover, however, with him scrutinizing her so closely.

"Have you anything to add, Miss Ladies' Gardener?" he said abruptly, and the class swiveled toward Agatha. He drew in a slow puff on his cigarette, the tip flaring red as if angered.

She exhaled sharply and stiffened. "I would add that if you're getting white salt deposits on your soil surfaces or stems, document that carefully. Make sure you test the measurement of the saline and the solubility buildup in the rhizosphere before you make any other documentation on your samples. I urge you to set aside a sample to test for flammability, so you can document if there is peat content as it dries." She snapped her notebook shut.

He puffed his cigarette.

She walked away, her heart pounding. Women's sewing would begin in twenty minutes. She'd sit in the dark until then.

౷

Olga met Agatha at the corner of Clinton and Market. Agatha nearly dropped the crate from her arms onto the dirt walkway at the intersection. She was sweating despite the evening chill, and her riding jacket was worn threadbare.

"I see you've prepared for the occasion," Olga laughed, taking the crate from Agatha. "Dolled right up. Brought your groceries. Watch out, wives! Life of the gala coming through!"

Agatha swatted her and stood still, doubled over on the walkway with her hands on her knees. When she got her breath back, she shook out her arms. "I can take it again," she offered for the crate. "Only three blocks, I think."

"I got it."

"You look lovely." Agatha touched the layered silk in Olga's dress.

"And you look like ... you're in mourning?" Olga hefted the crate up onto her shoulder and took Agatha by the arm, leading her down Market Street. "Can I at least plaster your lips with a wax stick?"

"No. If President Dean is there, he'd fire me at the door."

"Why hire a woman if you don't want her to be a woman?"

Agatha groaned. "I don't think he wanted a woman. I don't think I was anyone's choice. But they want to tout that they're the first co-educational public state college with equal merit, so someone had to teach those ladies domestication. That's the sewing, of course—the botany, I had to beg for." She lifted her elbows to air out her underarms. "I think I'm a little nervous. I've never met a professor's wife. What is one even like?"

Olga halted in front of 410 East Market Street, a large saltbox-style multi-level home made of beautiful smoothed sandstone. "We're about to find out." She dragged Agatha up the steps and pounded on a generous iron knocker in the shape of a steamboat.

A black man in coattails opened the door, and his mouth fell into an O. The house torched with oil lamps that sizzled loudly, and a piano played from the room beyond his shoulder. "Can I help you ladies with something?" He almost stepped out onto the porch to close the door behind him, but Olga pushed the door inward and thrust the crate at him.

"She's a professor," she thumbed over her shoulder, and she didn't wait to hear the man's reply as she walked in.

"I'm sorry for her etiquette." Agatha curtsied. "I'm an instructor at the state university. There's an employee party here?"

"Well, sure," he said tentatively, setting down the crate. "Well, sure, there is." He opened the door wide and let Agatha through it. "May I take your coat?" He was already sliding it off her as he said it, and he wrinkled his nose when his finger went through a hole.

"Thank you, sir," she said politely and patted the pocket to check that her notebook was safe. She fished through her coin purse for a nickel, looked at the piece longingly, and placed it in his palm.

He nodded at it and smiled, but it wasn't genuine.

"Bless me. Where are my manners! I thought that was a quarter," she said, her voice an octave higher, and she placed a quarter in his hand. She wanted to withdraw the nickel, but he closed his fingers around both coins. She curtsied again and walked toward what light emanated from the foyer. Of course Olga had gone ahead and left her! Oh, thirty whole cents! What that could have purchased. Her chest constricted. She pushed the fear down, forced a smile, and walked into the blinding light of the ballroom.

The piano stopped. Cigar smoke assaulted her face. She cleared the haze in front of her eyes, and looked around. They stared back at her entrance. A room full of men in studious suits, not a wife among them.

Shoulder to shoulder with black suit jackets and ascots. Not a spot of color save flushed wine cheeks. Some of the men chuckled and went back to talking. She let out the breath she was holding and turned for the foyer, but a drink tray came hurriedly through it, then seemingly from nowhere, Olga pushed her back into the room.

"Where were you?" Agatha squeaked.

"Waxing my lips," she replied and entered the room and laughed out loud.

Her dress was fashionably lowered in the front, and rolling off both shoulders. Agatha could see now that it was a pale pink with lace trim and airy sleeves, and the men eyed Olga very differently, circling like piranhas. The piano struck up "Whistle, Mary, Whistle" and was joined by a violin. Olga grabbed a scotch from a passing tray and another for Agatha and held it out to her.

"I cannot," Agatha said, holding her hand up at it. "It's in my contract." She watched Olga look sadly at the two glasses. "You go ahead. Have at it, love. It's a party, and you're now the center of it!"

They both laughed tightly as Olga drank from both glasses, and Agatha scanned the room that had gone back to its own business, already forgetting her intrusion in it. Yves Jolliet stood in front of a large hearth, one arm up on the mantel, his long fingers wrapped around a cigar. Every few seconds, he threw his head back and crowed at what the circle of men said around him. When he laughed so openly, so fully, her face tugged into a smile, then faded quickly every time. When the men would get to a long story, Yves would move his eyes slowly onto her, as if he'd already memorized every place she moved throughout the room. Then he'd slowly look back at the talker, Yves' face dragged down to the man against its will. She made her way to him, as confidently as she could muster, but naught could prevent her hands from shaking. Over her shoulder, she could hear Olga laughing, and men were chuckling in the armchairs, and bouts of it came bounding from the corners, and there she was, shaking. As she approached, Yves stopped pretending to listen to the conversation in front of him, and he blatantly studied her, as if she were one of his experiments, a soil sample, a zone of elongation. She wished she knew what he was thinking. But then, maybe not.

"Well, it's the woman," one of the men said, stepping backward as she neared the hearth. He put a hand on her shoulderblade, and she pulled away from it. He blew his cigar smoke into her face, and she breathed fiercely through it.

"Gentlemen," she said. "Dr. Jolliet." She curtsied to him specifically.

The men chuckled.

"And who exactly are you?" a bespectacled man from the Natural History Department added curtly. "This is the professors ball."

She waited for Yves to say something, but he shrugged. She drew in her brows. "All right, act as if you don't know me after we spoke on three occasions today."

"Ah, the ladies' gardener!" Yves said. "I didn't recognize you in that new dress."

She slumped her shoulders and turned. "Goodnight, gentlemen."

What a waste of a 30¢ tip. Had she gone home in the daylight, she could have walked the three miles. Now it was dark, and she'd have to hail a coach she couldn't afford to get through the black countryside. Yves had told her to come, knowing what it would be like for her, knowing she'd walk into a room of sniggering men. Olga schmoozed happily with a young man who held her drink in one hand as if he were a moveable endtable, and Agatha couldn't begrudge her that. She'd wait out by the garden until her friend had her fill, and they could go back to the grocer together. Olga lived in a room above the store with her aunt and uncle and two younger male cousins. Olga would ask her to stay, but Agatha needed to check on her moss, to record its change for the day. It liked to bloom with tiny ferns at night.

"I believe you had a proposal for me," Yves called from the hearth.

"No," Agatha replied tiredly. "I'm not allowed to marry, so you're in luck."

She walked through the men who parted in a lazy wave, and she made for what seemed like a back door to a patio or garden. When she stepped into the night, the cold lit into her. She shivered, but she wouldn't walk back through that room for her coat. She bit down on her lower lip and endured it. The flowers seemed to tuck in from the frigid oppression of night, and this always fascinated her. There must have been a wife at this house by day. Tulips and purple coneflowers lined a wrought-iron fence that had been painted white. Chips of the paint lay in the dark soil along the fenceline, and she bent and ran her fingers through the loam. It was rich from the river water, and when she brought her hand up, she noticed the dirt beneath her nails, how it never went away no matter how she scrubbed. What was she doing here? What had possessed her to come?

Just then, the door flew open and drunken men stumbled with laughter into the garden, their cigars swirling in spiral staircases above their heads.

"It's you!" one of the men hissed through his laughter, pointing at another man.

"She sketched you!" another almost couldn't manage around his bursts.

Agatha perked. "You went through my coat pocket?" She rose so suddenly from the dirt that the men jumped and snapped their mouths shut.

Yves Jolliet held out her notebook, open to her page from earlier that day. At the top, it read: PHYSIOLOGICAL CHEM. Below, the obvious sketched likeness of Yves, nicely shaded. "I thought you were taking notes." He looked at the sketch with something like affection. "Looks like you've discovered a new species." He pointed to her caption of him and read it aloud, "*Idiotus egotisticum.*" He closed the book and handed it back to her, amused.

"I *have* discovered a new species." She took the book. "And it's not you. You're the same old invasive species we've been uprooting from our lives for centuries."

Yves smiled. "You've discovered a species?" Now there was curiosity in his drunken tone. The men laughed beside him, and he raised his hand and shushed them. "Really?"

"Yes," Agatha said.

"Of?"

"A type of pleurocarpous creeping moss, like a feather moss, but with different patterning. It's the second bryophyte I've found and identified, but this one is … Well, I have a proposal for you."

The men chuckled again, and Yves smacked his hand into a professor's chest next to him. "Clamp it, you lice." He turned quickly back to Agatha, his eyes as bright as the oil lamps inside. "I'm listening."

"I can't—" She studied the men, more chagrined now that they'd been hushed for a woman. "The moss … is converting atmospheric nitrogen into ammonium, then into nitrite and nitrate, as if struck by lightning, but it's through some kind of association, perhaps bacteria of some sort. Not through fire and not from the moss directly, but through this relationship with a bacterium. It is fixing the dry soil and creating nitrogen availability for all the plants around it, even in a drought."

Yves stepped forward. "You've documented this?"

"I have. I mean, I am. It's in progress."

"Show me."

Agatha shook her head. "I can't quite yet, but—"

"Then tell me." He pointed to her notebook. "Is it in there?"

She clutched it to her chest.

"Keep talking, Miss Acton. I'm listening."

"Oh, *now* you know my name."

He reddened and pressed his lips into a thin pucker.

She looked at the line of men, their curious faces all in a row, arranged incidentally by height, like nesting dolls. "I'll take an arm."

Yves offered her one without hesitation, and she looped her arm through his, and he led her down the garden path toward Market Brook that ran beside the house and across the street.

"What kinds of bacteria is it associating with?" Yves asked.

"I don't know. I've identified the bryophyte species to certainty, but I haven't identified the symbiotic relationship yet. See, this is my proposal. I don't have the lab equipment to test it. My prairie lab is insufficient, and you've seen the university lab, murder."

"I thought you were a ladies' gardener? That is what I was told."

She stopped. "Dr. Jolliet. No." She faced him toward her. "I am a botanist and a chemist. I have the highest degrees in the field that I am able to get. Don't cast me off so easily because I'm not ... smoking cigars and drinking scotch in a frock coat."

"Speaking of which." He pulled off his coat and put it around her shoulders. "You ought to be in a frock coat. They've shut up the hells out here." He reached into the pocket of his coat near her breast, and she inhaled. "Would you like a smoke?"

"I would like one, yes, but I cannot contractually have one."

"My, they've got you on a tight leash, haven't they." He put one in his mouth and struck a match on the rough fence surface, and breathed it in and out slowly. "Can I get you a finger at Hotz & Geiger?" His lips bunched tight. "Can't do that, either, then." He lifted his cigarette, ashed it on a bed of stones, and pointed it at her dress. "They make you wear that dress, too?"

"It's the only dress I have."

He cocked a brow, took a long drag, then held the cigarette up to her mouth. "I won't tell."

She looked both ways, leaned forward, and took a puff on it.

The cigarette went back to his lip, and he talked around it, letting it hang. "There," he said softly. "Now it's like we've kissed." Her eyes went wide, and her lip quirked, and he grinned. "Relax. I kid. When we kiss, you'll know it. Now, talk to me."

From down the path behind them, the sound of yelling split the peaceful night, then pounding soles and laughing, then Olga's sharp

Swedish accent, always thicker when she was drunk. "Where do you think you two are going without a chaperone?" she said coyly, and Agatha could see that she lugged behind her the smitten endtable, still carrying her glass of scotch for her, mindful not to step on her crinoline.

Yves' attention went to Olga, and Agatha figured it would stay there, but he didn't even look her up and down before turning back to Agatha.

"Can't we be alone?" he whispered.

Agatha shook her head. "We really shouldn't. I could lose my job. And I need it."

Olga was listing, and she snorted. "Have you two kissed yet? Have I missed the kissing?" She thumped her young professor in the arm. "Darling, I think we've missed the kissing."

Agatha narrowed her eyes. "We've actually just picked up our knickers. You missed the whole canoodling. We went for a skinny dip in the river and a romp in the haybarn."

Olga stared. "I missed all that?"

"I'm a virile young fellow," Yves added. "We were just replenishing with a smoke before we set about to romp again."

Olga looked woozy.

Yves leaned in too close to Agatha's ear. "Let me take you home."

"Dr. Jolliet." His warmth traveled her spine like a prairie fire, and the answer had to be no, for modesty's sake. But ... if she let him take her home, she wouldn't have to spring for a coach.

"I mean, we'll split a seater, on me, and you can show me the moss."

"I need funding," she said bluntly. "I need a proper lab."

He stepped back. "So I am money to you."

"All of you are money to me."

Olga turned to her companion. "I'm feeling ill. I'm going to be sick."

Agatha winced. "I have to help her." She walked toward Olga and lifted her friend's arm over her own shoulder.

"I'll take her home," the young man said.

"*I'll* take her home," Agatha said sternly, and balanced Olga with difficulty.

"I'll take them both home," Yves said, setting the young professor back and escorting the ladies toward Market Street for a coach.

The young man yelled behind him, "You're leaving the party?"

"I've found a better one, Braham," Yves called over his shoulder, and he put his hand on the small of Agatha's back, his fingertips cosseting her waist.

After they'd deposited Olga drunkenly into her bed above the grocer, their coach turned east onto Jefferson toward the park. The Mechanics Academy was an outline of chimneys in the dark.

"That damn bell," Yves said.

"It is a wretched thing," Agatha agreed. "One wonders if the designer had a laugh on us."

Yves slid down on his benchseat and lifted one leg onto Agatha's bench in the cramped space. He lit a cigarette and laid his head back and studied the notebook he had open across his lap.

"Make yourself comfortable," she laughed.

"This all works?" he said, looking at her calculations. "How many times has it been tested?" He handed her the cigarette without looking up at her.

"It needs a second experiment. My lab is not sufficient, so it can only be a hypothesis until I can get a room that doesn't drop sod from the roof onto my samples."

"And you drew these, all these illustrations? They are incredible. We ought to get them in a book. Is there anything you can't do?"

She shrugged. "Play chess."

He smirked. "I'll teach you. Though I may soon find myself against a formidable adversary."

"You'll create a monster."

"Can I see it tonight? The moss."

"That's not appropriate, Dr. Jolliet. It's far too late for convention." She smoked his cigarette and pushed aside with her foot the crate of groceries that kept jostling closer to her leg. When she looked up, he was gazing at her, one hand propped on his temple, elbow out the open window.

"May I call you Agatha?"

"Well." She handed the cigarette back to him, and when he took it, he wrapped his fingers around her hand and caressed it so briefly. "We ought not to." She didn't know how to handle a scientist. He was an open book without any words on the page. His eyes roamed her; he assessed constantly. She imagined he looked for theories and equations on her skin, in the shape of her hips, and his blatant studying was unnerving and warm and shocking and marvelous. How could he be so unafraid to look, just to keep looking? She broke the gaze and picked at a chip of wood on the sideboard. "Not in public, then."

"Not in public."

"Not tonight," she added softly.

"Not tonight."

She watched Park Brook then Market Brook as the carriage rode over the precarious bridges, the ruts of Jefferson Street unholy on her tailbone. The rivulets of Ralston's Creek ran tiny under the street, slow-moving in the cold. The sediment was higher at the brook edge than it had been on her last carriage ride east, and she marked it in her mind to measure by daylight.

"Tell me about you, Aggie."

She looked from the brook to Yves, and the clever man was gone. In his place was a fascinated creature. She could have told him anything, any truth or lie in the known world, and he would have hung inside the words as if an insect ensnared in amber. She slouched unladylike in the seat, drew herself deep inside his frock coat, and he relaxed into her new position like it was home, with one ankle resting against her thigh. It was like an old couple reading on a loveseat, their legs and arms tangled in the small space, pretense gone through years of unraveling it, and she laid her head against the paneling and chuckled fondly. He was already so familiar, his starch and bear-fat pomade scent nesting in her, his sweat and coffee spills from inside his jacket, where the fabric wore softer at his underarms. When he smiled, his mustache rose unevenly on the left side. She lifted one leg up to his benchseat, over the top of his extended leg, and his eyes widened, then went hazy someplace far away. Not tonight, her words had said, but her body said yes to tomorrow and tomorrow and tomorrow.

"You go first," she said, as the coach rattled past Centre Market and over Johnson Street, much slower on these less-traveled parts. "You are a relation of the explorer."

"I am," he said. "He's a great-great something. My family were fur traders in the area originally, then more recently in the settlement of Napoleon, south of here. Traded with Meskwaki and Sauk before we drove them from the territory. My grandfather had a steamboat and made guidebooks that brought people here, all these immigrants." He waved toward Goosetown to the northeast. "And then my father set us up for life with his investments in the Mississippi & Missouri and the Lyons Iowa Central. I come from railroad stock."

The coach's lantern swung shadows across a mound of corncobs used for fuel in front of a log cabin surrounded with Osage orange hedges. Agatha thought about railroad money, how grand that must be, not to worry about a 10¢ block of cheese spoiling on the hot days. Governor's Square came into view.

"What got you into botany?" she asked.

"The hope of meeting pretty girls."

Agatha laughed.

Yves reached across and drew another cigarette from his inside pocket, yearning fingers against her ribs, the curve of her back, the side of her breast. He lingered too long, and she let him. He sat back and put the slim paper in his mouth with purpose. "You?" he said around it, nursing its stubborn tip that didn't want to stay lit by the window. "Past? Future?"

"My future is silly, but simple. I want a botanical museum up on Clinton Street."

"That's not at all silly. What a marvel that would be, out here."

"Other than that, I'm way too far north for anything. I 'visit Cordelia,' y'know?"

"Well, that's morbid."

"There's a lot of moss on her grave."

Yves laughed darkly.

"My father has a soddy on a prairie farm north of North, past Prospect Hill. We came with the Norwegians and Swedes from Ohio Valley a decade or so ago, hence Olga." She motioned back in the direction of the grocer, the way they'd come. "There was a flatulenta outbreak, and we panicked like the best of 'em. I had to leave behind my first notebooks. Father is not a good farmer, so I've parceled out his fields into study lots. If he minds, he doesn't say so."

"I would like to have a brandy with this fellow."

She smiled. "Much good it would do you."

The coach springs creaked and the old wood moaned beneath her like a ghost. She watched a three-story mansion appear through some stand oaks, and it blazed like the sun were rising in its parlor, as if the night had never happened, and now it was morn again.

"You really can't marry?" he said softly.

She shook her head and watched the house grow like a dry fire as they turned onto Governor Street.

"Will you come in?"

Her head turned slowly, involuntarily, toward him as if in a cloud. "That is *your* house?" she whispered.

"There's no harm in coming in. I have Hattie to chaperone us. I'll warn you she's Irish, in case you don't like Catholics, but she'll put you at ease. She's a sweet girl, if too fiery. She makes a mean toddy and will keep mum if you drink it."

"That's your house?" Agatha repeated. "From railroad money?"

"No, the university bought it for me. It was part of my starting bid when they were warring over me. Harvard wanted me to stay, but I thought I'd return to my roots. Not without some incentive, though," he laughed.

She stared at him. She didn't laugh. "How much do you pay Hattie?"

"$1.90 per week. And there's a stable and lands keeper in the barn. $2.77 for Barton, but he's worth it. Works twelve hours a day without a lick of complaint." It seemed to register that her joy was gone as the carriage rolled to a stop in front of the mansion. He quieted. "Come see my laboratory at the back of the house. You don't have to stay."

"How much do you make?" she asked him pointedly.

"Is that a marriage proposal?" he tried to laugh it off, but she didn't crack a smile. "Come, Aggie, we aren't supposed to talk about salary."

"I make $1.46 per week. It takes me two months to buy a barrel of flour if I starve myself of everything else. How much do you make."

"Jesus, Aggie." His eyes couldn't leave the crate of groceries at their entwined feet. The two hadn't moved, and now movement seemed impossible. "$24.37."

She gasped like he'd cut her.

"And ½."

"You make $24.37½ per month!"

Yves met her eyes. "Per week."

She dropped her leg from his seat and bolted upright. A hot rash crept up her neck. It made her lightheaded. She realized she wasn't really breathing, and she focused. He reached out, and she jerked back.

"Don't blame me for that. I fought for it, and they gave it to me. What fool would not take it?" He lowered his leg from her benchseat and tapped his fingers on the windowframe. "Come inside."

Agatha shook her head. "I'd better not. My mother will stay up for my return. She doesn't even know there was a party. Probably got the dogs on my scent trail."

Her voice was colder than she meant it to be, and she knew she was being stubborn. She could go inside. He would be tender. The house would be warm. There'd be a fireplace the width of one wall. Hattie would make toddies.

"Aggie."

"No, Dr. Jolliet."

He sighed and swung open the door and went around to pay the driver to take her up past the cemetery. She heard the exchange through the window. Yves was saying something about not accepting any gratuity from her, when her eyes blurred misty at the bright spots hung there from the house lamps. Her lip quivered, and she breathed in and out, regaining herself, centering. He came around to the window.

"I'll see what I can do about it in the morning." He squeezed her arm that rested on the frame. "Trust that I will." He tried for a smile, but she didn't give it. "Keep the coat. Stay warm."

The lights faded out the window. She watched his silhouette haloed then engulfed, and then the space between them deepened to a ravine until the coach rolled north past the land set aside for Judge Carlton's heirs, then the road to Davenport, then the Agricultural Society Fairground. They followed Governor Street past Goosetown and Oakland Cemetery, and the lines for the Lyons Iowa Central Railroad, until the parcels grew larger and wilder, and the prairies were vast, unbroken swells that rolled like a dark ocean. Her eyes still spotted from the house lamps, blinking into hazy white dots on her lids. Despite the chorus of rattling wood and springs and crickets, the howl of far-off coyote, the silence was paralyzing. She wanted to turn the coach around, go back to his lights and flit against them like a moth. She wanted to be home, in the damp dankness of the familiar soddy. She wanted to go back to life before the party, to what she didn't yet know. She wanted to lie beneath his body. One lone lantern shone behind an oiled-linen window when the carriage made the turn up her drive. She'd curl around her moss, watch the nighttime ferns grow, bury herself in his starch and coffee and soaped-wool coat, and let the dark prairie ocean drown whatever wouldn't buoy.

On the following Monday, Agatha was already sitting in President Amos Dean's sagging wicker chair when he came in. She ceased her slouch and uncrossed her arms. Dean was looking at a file and hardly noticed when he kicked the cuspidor into the side of his desk.

"Miss Acton," he said, pronouncing the name very clearly.

"You wanted to see me, sir."

"I did, I did. Yes. Let's see." He handed her two pieces of paper that were stamped APPROVED at the top. "73¢ for more potatoes." He pointed to the first. "And it has been brought to my attention that you need experiment bottles, so we've taken it upon ourselves to provide a set of those for you."

Agatha stared at the papers.

"We think it is very important what you are doing."

"What am I doing?"

Dean smiled. "That will be all, Miss Acton."

She rose, holding out the papers, as he walked behind his desk and sat, rooting around through objects in his drawer like a hog in mud. "I ... don't understand why you've given me this."

He stopped and looked up at her, smiled thinly. "Sure you do."

When he didn't say more than this, she turned and left the office, closing the door quietly behind her and leaning against it, cradling the budget papers against her chest. She drifted toward the shack as if an unseen pulley moved her forward, and when she opened the door, the darkness consumed her. Her eyes adjusted to the nothingness, and she smelled him before she heard him. Musk soap and pomade.

"Yves?" she said.

"Shhhh," he whispered. "Did you see Dean?"

"I did. What are you doing here?"

"It's the only place I can be with you without prying eyes." He came up to her. "That microscope is an archaic piece. Come use mine."

She couldn't see him, and she reached out, and his face was right in front of her. Her fingers grazed his lips, then she found the back of his head and pulled him toward her, and his lips met hers in the darkness.

"Oh, God," he murmured against her mouth, and he pulled away slowly. "That was not my intention."

"It was mine." Her eyes adjusted to the dark gray, and he circled his arms around her waist and pulled her face into his chest, across his racing heart. "Sewing starts in half an hour."

"I want to see your prairie."

"It's not in here."

"You're getting a raise. Did Dean tell you?"

She pulled back from him. "I got bottles."

"Yes, and you're getting a raise. They approved 50¢, but I bargained for $2, or else I walk out. We'll see what comes of that."

"You put your own job on the line?"

"I did," he said, "but it's nothing. They can take $2 from my salary and put it to yours if they won't budge. They won't let me walk out."

"I'll settle for the 50¢. That would buy me a good many crates of groceries."

"Carriage out to your place after sewing. Eleanor Blakely can chaperone. I won't take no for an answer."

The door to the shack opened in a spray of light, and closed to white darkness all over again, her eyes blinded by it, and he was gone. She leaned against the dirty walls and stroked the papers and smiled to the rotten potatoes, certain they had bred enough life to smile back.

౼

Eleanor Blakely was an old crotchety biddy, a secretary in the armory at the Capitol, and now sitting across from Agatha with hard disapproval etched into the railroad of her jowls. Every time Eleanor glanced away, Yves touched the tip of his pinky to the tip of Agatha's pinky splayed on the benchseat between them, and the two of them held their bellies in tight until they giggled, and Eleanor whipped her gaze back like a hawk homing in on two rabbits at once. Agatha still wore Yves' coat—something else Eleanor disapproved of. But it was cozy, and the wind was sharp through the drawn slats. Agatha saw the countryside go by in thin white lines, and she avoided looking at Yves at all costs. She was flush with embarrassment at her hasty kiss in the shack, and her lips burned bloodheat every time she thought of it. How foolish it had been, to invite him into her like that, to give him so much of what he wanted so quickly. And now to step back and pretend they didn't know what they knew of each other's bodies. The prairie grass looked white as snow. She listened for birds.

When the carriage came down the drive, Agatha wondered who heard it, who saw it. If someone from the homestead would come out to the fields. Her father, worn from chasing the new chickens her small stipend had helped him afford. When the wheels rolled to a stop, Eleanor was the first to step down, and Yves rose behind Agatha and pressed his mouth to the back of her neck. She stifled a laugh and stepped from the carriage with the help of Eleanor, and the three walked toward a tiny sod building in the middle of the field.

"That's where you live?" Eleanor pointed at the soddy.

"No, that's where I live." Agatha pointed far, far across the field to a miniature dot that was a second sodhouse at the curve of the horizon. "That's my father's house. This is my lab." She nodded to the junior version in front of her.

Yves laughed outright.

Eleanor made a sound like a grunting animal.

They came to the soddy, and Agatha suddenly spoke dramatically. Her parents could have heard her across the field. "This is it! We're here!"

Before her was a wide field cut into small lots with crude ditches between each, the numbers of the lots and the north/south and east/west ditchways marked with engravings on white paintsticks. Sections of the land were covered with wagon canvas mounted on tree branches, propping a weather tent over the top.

She yelled again, "We're here!" and stomped hard on the ground.

"I think everyone knows," Yves laughed.

"I want to make sure my ... father knows," Agatha said hurriedly, "so no one comes running with a pitchfork."

Eleanor found a grassy spot on the ground, checked for snakes with the toe of her boot, and sat. Agatha waved Yves over to the moss at the edge of a large mound. She got on her knees and rolled under one edge of the canvas. He watched her and followed suit on the adjoining side, and the two lay at an angle, head to head.

Agatha giggled and whispered, "I feel like a child on the brink of being scolded."

But Yves' face was on the moss, like hers always was, and inside their moment she adored that about him. The wind whipped up around them, and the canvas flapped, but he remained in place, ignorant of the dust that flew onto his face from the fields. He pulled out a magnifier from his pocket and held it to one eye. "*Pleurozium* or *Hylocomium* by the way it branches out from the ribs. Or *Ptilium*, though it's not big enough for knight's plume."

"*Pleurozium*," Agatha said.

Eleanor's voice rang out, "I can't see you under there."

Yves chuckled and whispered, "How naughty! And to think we're only looking at a little moss."

"She's not so little," Agatha said. "She runs through half of this mound. I've tested the mound, and it seems that its soil composition is no different from its environs. I imagine someone brought the spores on a wagon wheel down from Canada in the fur trade, or pioneering through here."

"Or there was a boreal forest that ran down the Iowa River that's gone now."

"Less likely. That was an initial hypothesis, but I've largely ruled it out, insofar as I can rule anything out. The roots don't appear to be structurally past twenty years."

"I like you," Yves said suddenly. "I like you when you talk like that."
Agatha blushed.

Eleanor said again, "I can't see you under there."

Yves sighed. "I'm not brave enough to kiss you in daylight."

"Tonight, then," Agatha whispered. "The ferns will be out."

He rolled out from under the canvas and dusted the soil from his
pinstripes. "The lab." He pointed at the door. "Let's see it."

"Well, wait!" she said, standing quickly. "We're entering the lab!"
she yelled loudly to no one, then turned as if to direct it toward Eleanor.

Yves stuck a finger in his ear. "What is it with you and all this hulla-
baloo?"

"I have to make sure they know."

"Who knows?"

"My ... folks. My family. So they don't think anything is amiss."

He squinted, but followed her into the soddy without protest, and
Eleanor yelled something behind them about keeping the door propped
open. Agatha didn't hear it because Yves let the door slam behind him.
The single room was one enormous table, rough-hewn from mismatching pieces of nearby trees. There were no chairs, not even a stump. An
old woven rug lay over one part of uneven flooring, and the room had
the generous windows that her university shack lacked. The table was
lined with chips of plate glass and ceramic, potato halves and strips of
bark, each containing sections of moss, crosscuts of soil samples, and
cutaway root systems in glass bottles of liquid.

"Beautiful," Yves said, and he bent to look at the samples, how clean
each one was, the notes beside them. As he stood over an open notebook to look at her species comparisons, a gust of wind rattled the little
sodhouse, and a clump of dirt shook from the ceiling and down onto a
root in a glass bottle. "Oh," he said absently.

"Murder." Agatha bent to the bottle notes and wrote across the page
with charcoal: CONTAMINATED 22 SEPTE 55. "Time?"

Yves looked at his pocketwatch. "5:09 p.m."

She wrote it down, then stood on her tiptoes and lifted a canvas
awning over the top of the table, about a foot above their bent heads. "I
told you the lab wasn't sufficient. Now you see."

"I do see. Would $163.73 fix it?"

She stilled, and a corner of the canvas flopped down to the table.
She pushed it aside with her hand and stared at him.

"No, I don't know every bit about you, but I've learned a few things,
poking my nose around where it doesn't belong. Museum spaces and

such." He snapped the cover closed on his watch. "Let's call it research. If I'm going to invest in my future, I've got to study it, no?" The wind picked up and rattled the door, and a scratching sound came from somewhere near the floorboards. "What is that?" He looked down at his feet.

"This soddy is in poor shape. There's an abandoned crawlspace beneath it, and it creaks like old knees when that wind gets going like this." She closed a shutter on the wind-facing window and stomped on the dirt. "I'm waiting for the table to fall through the floor."

"We ought to move this material to my lab."

"It would be just novelty for this material now. I've already written the paper."

"You have?" Yves walked around the table quickly and took her shoulders. "Well, let's get it published. Bring it to me, and I'll let the Society have a look. We'll see what we can do for it."

"You'd do that for me?"

He smiled. "I could try."

Eleanor flung open the door with one hand on her hip. The dirt had creased her frown lines deeper.

The night was dark black and cold and somewhere in the middle of itself, when Agatha heard the gallop. She hadn't known what to expect, but imagined him to ride only in coaches. When the hooves of a single horse pounded the ground, it beat into her spine where she lay, next to her moss. She didn't look. She pictured him there, in the dark, and when at last the beats were close, she could see his horse, its flash of white, the lantern pole that extended from the saddle mount with a lone lamp flickering. He hardly slowed the beast when he dismounted midstride, then he draped the reata around a row of hedges and carried the lantern to her. She lay on a blanket looking up at him. He came to his knees and flopped fast beside her, setting the lantern in the dirt at her head.

"Hello, stranger," she whispered.

"Fancy meeting you in a place like this." Yves scooped her into one arm and held her against him as he rolled to his back to look up at the stars. He pulled the edge of the blanket over her shoulder, though the wind had died to nothing, and the night, still unseasonably chilly, was at least calm. "Will your father see the light?"

She shook her head against his chest. The Milky Way crossed the sky like a healing scar, a purple-green that made the stars whiter. "Did you ever wish you'd studied all that up there instead of all this down here?"

"No," he said. "The land grounds me, quite literally. Gravity is a man's world. Up there is where you believe in gods and deities, comets colliding into balls of fire. Mount Olympus casting grand Titans into depths of hell. Down here, I believe in men. The power and simplicity of hands doing the work."

"And women."

He laughed and rolled toward her. "Pure legend and myth, women are." He put one hand to her cheek, and she closed her eyes. "Don't close them unless you want me to be someone else."

She opened them, and he was there. Her body was liquid where he pressed it, and she let his lips come down over hers and watched his mouth all the while. She wouldn't close her eyes then. Who else could he be? Who would she have him be? This organic matter made from the bellies of stars. The stillness of the night arced around them like a cave. They were so exposed in the field, but enveloped in a grotto that greened and bloomed for only her. When she finally closed her eyes at his lingering mouth, he wasn't anyone else, just a wisp of an idea that was hers but wasn't. A moment she could step inside of, touch its muscled walls, breathe in its breath, but could never live within indefinitely. When he pulled away, she opened her eyes as if they'd never closed, and watched his face soften to butter. His hands shook as he unpinned her hair and drew out long locks into which his fingers entwined.

"You've done this before?" he whispered.

After a pause, she said, "Yes," followed by, "I'm sorry." An apology for being a woman, for having to be pure and not being.

"No, that's relieving." He smiled down at her. "I'm too old to be teaching virgins how to cry."

She laughed, and he rolled and knelt before her, and the stars burned so bright, so vivid in their lanterns swung by the rider of Pegasus, the tender of Equuleus. She'd see the winged horse and not a square asterism, a quadrilateral, two crooked lines for legs and one for a snout. She wanted the wings, just this once, not to know what they were made of, but to fly them. They didn't make a sound. They held in their breaths for each other's ears, and he held her up from the rocks beneath the blanket, and their love was slow and quiet, silent to the night sky, silent to the witness on Pegasus' back. The grotto bloomed into sprigs of feral hyacinth and ramblers of star jasmine that vined around her skin like floss, and his heartbeat pulsed in her teeth. She never closed her eyes until he rolled to one side and she breathed him in. His new scent. And sweat, undeterred by the cold. Her body drummed with the stillness of the night, her heart yet moving wild in it. They lay there, looking up. He touched her pinky with his pinky, and they both giggled, giddy drunk on the fallen night.

Then, an interrupting thump came from the soddy, and this time there wasn't any wind to blame for it. "And now what was that?" Yves shot quickly to his feet and yanked up his trousers. "Is your father spying on us?"

"Wait!" Agatha said, and stood, pulling down her shift, but it was too late.

Shirtless and tousled, he'd flung open the door and held up the lantern, and there were gasps and cries, and he froze in place, the lantern casting light across the small soddy and the three black faces in the corner. The woman held out a knife in front of her, and two small children clung to her skirt.

"Jesus," Yves muttered low.

"Yves," Agatha said, coming through the door and in between them, pressing him back. "Please. Put the light down." She held out her hands in both directions, and the woman lowered her knife.

"You're …" he stammered, "you're runaways?" He blew out the light in the lamp quickly and let the moon fill the windows. "This is a … a depot?"

"Yves," Agatha clung to his arm. "You can't say anything to anyone. Please. I beg you. You can't speak a word of it."

"You never told me?"

"I can't tell anyone. No one knows but who needs to know. Olga doesn't even know."

"I'm so sorry," the woman said. "I didn't know you was. He … he was."

"It's all right, Minta. It's all right."

"Cloe had to relieve herself," Minta said. "I didn't know no one was up here."

"It's all right," Agatha whispered calmly. "Everyone's fine."

"I didn't know, and then I seen that lamp. Oh, Miss Aggie," Minta cried, tears streaming down her cheeks. "I didn't know. I near kilt him."

Agatha went to Minta and hugged her. "It's all right now. No one's in trouble. No one's mad. Of course Cloe can go relieve herself."

Minta wept against Agatha's shoulder. "I never meaned to put you in no danger."

"There's no danger." Agatha looked to Yves pleadingly, as if willing this to be truth.

He made a guttural sound and eyed the uneven floor under the rug. He kicked it back and saw the trapdoor that went down into a crawl-space. An inverted ring lay in the top of the door, and he hefted it up. By the light of the moon, they could all see the dark hole that went straight down. "I'll be," he whispered. He looked up at the crying woman. "It's okay. I won't utter a word. You ... do you need anything? Food or blankets ... or anything I can bring?"

Minta stopped crying, wiping her eyes with a tattered sleeve that left smudges of dirt above her eyebrows. "You won't get sweet Miss Aggie in no trouble, now, will you?"

"No, miss. I'll take it to the grave."

Agatha shook out her fingers. She had never imagined this. This was too much, too close to home. She breathed and held out her hand, steadied herself. "This is Minta, and the little ones are Cloe," she signaled the youngest one, "and Abernathia." She bent down to Abernathia, a girl of six with a slash across one eye from her forehead to her nose. The nostril that crossed the gash was split in two where it had resealed poorly. Her skin was too light to keep her secrets. "Abernathia wants to be a botanist, she tells me. She's had fun with the potatoes," Agatha laughed uneasily and inclined closer to the girl. "You might like to talk to Dr. Jolliet." She held out her shaky hand to Yves. "He's a botanist from the State University of Iowa. He got his Ph.D from Heidelberg University in Germany, the lucky sot."

Abernathia laughed and curtsied. "How does you do, sir."

Yves smiled, but his discomfort was plain. He patted his chest and seemed embarrassed to find it unclothed. "I ... do well, thank you." He looked up at Minta. "Do you have a lantern down there?" He gestured to the dark hole in the ground.

Minta shook her head.

"Take this one." He nudged it across the table and tossed beside it a leaf of strike-anywhere matches from his trouser pocket. "How long have you been down there?"

"The wagon ain't come."

Agatha held out her hand to Cloe. "Come on, sweetie. Let's go out back." She approached Yves and pushed him through the door and out into the night. Cloe ran from her grasp and out to the prairie dropoff behind the soddy, and Agatha faced him. "The wagon is late. It's never been this long before. I'm afraid for them, but I don't know what to do.

I don't know where they're supposed to go. Somewhere north of here, but they don't tell me where. I fear something has happened to the wagon."

Yves didn't respond.

"They aren't ghosts, so don't look as if you saw one."

"That little girl's eye."

"Yes. They all come through like that. Someone beats them; they run. We get them. Someone else takes them from here."

"All? How many have there been?" When she didn't answer, he added, "I said I'd take it to my grave."

"Eighteen, if these girls make it. Minta's just a child herself. She was eleven when Abernathia came. Eleven. It's just not right. You can't say anything, Yves." She took hold of him. "Swear to me on your very soul."

"I won't believe in souls until I can dissect one under a microscope, but I'll swear it on my heart." He took her hand and placed it over his chest.

Cloe came back from the dropoff, skipping up to Agatha, and Yves' face registered frustration. Cloe's arm was dead, dangling useless at her side, twisted like a pretzel stick. It was plain she'd been mishandled by someone.

"Minta was a housewoman," Agatha said, sensing his unease. "Not a field worker. When Cloe was born, she had the family's midwife." Agatha leaned down to Cloe and kissed her on the forehead, combed back her hair. "Go on inside now. It's okay to play upstairs. Just not too loud, okay, sweetie. The sound travels."

Cloe nodded and said some slow words that were indistinguishable. She struggled to get them out, but Agatha still didn't understand them.

"Once more for me," she said. "You want …?" The girl tried again, and Agatha thought maybe she understood. "… to bring up the dolly?"

The smile that lit Cloe's face made Yves turn away.

"Yes, Mama can bring up Dolly. Just don't let Dolly talk too loud to you, okay? Make sure she whispers." She kissed Cloe again, and the little girl ran into the soddy, holding the door all the way to the frame so it didn't slam. Agatha watched after her fondly. "The midwife dropped her. On her head. The child stopped crying instantly; they knew something was wrong."

"And the arm?"

"They didn't want a troubled slave. The midwife tried to drown her in the tub while washing the blood off. Held her down by her arm and snapped it right around. Minta leaped off that cot so fast, blood all over her. The strength of an ox, to hear her tell it, and I don't doubt it. I don't know what happened to the midwife, but Minta's been running ever since. It hasn't been easy with two small ones, and Cloe the way she is."

"What can I do?"

"Sew your mouth shut."

"I'll have to eavesdrop on your women's sewing class," he laughed mirthlessly. "I'd better go." He turned to his horse. "I may have brought attention. I can't risk that for you."

He walked away quickly and mounted and rode off without a lantern, shirtless in the cold, and the night swallowed him so wholly, so suddenly, he appeared to vanish. She looked back up at the Milky Way, and its scar still hadn't healed.

The sun streamed through the window of Park House, where Agatha stood in his shirt and nothing else, brushing out her hair as she studied the small people in the park across Jefferson, lining up for classes at the Mechanics Academy. They were only drab blurs from the third story. She didn't like facing this side; when they were on the north side last week, it had been much safer. The lot on Market Street behind them was still vacant, but to the south, in this view, the cupola of the Capitol loomed one block over, and she could see her unimpressive shack laboratory. Four nights ago, they'd been on the west side, and she could view the Iowa River from their window, watch the drawbridge raised for the steamboats. She realized she'd been counting the nights, documenting them in her mind like a notebook for an experiment that would reach no conclusion.

"Do you think anyone saw us this time?" she said.

"If you stand by the window, they will." Yves rose from the bed naked, holding the polished paper of her work and illustrations he intended to present to the Society, and he walked up behind her. With one hand, he held out the paper, looking over the calculations, and with his other hand, he caressed her hipbone under his shirt, which draped on her like a serape. "I hate this, you know."

"The paper?" she asked, turning only her face toward him.

"No. This." He gestured to the window. "I want those people to know us together. I want them to know. I want them to see what I've found, what I have."

"They won't be jealous of you," she laughed. She put one hand on the curtain and traced a moth hole in the velvet. "You promised."

"I want to stroll with you through that park. You on my arm down the Promenade. Laughing on the decks of a steamboat as we tour Bath Island, my arm around you in public. My hand on your waist. To kiss you where anyone can see. To walk in and out of the front door of a house we share, not sneaking in through the back lab at midnight."

She stiffened, and he kissed the back of her neck until she softened against him.

"I can take care of you. Say the word, and I'm at the courthouse in a boutonnière."

She turned to him. "I want the job. I worked hard for it. It was earned. To teach girls what I know, how to identify their natural world—is everything. When I walk into my museum, I will know that it's been earned. All this while."

Yves dropped his hand like an anchor and looked down. "You should ride out to the prairie and check on Minta, see if there's news of that bloody wagon yet." He dug into his coat pocket on the rack next to them and pulled out enough coins for her to take the carriage. "I've got to dress for work. Society today. But eavesdrop on Botany 2, yes?" He dressed quickly into a clean shirt and left her in his old one, wrapped an ascot around his neck, and pulled on his coat and tophat. "I'm picking up a *Bugle* in the lobby, so give me ten minutes before you come down. I'll save the list of captured runaways for you."

She said nothing as he stopped at the door, counting the lengthy pause in passing seconds. Her brain throbbed the room went so quiet.

"Someday I will want to marry," he said with his hand on the door-knob. "I would like children. To teach daughters how to identify their natural world. Is that not everything, too?"

A dog played in the park, absent of an owner. Running circles after its own tail, barking at a squirrel. Agatha watched it intently, the green of the park fading into a winter brown around its little white body. Where was its owner? She ought to have an owner. The door clicked behind her, and she closed her eyes. When she lifted her lashes, they were wet, and the universe had glassed over with its unshed sovereignty.

༜

When Agatha carried an empty crate back toward the grocer, it appeared there'd be snow by the afternoon. The wagons along the side of Clinton

Street were covered in their double canvases, and the men were checking the shoes of their horses, the ground now harder on them as the cold set in. Agatha hummed the melody of "Annie Laurie" and nodded to each passerby. At the wood façade of the vacant building, she put one hand to the window and stroked it gently, visualized it painted with the museum's sign. She tried the door, but it was locked. Never had she seen the inside but through the window. The whole world was a window, and she could only ever look into it from outside, never out from within—the interior a mystery, a constellation unknown to her, here, on the ground where men simply worked with their hands and no deities cast Titans anywhere. What did it smell like? Could she taste the limestone dust in the air? She figured it best that she not think about it. Most of her savings had gone to Minta, and would until a wagon arrived, no matter how late it was. That was the deal every depot made. The resident busker outside the grocer battled her tune with "On Top of Old Smokey," and she handed him a penny on her way into the store, then that song was immediately stuck in her head instead.

"Aggieeeeee!" Olga shrieked and twirled around the edge of the counter and kept twirling all the way to Agatha until she bumped into the crate and took it from her friend's hands. She kissed Agatha once upon each cheek.

"I have news," Agatha said.

"When is the big day? Please say you'll wear something brighter than that old thing." She waved at Agatha's black dress and set the crate on the stack of them. "I want to be your maid. It's only fair. I've known you longest."

"We're not together. For the last time."

"If you want to lie to them, that's fine," Olga said crossly. "But don't lie to me. I can see when you're hiding. Don't you read me a headline, dear."

"We're not together," Agatha repeated with less conviction. "No, I have real news."

"Well, I have news!" Olga said.

"All right, you go first." Agatha knew that Olga would anyway.

"Aunt Freja thinks it would be a good idea for me to have my own land. For when my own big day comes with Dr. Braham or whoever."

"Are you still with Dr. Braham? From that horrid party weeks ago?"

"Sometimes on weekends. Listen, though." Olga rifled through a basket of onions. "These yellow ones is on sale." She put one in Agatha's hand. "Freja says I need a land plot, and she's urged Ira to purchase the one right next to your father's prairie, on the cemetery side, nearer the city. We wouldn't be right side-beside, but I figure you'll be at your da's until you're an old spinster, so we'll be neighbors!"

"That's ... capital."

"Capital!" Olga laughed heartily, and a clean-suited gentleman peeked from the powdered milk cans and frowned at her. "Oh, you go on! Rattle your cans, old man!" She plugged Agatha in the rib. "Capital! Listen to you. When you tire of your da's do-this and do-that, you can come over and sew bootlets with me and be a godmother to a bunch of squirmin' Swede bubs." She'd affected the accent for laughs, but she dropped it when a handsome gentleman came into the store. "Good morning to you, Mr. Strohm." She turned back to Agatha. "I'm done. What's your news?"

"They're publishing my paper."

Olga's eyes flew wide, and she squealed loud as a child's whistle. She grabbed onto Agatha's shoulders and jumped up and down, forcing her friend to jump up and down, too. "That is ... oh, Aggie!" She kissed her again on both cheeks. "That is licked cream, I tell you. I thought the journal didn't allow ladies? Is it a different one than that, um, letters one?"

"No, it's the *Journal of Letters*. They don't allow ladies ... *yet*." Agatha smiled and almost choked on her words. "I'll be the first."

"Oh," Olga rasped out. "Oh, oh." Her face crinkled like a newborn's, and tears escaped her eyes. "Oh, Aggs."

"Stop that." Agatha swatted her. "You'll get me started on it."

"How?"

"Dr. Jolliet is a member of the Society. He showed them my paper and illustrations and brought in my samples. They looked into taxon experts, and found that mine appears to be a new species, with acceptable measurements and details, and they're excited about further study on the potential bacterium. This paper could get me funding to investigate a possible nitrogen-fixing parasite that causes the soil nutrients." She waved a hand. "That part is high talk. Unimportant. The point is it's nigh impossible for women to get considered, but they were all hopeful and agreed it should be published right away. It should make the November issue."

Olga still cried. "What do I say to that? That is an ace." She wiped the tears with her sleeves. "I mean, it's ... capital."

Both women laughed and embraced hard and Agatha held the yellow onion tight in one hand. The men in the store stared at them, but

Agatha didn't care. How could she care? She'd be their equal in weeks. *Weeks.* She wanted to tell them that. To wave the paper in their smug faces. Weeks that would both fly by on the tail of a swallow and crawl on the belly of a snail.

☙

Those weeks did not fly on any tail. The wagon never came. Minta was losing her mind with fear, and Agatha's message to the conductor was unanswered, lost somewhere in the ether. Had he been found out? Lynched? Had it been intervened? For the last two weeks, she'd given her entire $2 raise to Minta instead of investing it in the museum, and Yves delivered baskets of fresh bread and soup stock on his personal carriage well before dawn, to avoid detection. But Agatha feared the patterns. Every time she saw the Jolliet family crest on the back of his carriage, her heart slapped her ribs with dread. Whenever she heard a bloodhound in the city, she looked northward to her homestead, her stomach in her throat. The Fugitive Slave Law had been in place for the past five years; to harbor them meant a trial, confiscation of land, losses of jobs and wages and possessions. Sometimes there wasn't a trial at all if the wrong finder got there first. And the slaves were shipped back on wagons. Hundreds of dollars to track them down, just to bring them back to kill them as an example for others who thought about following their fateful lead. There was reward in being an informant. Someone would take notice of the patterns.

But today, Agatha let this go. She knew Olga sat outside the door to the university shack, holding a copy of the *Journal of Letters.* She'd given her $2.03 to fetch a copy, and she could hear Olga cuss at passersby who scoffed at her for eavesdropping on the sewing class. Damn the Mechanics bell for not being early today. Some pranksters had upturned it in the night, filled it with water, and let it freeze and crack. Now the tinny, shrill thing wouldn't ring, so it couldn't be early. Yves had left their Park House hotel room before she woke up. Last night, they'd slept on the west side again, and they'd watched the cold river burst into whitecaps along Bath Island from their high terrace, where they'd wrapped together in one single hotel robe and laughed at the walkers on the Promenade who never knew their silly antics were being witnessed. That was as close as they could come to being public. She knew he'd already been the first to read the journal that morning, and she admitted disappointment that he hadn't rushed right to her with his copy. He must not have truly known what this meant to her. Which was fine, she reasoned. How on earth could he know? Or he was embarrassed for her that the university made her purchase a copy with an entire week's wages, and wouldn't foot one for her. As the girls made their last brocade stitches on their baby blankets for their future hope chests, the Capitol bell finally rang, and Agatha ran around blowing out the candles before the rush of bodies could knock them over.

"Wait for your chaperone!" she called as they went toward the Capitol. She popped her head out at Olga, and smiled wide. "Well? Did you find it? It's called 'Identification of a *Pleurozium* cryptogamic species and study of nitrogen-fixing parasite associated with feather moss varieties of the Iowa prairies' or something like that. Dr. Jolliet said the journal decides the title, so—"

"Yes, I found it," Olga said flatly. "'Identification of a new cryptogamic bryophytic species, *Pleurozium actonius*, and the study—'"

"*Actonius?*"

"Yes. 'Commonly named Actonia,' it says."

"The journal named my own species after me?" Agatha creased her forehead.

"I don't think the journal did." Olga held the page out for her. "I think the author did."

"But I didn—" She stopped when her eyes landed on it. Her lungs slipped through her pelvis. Underneath the title, the author: DR. Y. L. JOLLIET, F.R.S., PH.D, ESQ., and furthermore: DR. E. P. BRAHAM, F.R.S.; F. F. HARTZFELD, ESQ.; &C. Agatha stared at the printing. She willed the words to change on the page. "No," she muttered. "No, no, no." She shook her head and looked up at Olga, and a tear was streaming down her friend's cheek.

"I won't be marrying Dr. Braham," Olga said angrily.

"This can't be," Agatha said, her voice so shaky that the words barely left her. "This is my work. These are my words, verbatim." She held it up. "I wrote this!"

"I know you did. I seen it in your handwriting."

"This is not real. This is not real." Agatha pinched herself on the arm. "They can't do this to me."

"They can, though, love," Olga said, rubbing the spot on Agatha's arm where she'd pinched hard enough to turn the skin purple. "They can, and they always have, and they will keep doing."

Agatha looked at the tears in Olga's eyes, how long she'd been sitting there crying while Agatha reveled in possibilities in a dark shack.

She snapped the journal against her thigh like a gutwhip and turned for the Capitol. She took the steps in twos, petticoat be damned, and she launched past the reverse-spiral like she'd found Pegasus' swift wings dragged down from the stars to her own heels. At the bend of the hallway, she swept a bucket of softsoap off the table, and it clattered onto the floor, and she didn't even stop at the door to his classroom. In one motion, she flung it open, and it smacked against the limestone. The boys in the classroom jumped, and she stormed in.

"You son of a bitch," she said, raising the journal toward Yves.

"Class dismissed!" he said brusquely, clamping his textbook shut, and he spun toward her and held up his hand. "You will wait." The boys filed out, and he watched them leave, never looking at Agatha. He passed her and ran his hand down the crumbled hole she'd made in the wall and closed the door quietly. He turned. "Now, you may light into me."

"Oh, may I? I have your permission, do I? You've been planning your retort, your calm, all day, yes? For weeks?" She held out the journal at him. "This is mine. You are nowhere in it. And Braham, Hartzfeld? What in Columbia did they have to do with it? I don't even know them!" She choked on a lump in her throat, but she wouldn't cry. "You ... slept with me ... by my side for weeks. And never said a thing. Never tried to reason this, or prepare me ... knowing what this moment would be. You knew!"

"Aggie."

"Don't you call me Aggie. I am Miss Acton to you. Show me some goddamn respect. I've never even met you. I don't know you at all."

"You have nothing but my respect," he swallowed with seeming difficulty, "Miss Acton."

She lifted the paper again, right in front of his eyes. "And this is your respect? This is how you repay me for letting you into my life, into my notebook, my bed? You can take your respect and jam it in a shoe on its way up your ass, is what you can do with it."

"It wasn't about you. It was a decision I wasn't in the majority of. It was not meant to be personal."

"Not personal? Well, it feels mighty personal to one person in this room." When he looked away, she yelled, "Look at me! I am a person. A real, alive person. What I feel *is personal*. Don't you see me as a person?"

Yves didn't answer, then he took a deep breath when she didn't follow it up with anything else. "Are you done? Will you hear me now?"

She lowered her head, and a sob came against her will. "You took my work. You put your own stamp on it. Can I have nothing that is mine? You had to make it yours, a man's. Just like every other man's idea in all of time before us." A bigger sob came, and she bit her lip to keep it in. She would not cry in front of him. She would not give him that.

He was quiet and waited for her to get anything else out before he leaned against one of the student desks, crossed his arms, and tucked in his chin as if studying the legs of his own desk in front of him. "I don't know what you expected me to do. You gave me knowledge the world needed. Knowledge it needs *now*. The Society doesn't admit women. They don't promote the ideas of women, nor do they particularly like them when women come up with them. I pushed this past them because it is new and fresh, and they took it and marched it out under their flag. The journal doesn't print the studies of women. Ladies studying botany is considered a frivolous activity for those with too much time. Your work wouldn't be taken seriously with your name on it. This school didn't hire you to teach botany! They hired you to sew! This," he gestured at the journal in her hand, "is the best that can be offered. Or you could wait a hundred years for someone to find it in a drawer after your death and maybe publish it then ... or maybe not? Maybe the Society admits women in a hundred years, maybe not. Who knows. Who cares! This is now. This is it. That it's out there for the world."

"And you got a check for it?"

"Ack, money! It's all that's important to you."

"Money is only unimportant if you have it."

"I offered you a life of it!" he yelled. "You can have the check. I don't want it."

Agatha snorted. "How noble of you." Her voice fell to a whisper, "I gave you my heart."

He looked hard at her. "You didn't, though."

She stilled.

"I won't say the word to you, Aggie. It does me no good. You're not mine. You never will be. You won't marry me. You won't be seen with me. I won't father your children. What does it matter?" He shrugged. "What does it matter if I'm awful? If I lied? If I knew something I didn't tell you? If I'm the wretched of the earth? What does it matter if I held on to the little sliver of you that I had as long as I could because I knew it would be gone in one flash of a second? What does it matter if I love you or don't, or did, or never or ever will?" He stopped leaning and pulled himself upright. "You chose $2 over me. You chose that paper," he thumped his finger on it twice, "over me. So there it is. I took it from you. I took what you wouldn't give me. Because I can't sneak around in one more hotel room. Because I can't keep loving a secret. Because that paper was demanded and expected of me, and all you ever demanded of me was to keep my mouth shut. So there it is." He thumped the paper again. "My fucking shut mouth. I'm sorry. It's there, and I can't take it back. You can have my broken heart, and I can have yours, and we'll call it a draw."

She stared at him, her jaw tight. "Your whole Society knew, and let it happen?"

"It was their idea."

Tears finally fell, but she wiped them away.

"I didn't have a choice."

"You did," she said unsteadily. "You have never had to do a thing in your life without the luxury of choice. You don't know what it means not to have a choice, to have someone else decide for you." She spread out the page of the journal she'd been crunching. The copy she'd purchased with her own wages. She laid it down on the desk in front of him, and smoothed it out with one hand. "Now you get to choose how to live with it." She stood straighter and came to him, his face she'd once wanted this close, the smell of pomade. "Goodbye, Dr. Jolliet," she said softy. "I wish you luck." Then she turned and walked through the door and didn't slam it, and behind her, she heard his heavy sigh and the thud of a chair as he slumped in it.

She decided to be calmer. If she wanted President Dean to listen, she'd be calmer. Her knock on his door sounded civil, she thought, but no one inside told her to open it. She stood there and knocked again. Finally, she opened it quietly and stepped inside.

"You didn't hear me knocking, sir?" she said.

"I heard you," Amos Dean replied, not looking up at her.

"I would like to file a formal complaint against Doctors Jolliet and Braham, and Mr. Hartzfeld. I'm sure you know why. It seems I was the last one to know."

He looked up at her. "You don't want to do that, Miss Arton."

"It's Acton, sir."

"Sit."

"No, thank you, sir, I'd rath—"

"Sit," he said louder.

Agatha sat. Her leg shook, and she crossed her hands in her lap to keep them from shaking, too.

"Miss Arton," he said, leaning back in his seat. "You've caused us a great many problems this school year. We've tried to be accommodating. Gave you a raise, ordered your supplies, though it put us over budget. Gave you a bot-a-ny class," he said sarcastically. He stood and came around his desk and sat on the edge of it. "Look into my eyes."

With great effort, Agatha did.

"You don't want to file any complaints against Doctors Jolliet and Braham, and Mr. Hartzfeld."

"They took my work."

"That's not how I understand it. And that's not how the Royal Society understands it. That won't be how the board or the courts understand it." He opened the copy of *Journal of Letters* that he had on his desk, the page already bookmarked. "It says here, plainly, '&c.' You are in the &c., so no one will see your grievance as anything other than selfish. Unladylike behavior. Caterwauling. You'll bring a lot of shame to our university, which took a chance in hiring you. You aren't as experienced as Dr. Jolliet. We aren't going to fire him and replace him with you, if that is your fantasy."

Agatha drew in a breath. "I only want what's fair. I want this piece redacted, and I want my name on it. If I have to split authorship with Dr. Jolliet because I'm female, then ... fine. But Braham and Hartzfeld? I don't even know them, besides two passing scowls."

"They are earning publication credits. It was a favor from the Society."

She jerked her head up. "Perhaps I would like to earn publication credits, sir, for my own work?"

"Miss Arton." He stood and loomed over her, then came uncomfortably close to her face with his own. "What do you think the board would say about you smoking cigarettes in dark carriages with your male colleagues?"

She exhaled sharply.

"Attending a professors party, when you are not a professor?"

"That's not fair."

"Life's not fair, dear. Surely you've heard that adage." He walked back around to his desk. "Drop this little grievance, or perhaps the board would like to know about certain goings-on in various rooms of the Park House? Do you think they'd be sympathetic to learning of your affair, your very intimate partnership, with the distinguished colleague you are now trying to say was not a partner?"

Heat crept up Agatha's neck.

"Or what if they learned of certain ... other things?"

"Other things?" she asked fearfully. "What other things?"

"Perhaps you can fill in some of this picture on your own. I'll let you think about it before I give you the complaint form."

"Other things?" Oh, God. Minta and the children. The soddy. He knew. Someone had found out the patterns. Someone knew. Her heart slammed against her insides, and her breath grew ragged. Her eyes flitted about the room, seeking something to land on that made sense. Dear God, not the children. Sweat formed on her palms, and she stepped backward toward the door.

"Do you wish to file a formal complaint now, dear?"

"No." Agatha stood stock straight. "I wish to ... I wish to turn in my formal resignation. I will no longer work for men who do not support my work. You can't threaten me. You can't chase me out." She breathed fast and hard and wiped her palms on her dress. "I quit."

"You what?"

"I quit."

Her back was at the door, and she threw her butt against it and pushed it open and was through it like a shot. She tore down the hallway toward the entrance, not even registering that Yves came down the hall after her. He caught her arm and turned her to him, and she clawed at him.

"You said you'd take it to the grave!"

"That I'd take what to—oh, God."

She slapped his face, and he caught her hand. "How could you tell him?"

"Dammit," he seethed, "I said nothing! I've never told anyone anything at all about you, or them, or any of it! Listen to me," he took her in his arms like he used to do so softly, but now it was desperate. "I've done a lot of despicable things. And I'm not too proud of myself today. But I've never told your secrets. Or *our* secrets." He shook her. "You think what you want about how I am and how I feel, but whatever anyone knows, it didn't come from me. I swore it on my heart, and that's something you still own."

"You told them about the hotel," she said.

"Never."

"They know about Minta! Oh, dear God, dear God!" She broke from him and ran for the door. She heard him curse behind her, and his footsteps pounded down the hall, and she was out the door and down the steps and running onto Iowa Avenue.

Olga yelled for her and ran behind her, but Agatha couldn't stop. She heard Yves shouting from the Capitol steps, but her brain screamed over the top of him, and she sprinted. She would run the whole three miles. She wouldn't stop until she died on the street. The cold icepicked her lungs, and she cut through the park and onto Jefferson, over Market Brook and through Centre Market. Her heart was bursting. Her lungs burned. Carriages passed her, and she patted her pocket, but she had nothing. She'd left it behind, all of it, all of him. She stopped and panted at Johnson Street, her head between her legs, and she vomited on the dirt path. Her guts tightened, and she gasped with the agony, but she sprinted again. A carriage would be faster, but there were no carriages in sight now, even if she had money. She took a shortcut through Thomas Snyder's yard and Arbor Square, then through Secretary of State McCleary's pumpkin patch. Shriveled pumpkins twisted beneath her footing, and she fell knee-first onto a sharp one. She swore, and her lungs heaved vapor, and she hauled herself up. There was blood on her palms, and her knee cramped, but she made it onto Lucas Street and through the alleyway of Goosetown. Her cramp hit her hard on Church Street, and she dropped to both knees and pounded the dirt, then seethed at her split hands. The afternoon sun blazed and reflected off some residual drifts of snow, and she put her hand to her stomach. She'd be sick again. Minta. How could he? she asked. He didn't, she answered herself. He didn't. Someone else did. Eleanor Blakely? Who? Who followed them? She jerked herself up on a wooden fencepost and limped slower through the cemetery. *No, please.* She crossed Ronalds and Brown and North at a drag, but she'd keep going. Keep going. *No, please.* She vomited again on the prairie and could see far out into the white oceans of grain that waved as if they weren't witnesses to a single thing. How long had it been? Had she run for half an hour? Where was her land? She saw shapes, and then she heard it. Bloodhounds, still far off. Still far off? Voices. She swooped to her good knee and lifted her dress, and her bad knee was torn, bloody at the crease. It ached. She ran. He hadn't told. Were there bloodhounds? She screamed in her throat, and it was lodged in her head. She loved him. There were bloodhounds. How could he? Locusts leaped on her dress, her hair, into her split hands, and she swatted them away. Her ears were white hot and bleeding, and she ran.

And then she saw the soddy laboratory. The shapes moving. Maybe a gunshot? Or was that her bones smacking against the resistance of winter dirt? She came up again, and the shapes moved swiftly, and she couldn't see them plainly, but she could hear hoof beats. Behind her. Mounted riders? In a blink they would be there before her. In a blink. But she saw the shapes moving, a carriage. Someone running. Who had told? Eleanor? She fell into the dirt and vomited again. Minta. Cloe. Abernathia. Their forms were gone, and a carriage had kicked up dust, and her father stood outside the soddy with an Enfield rifle-musket. Agatha crawled toward him on her hands and knees, sobbing, and a woman—her mother?—threw buckets of well water onto the kicked-up dirt. The great white wave of the prairie drank them down, and a red-headed teenager blocked the sun on Agatha's face, and helped her to her feet. Agatha's hands went to her stomach.

"What have you done with them?" she rasped.

The girl answered in a thick Irish brogue, "They're gone now. They are safe."

"Gone where?"

"North, lass," she pointed. "To Canada."

"But there's ... bloodhounds," Agatha panted and couldn't let go of her midsection. It was like a mule had kicked her. "Riders."

"Aye," the girl said, "for some unfortunate others. Not comin' this'a way. And won't find nothin' but prairie. We made sure of it. They're in a hidden benchseat. No one will ever see 'em crossin'. They'll have to get through me granny first," she laughed. "Good luck."

Agatha looked for the coach, but it had disappeared into the stand of trees at the edge of the prairie, and from there, it was wilderness. Wheels could turn anywhere. Streams would part tracks, and winds would blow grasses back in place. Agatha's mother still fanned the dust until it settled, and her father now scraped the tracks with a rake.

"Who are you?" Agatha asked.

"I'm Hattie."

Agatha put her hands on her knees and bent and vomited and stood and gasped out a laugh. "Of course you're Hattie. Of course you are." She dusted off her dress, wiped her mouth with the back of her hand, and looked at her split palms. "I'm sorry if I got some on your shoes." Off in the distance, bloodhounds and horses still sounded for some unfortunate someone else.

☙

Agatha Acton discovered the moss in 38-Lot the day a band of slave-holding Missourians laid siege to the Wakarusa River Valley, over the Territory of Kansas entering as a Free State. She read about it in the *Bugle*, and then squatted over her prairie grass and identified a new species of moss growing in the turkey foot. Olga recorded 5:32 p.m. in the notebook between them, followed by Agatha's best guess at the coordinates, 41.67, -91.52. Agatha came within an inch of it, her eyes wide, one pupil nearly touching it, and then she marked the moment with a hand on her abdomen. The movement inside was only a flutter that did not have a name, a secret in a life of secrets, a heart beating in a trail of broken ones. *Spreading prostrate growth habit. Unbranched. Little mounding in the colony.* Her insides swelled like they were pumped with air, and she dragged her fingers through the crumbly soil. What a beautiful little creature.

"And do you know what I think?" Olga said. "I think it is better this way. I know it's not what you want to hear, but here is what I think."

"What do you think," Agatha said, half-listening.

"My father used to say, back in Ohio, that it didn't matter who got credit for something, as long as it got done. And I sometimes imagine, how wonderful a city would be, a world would be, you know?—if no one cared who got the recognition for what was accomplished. If we just did it for the good of mankind, instead of the pride of it."

Agatha looked at Olga and watched her measurements carefully.

"I mean, it's out there now, and think of the good it will do. It's named Actonia. Think of that! No one will ever care who discovered it, but generations from now, people will look out at their fields and say, 'My, what beautiful Actonia!' You're the one they'll remember."

Agatha laughed, "It's a moss, Olga. Generations from now, people will be stepping on it."

"Then what does it matter anyway?"

"Well, we can say that about everything."

"But the good of mankind—"

"—is not in who gets credit, but how we use what we know for the knowledge of all. I know, I know. You are right. I gave it to the world; that's all that matters. If it had to channel through a man to be heard, then, well. That's just where we still are." Agatha wiped her brow. "That's why I miss teaching the girls. Because I believe that someday this will not be where we are. And if I can't get there, then I want to push them there instead. A little closer."

"Have you heard back from Female College?"

Agatha shrugged indifferently and stared down at her new moss. "Well, it's something."

She nodded. "It's something. I can't imagine there's a better candidate."

"No, though they do like to avoid scandal."

Agatha looked across the prairie and watched the glumes of wheat dip then stand, dip then stand. "Odd that I'm a scandal, isn't it."

Olga laughed. "It is, a bit. Though I know you too well to think it's not been a long time coming. I got to get to the store. You?"

The two women pulled a canvas over the research area and walked toward Governor Street, dirt on their coats that they didn't bother dusting off. Agatha felt queasy, but she hid it behind a little cough, and two miles in, Market Street was bustling, and then Clinton Street was full of Mormon handcarts and wagons offloading supplies for the reconstruction of the new Presbyterian church in place of one that had recently burned.

The women parted ways at Market, and Agatha walked to her empty storefront. She meant to put her hand to the glass, to feel its lifepulse through the old limestone, but she stopped short. The sign in the window had flipped, and it now read: SOLD, and she felt the vacancy inside her like it had been carved out. She put her fingers on the glass, and nothing moved but the flitter inside her. It had been weeks since she'd been here. She didn't have enough for it anymore, without income, and now someone else would paint a sign in a fancy arch across its window. All for the best, she reasoned. Dreams could start over in a different time and place. Futures could happen anywhere. As she turned to go, she noticed shadows inside, and she looked to the door, and it was propped open with a rock. Work had already begun on the new interior, and she smiled to herself, hummed a line of "Annie Laurie," stepped over the rock, and entered the world she'd always seen from the outside looking in.

Boxes lined one side with light fixtures, small chandeliers covered in sheets to keep the dust away while the limestone ceiling was sanded down in the rough spots. She looked up at it, the dust in virga shafts like slow rain. On the other side of the room, glass display boxes lined the wall, some stacked precariously where a mover had set them. A light glowed from a rear room, and she realized she'd never seen what was back there. She walked toward it, and her foot hit a tin sign leaning against the table mount. She turned it and lifted it. Her chest felt riddled with buckshot.

"I know it's not much to look at yet," a voice said from the doorway, "but it's owned free and clear, and there's a generous funding grant coming through for the monthlies, so you don't have to take the money from me if you want nothing to do with me."

Agatha sucked in through her teeth and kept looking at the sign. A cane clicked on the floor behind her.

"There's nothing I can say to make anything right again," he said, "but there's a classroom in the back, and you can hold workshops and teach girls how to identify their natural world." He cleared his throat. "I hear that's everything."

Agatha finally unfuzzied her vision and read the sign in her hand. ACTON BOTANICAL MUSEUM.

"I won't come around." He clicked his cane again. "Unless you … want me around."

"Are they safe?"

"They're safe."

"So it was your coach."

He walked up behind her and held out his hand. "I've got something to give you."

When she pulled her palm away, it held two keys.

"The door sticks, but it works." He sighed. "We both know I've … made some bad choices. But you were never one of them. After you left the university … I just. Well, I figured I'd just pick a place to start, and start. Give something back to you that I took."

In the one glass case that had been mounted, she saw a tiny fossilized moss, alone in the center of it.

"I wanted to make the first contribution to the museum," he said, pointing at it.

She didn't know what to say to him. The man she'd known was gone, or hiding in the sheets of a hotel room somewhere far off. She heard him light a cigarette behind her, and she smelled the smoke of it as it curled the room like a parade streamer. The next thing she knew, the cigarette was held out to her, and she took it and put it to her mouth, and she tasted his sour-sweet again.

"And the other key?" she said.

"The back door of my laboratory off Governor Street."

She smiled faintly. Always the back door. But there didn't have to be any back doors now. She could walk into any land through the front door with her head held high. She could love him. She could hate him. It didn't matter. All that mattered was the good of mankind in the end, the knowledge she gave, no matter the channel. She felt what he'd given her kick inside her, and she could tell him or never tell him. She stared into the glass and saw their two reflections in it. Her, over here. Him, over there. A space between them only feet apart. It could grow wider. It could be crossed. A tiny pinky could make a bridge. A step to the left could coulee a river. She squeezed the keys in her hand, his olive branch, and slid them into her pocket. The back door to his laboratory entered through into the parlor and then into his bedroom. And then out the front door again, forward. Or back. And there, two reflections muddied into a glass, and she imagined it, rows and rows and rows of them on display, the two of them, in miniature, replicated, and Actonia with labeled placards, and a workshop where she'd teach her daughter how to identify her natural world. There, his feet a moss that branched outward, and hers a bacterium that bled lifegiving nutrients to the soil occupying the space between them. Empty, but she could cross it. Or she could not. This time, the choice was hers to make.

ONE NIGHT, WHEN THE
BREATH OF AUGUST BLEW HOTTER

"It isn't as if you liked him. I hardly think you can feel sorry that he's lying six feet under."

"He's not exactly six feet under," Richard said to the haughty woman, as he tugged on her dead husband's limp arms and battled to keep the overcoat sleeves from slipping free. The battle lost, the dead man's arms dropped from the sleeves, and a pocketwatch fell from the pocket, bouncing off Richard's polished wingtip, splattering mud droplets up his spats. Its *tick-tock-tick-tock* amplified in the darkness, the sound thudding against Richard's chest like Elda's heartbeats.

Elda. What a dame. Any man would die for her, and one did. *What a dame; what a shame*, Richard had always said. Yet, here he was, lifting Elda's fourth husband into an early grave without the bravery of questions. He watched her clench the shovel like she would a man's heart, twisting its handle, jabbing it into the ground with repeated blows. His heart hurt from the careless repetitions, hurt like a heart would hurt if she squeezed it or drove a shovel through it.

As he turned, he glimpsed a flat object leave her hand and wing through the air and land with a soft thud inside the grave. He squinted to make it out, a shadowy square, then looked at her, and one eyebrow rose on the face that lit like a hovering star.

"What was that?" he asked and threw a shovelful of dirt on it, then another.

"A souvenir."

Dawn creased the horizon by the time he'd kicked the last batch of dirt and leaves over the hidden grave. Streaks of light parted the trees like physical fingers, and Richard panted, wiped his brow, and could see the sweat on the back of his hand. They had to leave. The spot had been carelessly chosen, he saw now, the road rather closer than he'd remembered.

"You didn't like him," Elda whispered again.

"No." He mopped his face with his cuff. "No, I never liked the man." There again, the *tick-tock-tick-tock* repeated like a creature scratching initials into tree bark, and Richard eyed the timepiece resting near the toe of his shoe. "Might I have this watch?"

"For memories, Rick?" she chuckled coldly. "Old times' sake?"

"For payoff," he returned. "Lord knows I'm not getting what was promised from you. So you oughta think real hard about keeping me quiet."

Elda raised a brow and her pretty lips curled. Void of thought, her hands clenched tighter on the shovel. She liked that pocketwatch.

"I'm going for my coffee at the Depot. Have to keep routine." He dropped the watch in his coat pocket and patted it, then patted his pockets further. His face scrunched. He felt his breast pockets, then his inside pockets, then his outer ones again. Only the outline of the watch, but not ... Where was ... It was empty. He dipped back into the pocket where it should be, then looked up at Elda.

She winked, then dropped the shovel, turned, and stepped lightly through the woods until her form disappeared. He stared at the mound like it would awaken, so much more obvious in the brightening light, and the blue of an Amilcar passed through the mouths of trees along the road. He stared and stared down at the grave. *A souvenir.*

IN NAME ONLY

*P*rologue.

The last straw was the night Molly Sleight's uncle informed her that the paper was filed, and she was now his wife. Her father's brother said such as she stood vulnerable in a stall, her soft shoes ruined in muck, and a muckrake tight in her hand. He said she ought to have known it was coming, the way he'd taken to her. He said she had no other prospects, out there, a hundred miles from anywhere. He said she was nothing since her family had died of the scarlet fever. He said she was a heretic so didn't none of it matter. He said a lot of things while she stood there with her muckrake, gripping it as if it were the broomstick she wished would whisk her away like the heretic she was, then, if she was.

It had been a hard season for soil. Beans were stunted and worthless, and he said he needed children to labor the fields to come. It didn't matter where they came from, whether ordered in catalogs or from the only surviving daughter of his dead brother. Her uncle had already kidnapped a boy from some town, evaded the law and the papers in the middle of this nowhere until it became a nonstory, the grieving parents abandoning the search and blaming Indians. As Molly stood in the stall, the boy Antrum picked stunted beans in the blighted field. She'd been told to pretend Antrum was her son, though Molly would have had to have birthed him at nine for the ploy to work, for the boy was nearing nine himself. He couldn't run off because he didn't know where he was. Neither did Molly. There wasn't a town in any direction. There wasn't anything in any direction but sunset and sunrise again. She gripped the muckrake.

Damn, but they were suspicious of him, Nathaniel Rounder thought, sloughing off another stinkeye with a grimace. There had been a slew of goings-on: A robbery at Marter's Savings & Loan. Someone picking clean the shelves of the general store. Walker Stout had invested in three expensive mirrors to keep the pickers at bay. Did anyone know how hard it was to procure mirrors out here? If they didn't know, they soon learned after talking to Stout for any minute longer than the length of a salutation. And maybe they were all suspicious everywhere, and of everyone, but for some reason, they were most suspicious of a man who wasn't yet married. Like he didn't have the guiding hand of a good woman to set him right. Nat assumed he'd have to remedy that soon, but wasn't a girl in town he didn't already dislike.

He watched the coach from the feed trough where he filled his old nickelsack. It was the mail coach, but it held two passengers. *Must have picked them up in the desert,* he assumed, and he watched a young woman step down with a child too old to be hers. Scarlet fever, no doubt. She was now the caretaker of a young brother straggling along behind. They were both a mess. But then, so was he. He lifted his nickelsack and walked a few steps closer before deciding better of it. A woman would be bad enough. He didn't need a boy to care for, too. And he hadn't paid his nickel.

Molly stood before the clerk in the courthouse, one large dilapidated sod room with a dozen straightbacked wooden chairs, his interlocking-log desk in one corner, and a wooden crate of papers on the floor next to it. Tabs stuck from the stack with letters of the alphabet, and he sat in front of her, going through the S's for the third time.

"Ain't here," the clerk said again, also for the third time.

"Well," Molly said, hiking a finger over her shoulder, "supposing a girl was married out there, way out there, where would that paper'a been filed?" She stared at his stack. She wanted to burn the whole lot of them. How many of those poor girls had been married by proxy?

"'at depends, miss. What county?"

"Out there." She waved past the door. "Out where there's nothin'. Nothin' County."

"Could be filed anywhere, then."

"There another town nears here?"

"Maybe. Out that way." He pointed. "And that way." He pointed. "I ain't never seen 'em."

Molly sighed. "Where would I find missin' persons?"

"Hell, if I could answer that, they wouldn't be missin', now, would they?"

She glared at him.

"You a missin' person?"

"Not me. But I know someone. Been kidnapped."

The clerk perked. "Now, hold on. Who's been kidnapped?"

"I just asked where I might find missin'-person papers."

"Now, hold on now."

Molly grunted and backed slowly toward the door. "Forget I said nothin'. You wouldn't know anyone hirin' out, would you? Governess or something?"

The man stared, tugging at his beard.

"You've been a real big help, mister," she said as she walked out.

❦

Nat saw her again the next week at the smithy. The little boy was playing with a rawhide of horseshoes hanging by the door, clanking them together, much to the unnerving of Robert Mackey. Nat needed a shoe but didn't want to get in the middle of that, and negotiating with Mackey when he was in a mood was a trying prospect. She was asking for a job. What job was there for a woman in a smithshop? Nat tipped his hat to the town crier when the man walked in, made certain to tip his hat to two ladies behind him, and then Nat was in the street. Bartleby Shenk scowled at him. Nat glanced away and gripped the bent horseshoe he'd brought to the shop for exchange, in case things got to shoving.

"Hey. Mister," her voice came from the exitway of the shop.

Nat turned.

"Know anyone missin' a kid?"

He raised his brows, but it was an odd question to process.

Molly puffed out her cheeks like an uptight horse and stepped off the porch. "A proper 'no' would do."

܂

"I … I need a job. Please, sir."

The voice sounded less proud, but Nat Rounder still recognized it another week later. Her eyes flicked about, and she toyed with the shop-worn frills of an outgrown dress that he could just make out in the mirror's reflection. He wondered where she'd found it. Perhaps she'd raided some child's closet. And she'd cleaned herself up to look pretty enough. He thought of Walker Stout when he looked back in the mirror and sipped his drink, surprised to find himself interested in the bartender's stalled reply.

It was plain the kind of job this tavern offered a pretty-enough girl, just as it was plain this pretty-enough girl had never before taken that kind of job. He found himself cursing scarlet fever, but that was an odd thought because wasn't a soul around who'd bless it. Maybe now she wouldn't be so cocky. He drank slowly, knowing the tender wouldn't give him another one until everyone else had been served—if he didn't simply tell Nat that they were all out of liquor, like Wilhelm liked to tell him, the sot.

"You done this before?" was Wilhelm's reply, after he'd looked her up and down more than amply.

Nat watched her shake her head in the mirror over the bar. He picked at a corner of the rough-hewn oak countertop, just as she had been picking at her dress. She didn't look comfortable in it, and it didn't suit her, all those frills. And where was that boy who had been hanging on her? What unlucky bastard had she pawned him off on? He shook his head but stayed out of it. This place would chew her up and spit her out, but it wasn't his problem. It wasn't his problem.

"Wait here," the bartender replied shortly, and then he left, and left her there. Standing in the middle of a bar of drunken fools and gamblers, miners with halitosis, cattlemen with wandering hands.

It wasn't his problem. *Better get used to it,* Nat thought, but his lips said something else: "You don't have to do this. Do you have a good reason why you are?"

"I had a real bad month," came her terse response, and her cockiness was back. "Hey, you're that poke don't know how to just say no when asked somethin' simple."

Nat snorted. "It weren't nothin' simple. I thought you was gonna hawk me that kid."

She chuckled. "Well, you wanna buy him?"

Wilhelm was coming back. Nat could see him in the mirror. Nat reached out and took her elbow and brought her in close to him. She didn't blanch.

"I got a ranch a bit down the road," he said. "Out of this place, out of here. If it's shelter, food, some decent things you need, then, it's better than here. You can come on with me, and we can be halfway to the Bent R before Wil gets back."

"Why would you do that for me?"

"'cause I wish someone had done that for me a time or two."

"I can't pay you."

Nat chuckled softly. "I don't need pay."

"I'm all right with a muckrake."

He grinned. "I'll bet you are." He stood and dug out some coins from his pocket and handed her his glass. "I'll bet you're all right with this, too."

She took it and slugged it down and hauled on his arm. He let her touch him but didn't touch her in return. She might have dolled herself up, but he could see the caked dirt under her cuffs. She needed a bath.

"Oughta get you some new clothes," he said, when they'd stepped out to the street, "and then you oughta marry me, too."

Her intake of breath was audible.

"Well, you don't got to, but if you take up at the ranch, you're gonna set this town to talkin' if you's unmarried, livin' under a man's roof. It's up to you." He cleared his throat.

She nodded. "Well, I ain't unmarried. I don't know how to get out of that mess."

"Oh," Nat said absently. "You wasn't wearin' a ring. I just assumed."

"And you wouldn't'a been no Mr. Adonis if I was wearin' one?"

"Mr. Adonis," he laughed. "Shit."

"How do I get out of that? Can you tell me? How do I find that paper?"

"Look. Do you even know there is a paper? You don't want to be married, you just say you ain't married. Burn the trail. Change your name to Matilda. If it ain't this county, then ain't no one gonna know, less he comes lookin'.'"

"Then, I ain't married."

Nat sighed. "Well, I need to be." He looked off to the west, his hand shielding his eyes from the sun. "Real quick."

"Never heard of no kind of trouble that bein' hitched real quick could get you outta."

"Then you ain't heard of my troubles."

"Maybe you could just ask me my name?"

"Oh, right." He had the good grace to look chagrined, although he wondered if it really mattered to either of them. "What is it?"

"Molly Sleight."

"Nathaniel Rounder. Nat, to everyone but my mama. Adonis, to you."

She held out her hand, and he shook it like a man's. "What do I do with my ... son?" She nodded toward Antrum, sitting in a swing on the tavern porch, trapping a horsefly against his knee.

"Hell, he ain't your son. You don't want folks askin' questions, don't spew lies that a soddee could bust faster'n dirt."

"All right. He's kidnapped."

Nat ducked her under the cover of the tavern awning quickly, away from the eyes that all suddenly turned on her. "Hell'd you say?"

"My uncle 'napped him from somewheres."

Nat held a finger to his lips.

Molly lowered her voice. "I been tryin' to find from where. Antrum ain't my brother or son or nothin' related."

"His name is Tantrum?"

She grinned, thought of correcting him, then said, "Yes. Call him that."

"Hey!" Wilhelm said, sticking his head out the tavern door. "You want a job here or what?"

Nat took her hand and pulled her into the street. "She's working for me now." He led her in the direction of the justice of the peace.

Antrum caught the horsefly and raced after them, cupping it in his hands.

☙

The ride to the ranch was long and dusty. Nat wished he'd thought of that before Molly changed into new clothes. She sat squeezed between the saddlehorn and his groin, rubbing against him with each bounce, and Antrum sat squeezed in the pinion behind him. Nat hoped she couldn't tell his discomfort, nor his relief when they arrived at his ranch. As his workers approached, he scanned them hesitantly, then waved a hand at Molly.

"This is my wife, Molly Rounder," he said, seeming somewhat embarrassed. He knew it wouldn't go over well, the suddenness of it. It wasn't like they were a real fit.

Molly was dumbfounded at the reception. Some of the men scowled. Some of them took particular interest in their own boots. Some smiled, but it didn't seem genuine. One man saw apple-red, and Molly frowned at him. Nice welcome wagon.

"Congratulations," the man muttered, and turned and walked away.

Nat's eyes followed him. "Eddie!" he yelled, but the cowboy didn't stop. Nat waved it off and helped Molly down. "They'll get used to it. They know I've only gone and done the thing to stave off some pressure. It ain't the noble way to go about nothin'."

"Well, don't bother with impressin' me. I didn't fancy you the noble sort."

He laughed, but when Antrum was down, he left her there, and followed after Eddie. She shrugged at his manners and took Antrum's arm, and a ranch hand led the boy to a room in an oversized house. Hours later, she learned that Nat would stay out in the barn until well after dark, and another hand showed her the kitchen and a rustic, unused bedroom. He blushed as he beat the mites out of the quilt, wiped the settled dust off the top of the bureau with a corner of his chaps, and pointed his finger out the dirt-smudged window toward the backhouse. Then that man was gone, and Molly didn't see another one until after nightfall, when Nat rapped softly at the bedroom door.

"You settled in good?" he whispered, not wanting to wake her if she were already asleep.

But she wasn't asleep. She'd bathed and prepared herself for the duties of a marriage night, whatever those duties might be, relieved that this time they didn't involve muckrakes and trowel handles and running half-naked through fields of beans in the pitch of night.

"Come in," she said.

He hesitated and opened the door slowly, first peeking only his head in. "I don't need to come in, just checkin' that you had everythin'. I got my own room across the hall if you need anythin'."

"Your own room? But …" she paused, "I thought …"

"We're married in name only, sweetheart. I ain't holdin' you to nothin'. Just givin' you a place where you don't earn your keep with drunks. Ain't no rush to get acquainted."

But she startled him out of his next words when she approached him and drew her arms around his neck, pulling his face to hers. It happened so quickly in the dark room that he hadn't expected it. He stiffened. A sound left his throat like he was choking, and he broke her contact and stepped backward toward the door.

"There somethin' wrong with me?" she snapped, near to slapping him. "You act as you swallowed nails."

"No," he said quickly, but his hands were still withdrawn. "No, I'm just. It's not." He said it softly, "Not yet."

"Then there is somethin' wrong with me. Am I ugly or somethin'?"

"No, Molly," he said. "You're lovely. It's me. I'm slow to this. There's something wrong with me, not you." Shame entered his voice. "We'll talk some tomorrow. We'll go slow. I can't … yet."

She furrowed her brows. "Can't … get it up?"

He snorted and smirked. "Sure."

She stared at him, but stepped back. *Fine, he was slow. Or maybe impotent.*

"In name only," he repeated, tugging his hat down over his eyes. "It's just for show." And he left the room, closing the door behind him.

Sleep didn't find Molly Rounder. The blankets strangled her as she tossed under them. Antrum snored in the next room. Molly could still smell the stunted beans, the bitter scent of rotted fruit and oxidized copper. She'd seen Nat go out to the barn hours earlier after he'd left her room, and he was still out there. A light glowed beneath the large wooden door and shadows moved back and forth in the glow. Her eyes were glued to the shadows through the dirty glass, and as the hours passed, she wondered what kept Nat Rounder awake. *Didn't he need some sleep?* Weren't cowhands up at dawn? She knew there were cows somewhere in the fields. She could smell their leavings, though she hadn't espied them. Perhaps this insomniatic behavior explained the darkened circles that cursed Nat's eyes into aging much before their time.

Unheeding the advice of the ranch hand who had first shown her to her room, Molly walked out of the house barefoot. Her nightclothes wrapped silkily around her, revealing everything, and her long hair fell loosely down her back. If another man had seen her, he might have thought her irresistible, so why had Nat Rounder not come to her bed?

The door to the barn slid open easily and quietly. But when she stepped into the lantern's light, her eyes adjusted well before Nat and Eddie flew apart from each other and fumbled with shirt buttons.

"What in boot hill is she doing out here?" Eddie yelled, aiming his anger again at Nat, then facing away from Molly to buckle up.

"Molly, please," Nat spoke in a strained voice, knowing she'd seen more than her expression let on. "Go back inside, please. This is not … how it looks."

"Isn't it?" Molly and Eddie asked in unison.

Molly could see that Eddie'd had enough of pretending. She didn't need to know him in the slightest to know he was at the end of some invisible rope, tired of hiding, and Nat was a crumbling wall of confusion. Her heart went out to them both. In the span of seconds, everything was understood.

"Eddie, please," Nat pleaded. "Not now. Not like this."

"It's all right," Molly said, half-grinning. "It's good to know that there ain't nothin' wrong with me, then."

Nat laughed shortly, then held it.

"There's no reason to be afraid of what I'll think."

"Molly," Nat tried again, "it's not what you thi—"

"Yes, it is, Nat," she said. "It is, and it's all right. I'll go back inside now. I just saw the glow of your light under the barn door, and I didn't know what …" She cut off her own words. "I'm glad I know." She looked back and forth between Nat's nervous eyes and Eddie's hopeful stare. "I won't let you down. It'll be between us." She suspected most of the ranch hands already knew, which is why they'd felt so embarrassed for her, but she wouldn't make that assumption openly. The rest of the town, however, didn't need to know. That was Nat's fear, she could tell, what encroached upon him daily, why he had to marry in a crack, and that was where she entered the picture. "It'll just be the three of us."

Eddie stepped closer to Nat and put a hand out, and Nat let the hand find flesh. Molly nodded and stepped backward toward the door, watching closely as the shame left Nat's eyes. It turned to relief. She closed the barn door behind her and settled against it, softly laughing. Then, the serene night burst with hooves, and lanterns lit the horizon like flickering meteors.

Men shouted from horseback and pounded the road in the dark and flew through the archway of the Bent R. Molly peeked around the corner of the barn, then swung back. Nat ran out, still buckling his trousers, and a horseman pulled up short in front of him, swaying a lantern into his face. Nat wished for a wagon iron. The man spat on the ground.

"You kidnapped a boy, you queer childfucker?"

"Hell'd you say to me, Stout?"

"Boy gone missin' some months back, next county, and tales told'a you and kidnappin', Rounder, you damn queer bent faggot. You touching a boy?"

"That's enough, Walker," another horseman said, but Nat couldn't make out who it was through the lanterns' swinging shadows. "You got a kidnapped boy here?" the man said, calmer.

"Who's askin'?" Nat said.

"I am." A roughshod woman pulled her horse forward. "I need to know if it's my son. I swear I won't ask what you done to 'im, so long as you just give him up to me properlike and let the law deal with you from there."

"Hell, that's some judgment," Nat mumbled.

"Damn faggot nigger raped a little boy!" Walker Stout yelled again, and were it not for Bartleby Shenk restraining Stout, Nat might have panicked about fire being set to the barn.

"Well, I sure ain't a nigger," Nat laughed. "I'm a lot of things, but you oughta have Doc Dray check your eyes over you can't tell that much, Walker, you foul-mouthed shit."

"But didn't say you wasn't a faggot! Can't argue that one, can you?"

The barn door creaked and a gun cracked, and Molly walked out of the barn holding up a rifle. "Next man calls my husband queer faggot gets it right between the eyes." She raised the gun toward the dozen horsemen and dug her bare feet into the mud. "Go on, say it. I'm itchin' to shoot one'a you sonsabitches."

"Husband?" Robert Mackey brogued.

"Yessir." She looked down at her nightgown. "You just interrupted my honeymoon hay-tusslin', so this'd better be worth my buckshot. You oughta learn the name Molly Rounder 'cause one'a you plants backside here again, it's gonna get branded with my R."

Nat chuckled, and more of his men came out of the bunkhouse, some clutching farm tools.

Molly turned in the darkness and yelled toward the house, "Antrum!" but the boy was already running out.

"Holder!" the mother cried and slid from her horse.

"Thought you said his name was Tantrum," Nat said.

"His name is Holder!" the mother shouted.

"Mama!" The boy ran to her.

"Husband?" Robert Mackey brogued.

"The man who took that boy," Molly said, "can be found in a stable way out that'a ways, but he ain't gonna be too recognizable now. Just don't go blaming no kidnappin' and rapin' on my husband. Antrum will tell you."

"His name is Holder," said the mother, hugging him, inspecting his backside.

"Husband?" Robert Mackey brogued.

"I'll be damned," Bartleby Shenk said. "Hay-tusslin' with a woman."

Walker Stout added, "I coulda sworn you was a—"

Molly raised the rifle.

Eddie laughed at the edge of the barn.

"Kindly to meet you, Mrs. Rounder," Stout added more cordially, and he tipped his hat, kicked his horse in the sides, and about-faced.

The mother lifted the boy into the saddle and rode out after Stout, and the rest trailed behind, slower now, contemplative.

Nat looked at Molly. "If he's rottin' in some horseshit, why'd you worry about the paper?"

"In case he rises up, y'know? Burn the trail."

"Well, I'll watch your back for ghosts; you watch mine for stick-burners, yeah?"

Eddie laughed at the edge of the barn.

"You know how to fire that thing?" Nat asked.

She finally lowered it when the horsemen were tiny specks of light that no longer appeared in motion. "Reckon their mouths were big-enough targets I coulda learned real quick."

Eddie laughed at the edge of the barn.

"It's nothin' I ain't heard before," Nat said.

"I'm better with a muckrake," Molly said.

"I'll bet you are," he chuckled. "I'll bet you are."

YELLOW FLOWERS

*T*he yellow flowers reminded her of the fever. Anna had watched her mother's eyes fill with the same dreaded yellow color overnight, and now the flowers that dotted the Pennsylvania countryside through the coach's rolltop window brought the memories back. To a seven-year-old girl, the blood from her mother's mouth and stomach had been shocking, but the image of those jaundiced yellow eyes, so empty and lifeless, is what would forever haunt Anna.

She'd been living with her family in the nation's capital, bustling Philadelphia, in the summer of 1793, when the fever struck. Her father—a sailor at Arch Street Wharf, where thick swarms of mosquitoes and the stench of waste permeated the air—succumbed after only three days, but not before bringing the devastation into their home and plaguing Anna's mother and two infant cousins. The babies, their insides so fragile, died quickly; but her mother held on for a while.

Anna dripped wet cloths over her mother's forehead for two days before the young girl was whisked away by a neighbor, enclosed in a lightless root cellar until she'd lost track of time, and finally stuck on a coach headed away from the city and into the countryside. The yellow flowers caught her attention again. The buds reminded her that she'd never know what her mother had looked like when she'd died, never hear her last words.

"Remember, don't tell them you're from Philadelphia," a voice spoke over her shoulder as the coach approached the Maryland line, "or they won't let you in. They'll think you're diseased."

The voice belonged to a black man from the Free African Society, but Anna hardly knew him. Thomas: that much she did know. He'd been sent in to help at the request of President Washington because the black men of Philadelphia were immune to the fever, she'd heard. Thomas was the one to find her in the root cellar after her neighbor had disappeared—died, more likely. Anna still had several roots and canned meats from that cellar in her overnight carrier; she'd been thankful her hiding place held provisions, and Thomas had been thankful that she'd shared the meats with him. Touched by her plight, he took the great risk of escorting Anna out of Philadelphia before the fever could claim them both. Apparently, he hadn't been so convinced that black men were any more immune to the fever than whites.

Just over the Maryland line, families gathered to find their panicked loved ones and to band together to build shelters for any unaffected evacuees. Thomas knew this, but insisted they pass by this camp to avoid detection. The bordering states quarantined refugees and refused to let them cross the state lines. Many of the evacuees were infected, spreading the fever, so traveling farther onward would keep Thomas and Anna alive.

More yellow flowers sprinkled the meadows as they passed, and the sun blazed violently, blinding Anna. Her forehead felt moist; was she sweating? Her eyes fuzzied. When she could see clearly again, a figure moving among the camp stole her attention. She knew that figure. She knew those arms, the height of those shoulders, even that floral apron she'd seen for all her life.

"Stop the coach!" Anna cried. "It's Mama!"

Thomas squinted in the sun, contemplating. To stop the coach could mean death. He looked back at the little girl, knowing this, but knowing that if he didn't stop, then that also meant death. He'd risked life and limb to bring them this far, but. His heart sped up, and he worried his bottom lip with tight teeth, a tight jaw.

"Stop the coach!" he called out, pounding the wood behind his head. "We're here."

A LIFETIME OF FISHES

*G*race Hewitt expected to be bound and gagged when she opened her eyes and saw the savages rushing toward her, knives splayed. Grim, taut lines for mouths. She closed her eyes again, squeezed them tight. With her leg twisted beneath the wracked remains of her father's rowboat, she could go nowhere. Her father folded around the battered wood in a shape one could not have survived. Her brother was gone, lost somewhere at sea along the islands of Massachusetts Bay, a place these primitive people called Canopache. Thomas Baltreaux would not know where to find her, would never be her husband now. No one would rescue her or would ever learn of her fate at the hands of these butchers. She clenched her teeth to face her death.

When Grace opened her eyes, the glint of a knife sparkled in the sun, and she whimpered. At her sound, the blade withdrew, and a figure, blocked by the cruelty of silhouette, came down to her where she lay crumpled under the broken wood. When he reached her level, the sun worked with her, and she saw a light deerskin mantle draped loosely across one broad shoulder and halfway down one arm, open across the other and cinched at the waist with a fibrous belt. A leather necklace of shell and bone hit Grace in the cheek as the Indian bent over her, and he made a muffled sound of words she didn't know, the tone apologetic. She tried to move her mouth to speak, but her throat went dry.

"Pooneam, netop. Nutussawes Ishkodhonck," he said, pointing to himself and saying it again, "Ishkodhonck. Ishkodhonck." She shook her head in confusion, and he seemed frustrated, but let it go, pushing her back down to the ground when she struggled to rise. "Appish, ap-pish. Wuttattamwaitch, nippe," he insisted, pouring fresh water from an ornately carved Eastern Elk horn into a cup of sewn bark strips.

A shudder rippled through her as his hand touched the base of her skull, but she relaxed when her mouth met the clean, welcomed water. The cup left her lips too soon, but she reluctantly allowed him to control her sips, so she didn't consume too much too quickly.

Another Indian called out to the first, "Ishkodhonck, neemat, how-an no eshquaw?" and a realization swept over Grace.

His name was Ishkodhonck. That's what he'd been trying to say. She took a calming breath. *A man does not reveal his name or offer water if he intends to kill.* She watched curiously as the two men spoke in a fast, difficult tongue, indicating her leg with a repeated word: chohquog. Grace had given no thought to her leg. It was purple and green and numbed, sliced in several places, but causing no pain. These men, however, focused on it specifically.

In the brilliant sun, Grace studied the one called Ishkodhonck. His hair was black, chopped in short, uneven chunks around his face and eyes, but long and loose at the back, hanging past his shoulders and tied behind his ears with a strand of cordage and turkey feathers. The bone and shell necklace that had thumped her cheek was only one of many, each hanging long around his neck, some down to his waist—the grand-est containing an animal claw. In one hand, he clutched a robe of rac-coon skins, strung together with leather cord. In the other, a bone-handled flint knife, which had been sanded sharp, shimmered in the light. Its empty sheath dangled from a cord around the Indian's shoulder and lay against a deerskin breechclout wrapped between the man's legs and tied with fiber about the waist, leaving the animal hide to hang down in the front and back like a short apron. Thin deerskin leggings covered him from foot to upper thigh, the fitted hides secured to his legs around his ankles and knees with strips of woven hemp, and then secured at the thighs into the same fiber that held his breechclout at his waist. Thick mooseskin moccasinash cradled feet too small for the tall man. A tattoo of a claw, reminiscent of the one that hung about his neck, was emblazoned upon his chest like a military medal; and encircling his upper arm, the faint tattoo of a thorny bramble design seemed meek in comparison. By the time Grace's eyes traveled the man, the two Indians were engaged in an argument.

"Ish-kod-honck," Grace spoke in her best pronunciation, and two sets of dark eyes turned to her with surprise.

Ishkodhonck arched a brow and fell on his knees near her head, tilting the cup—the wuttattamwaitch, as he'd called it—back to her mouth, and making the soft shushing sounds of a mother relaxing a baby. Pity shrouded his face, and she scarce could move as he dug through a small pouch she hadn't noticed and pulled from inside it a second smaller pouch. The tiny drawstring dwarfed in his long fingers, but he dug at the string until the deerskin parted. He dabbed inside, then drew forth a powder coating his finger.

Grace's eyes widened, and she thrashed her head from side to side, despite his shushing and his murmurings of words she didn't understand. With his other hand, Ishkodhonck pulled her mouth into a pucker as she forced a scratchy scream through her throat. His brows furrowed above her, but she fought him, flailing her arms, until he straddled her chest to still her. When she again opened her mouth to scream, he stuck his finger in it and twisted the powdered mixture along her tongue and gums. She bit down on his finger, cutting through his flesh, until he yipped and pulled his hand away. His gaze darkened while he shook out his fingers, but the look fled quickly, replaced with one more apologetic. In her mouth, the taste of something, and his blood. His blood mixed with something, something. She stopped thrashing, feeling a tingling course, then drip, slowly through her body. She stared up with a helpless look of defeat into his returned face of pity. Only pity. *Why?* The question seemed to slip away just as the world did.

The rocking of the canoe and the quiet murmuring of male voices swayed Grace awake enough to make out Ishkodhonck's face above her, peering at the water of Canopache Sound. Odors of birch bark, cedar, pitch, and spruce from the wet boat filled her senses. The realization that she lay across the Indian's lap in no way eased her comfort, and as she shuffled, aches shot through her stiff body. She gasped at the pain of it, and he looked down at her, moving to cradle her shoulders in the sticky warmth of the raccoon robe he'd draped about her. The canoe's murmuring voices quieted, but her eyes curtained over again with blurry vision. She waited for someone to say something to her, but it seemed that Ishkodhonck's finger dabbing back inside his powder pouch would be the only reply. The sharp stabs that stole through her thigh spoke of why such pity shone back in his face. *She would not look down at her leg. She swore she would not.* But her eyes trailed his to a wad of hides that he held steady in the space just above where her knee had once been. Her skirt was ripped in shreds away from its wet entanglements, and below the wad of hides, there was nothing. Space. And the bloody mess of animal hair bunched in Ishkodhonck's fist as he pressed firmly into her naked, stumped thigh to slow the bleeding.

Her lower lip trembled, and she knew nothing else to whisper but, "Grace. I am Grace." She managed to point to herself, and he nodded without expression.

"Grace," he repeated, dragging out the 's' sound, its hard-consonant placement coming with difficulty to him. He raised his finger, and she opened her mouth, sliding forth her tongue, welcoming the powder that would take her away from this a second time.

The jostling of men lifting her—a canoe dragged to land, shouts of greetings and orders, and fish flopped onto beds of seaweed—sent Grace into spasms and in and out of consciousness. She clung to Ishkodhonck's voice and seemed to trust the space in the crook of his neck to rest her head each time it swam as if underwater. Her sweat and tears pooled against his deerskin mantle, and she muttered tiny gasps that coaxed from him soothing words she did not need to define in order to understand. He hurried with her up the beach, her head throbbing with the vibrations of his shouts of "Noot! Wiaseck!" and as he laid her down on the raccoon robe, he fumbled again for his pouch of anesthetic sleeping powder. She shook her head and pushed his hand away. Words flew all around her, but none she recognized, except Ishkodhonck's name, and another word he kept muttering softly, "Wompsooksy." When he pulled away from her, she saw that he was coated in her blood, from his mantle to his leggings to his mooseskin moccasinash. He was offering her his powdered finger once more as a knife circled her head, but fear overcame her, and she pushed the powder away, needing to know what was going to happen to her. In an instant, her questions were answered. Ishkodhonck tore the remains of her skirt and the raccoon skins away, and before she could scream out, he held a white-hot, burning blade against her wound. The pain was lightning fast. Everything went dark for the last time.

🍂

When Grace came-to, she was staring at a curved ceiling of matasquas bark strips and woven reeds of cattails, cornhusks, and bulrushes. A mat of woven bark covered with soft bearskins lay beneath her, and she shivered beneath the raccoon robe that smelled of dried blood and Ishkodhonck's sweat. Before the Indian had realized that she'd opened her eyes, she watched his busy hands at her waist and recognized the smell of urine as he removed the soiled beaten-deerskin rags between her thighs. A wave of embarrassment washed over her, and she didn't dare say a word to be caught staring in the awkward moment. She closed her eyes and felt his fingers brush against her, wash her delicately with warm water, then shift her carefully to wrap new rags between her legs and around the woven hemp ties at her waist. When she peeked at him again, he did not appear embarrassed, dutifully continuing to clean her and apply a poultice to the wound she now could see clearly for the first time.

She had no right leg from the lower thigh down. It had been severed just above the knee, and the space that once connected to the kneecap was now black, the smell of burned flesh the only thing remaining. *What would Thomas Baltreaux say to me now?* she found herself wondering. *Surely, he'd find some reason not to marry a woman with one leg.* Sweat dripped from her forehead, and she was thirsty, eying a large shell filled with clean water that sat beside her head. She wished she had the strength to reach it.

As her mind came back to her, she took notice of things. Today, Ishkodhonck's hair lay in two tight braids down his shoulders, and his torso was bare, except for the necklaces that hung down the center of his hairless chest. His breechclout was the same as the day he had rescued her, still spavined in dark splotches of her dried blood, as were his leggings. She, too, was dressed in deerskin, a long mantle covering one shoulder and her torso, cinched at her waist with the hemp belt that also tied her breechclout-style rags into place. Beside her bed, she saw that he was sewing an elkskin moccasin for her, using sticks to measure out the shape of her remaining foot. She willed her mind to remain blank, not to think of rescue or what her future back on the mainland would hold for her now. She knew she must have been missing for days, maybe even for a week, or weeks, although time had slipped from her as often as her consciousness. Surely they'd come searching for her father; but if they found him wrapped around the rowboat, they might look no further. Her brother clinging to a reef that sliced his arms was the last image she had of him, the blood turning the foam pink. The waves had come so fast, and nature had been indifferent to his desperation. It swept him away before she could even call out to him. Her father washed up seconds after, knocking the boat onto her with the driving force of the sea behind him, half burying her beneath it, down into a beach that turned to quicksand with each wave. Her last thought of him had been a hope that the carrion birds circling his body would alert someone from far off. She'd waved the birds away with a small plank until her waning strength made it impossible to continue doing so. Then, she'd refused to look. Held her nose for hours. Remembered the pink foam. Perhaps no one was coming to her rescue, but at least for the moment, she had learned she was safe enough.

Her thoughts sank back to Mr. Baltreaux, sitting in his Boston office—Shawmut, these people called it—figuring what his fellow lawyers and he could do to learn the fate of his betrothed, his fair Grace Hewitt. *Whose knowledge could he buy? Whom could he pay to send a search party?* Along the hedges of her father's home, tall ferns grew that brushed her thighs when she walked by. Soldier, the terrier, circled her feet—one leg, then through, and around the other. She'd always run to the corner of Wax and Lumberstock for the letterboy. Stones beneath her feet, limestone goatsheads lodged in two soft leather soles. She wanted a Boston Saltbox set back in the country, stairs of brick leading down to the cartway.

"Wompsooksy!" Ishkodhonck broke her trance when he finally saw she had opened her eyes. "Wompsooksy, teag k'meech? Nasaump, sobaheg? Nammossuog?"

He flung his words at her, but she didn't know them. She nodded meekly when he raised a plain-pottered bowl from where it had been warming over a firepit, the smoke trailing up through a hole in the roof, called a wanachikmuk she would later hear, that she now followed with her eyes. He held out a wooden spoon, a kunnam, and the bowl full of a dried corn, berry, and nut porridge. Nasaump, he had called it, followed again by Wompsooksy, which she now could assume was his name for her.

And so the days passed like this. Ishkodhonck left her side only when the medicine man visited, and he'd go off to fish and hunt—nammos and atchanam. To gather pootop, mesquashcoo, quahog, meeshyog, ashontyog. To tend to anacooonk—farmwork. She quickly learned his words as he pointed and repeated, always followed by Wompsooksy, sometimes Wunnysu Wompsooksy.

When she'd gained some strength, he bounded one day into his wetu, bearing an armful of fish that he threw onto a mat of dried seaweed. She was sitting on the edge of the bearskins when he turned to her, his face brightening to see her strength returning. He had an easy smile; she instantly liked that about him. His teeth that he cleaned with pine needles and mint leaves were white against his bronze skin, like they glowed.

Through his smile, though, he looked anxious this day. An icy chill raced into her. No one had come to rescue her, and every day that she lay in bearskins felt more permanent. *Was she his wife now? Is that the way it worked here?* He'd never lain with her, yet she remained solely in his care. *What did the others say of this arrangement? Was she a prisoner?* She remembered how he'd won the argument with a man she'd later learned was his brother, Aiyesonk, to bring her here.

Ishkodhonck's smile didn't waver when he saw her apprehension, and as had become his custom, he slid his arms beneath her back and thighs and lifted her. She didn't fight it anymore. A fitted stick had been carved by his deft hands, but she'd yet to use the crutch, finding the sling of his arms easier for mobility when she had none yet of her own. Pain still racked her severed thigh and weakness still claimed her, but soon she'd be strong enough for the crutch. She had come to rely on him for the fish he brought to her daily and the clothes she now wore— the full mantle, breechclouts, and legging he'd fashioned her, and the elkskin covering that wrapped around her thigh stump. Her eyes were drawn to two slits across his palms, where his skin had recently been cut, but she didn't know enough of the language to ask him about it.

"Taubut," she whispered what she did know, and he seemed pleased that she'd learned his word for thank you.

๛

Ishkodhonck carried Grace to what he called a nush wetu, a longhouse containing three firepits that appeared to house several families of importance, all of whom exited out the tiny square door after Ishkodhonck carried her through it. Whatever was to happen, those people were not invited to stay. And then, neither was Ishkodhonck, it seemed. He set Grace upright on the beds of raised animal hides and wood that lined the walls, muttered, "Wunniish, Wompsooksy," and vanished through the hole of light from which they'd entered.

"He admires you," a woman's voice spoke in stilted English, and Grace nearly leaped from her skin. "He has taken care of you?"

Grace found her tongue with difficulty, and muttered, "Y–Yes, he is kind. You speak English. Who are you? Why am I here? What is going to happen to me? Am I married to Ishkodhonck?"

The woman chuckled. "Your people have called me Mary. You may call me Mary. I am sonks, the sachem's wife, an elder of this clan. You have learned Ishkodhonck's name well. Most of your kind would call him Fire Goose. You are here with the Wampanoag because your boat crashed on an island, and for no other reason. Nothing is going to happen to you; you are free to go or stay. I have been consulted, as my family holds many plots of land, and Fire Goose has asked you be entered into the people. My husband has met with the councilors and pniese, and we decide it would be all right for you to remain."

Grace looked hard at the older woman. "You did not answer the last question."

"Perhaps because you ask too many."

"You don't think I have a right to know if I am married to my captor?"

Another smile crossed the woman's face. "Fire Goose is not your captor. We do not take captives." Mary stood from her spot and walked to Grace, taking a seat directly behind the young woman. The sonks drew Grace's blond hair through wizened fingers, then plaited the locks into a braid down one shoulder, as natural as day. "Do you feel like his captive? You said he has been kind."

Grace's cheeks scarleted. "He is. It's just—"

"As I've said, you are free to go. There may be others of your kind looking for you. You may go to them, if you choose. If you stay, you will work. Fire Goose will give up a land plot to build you a wetu now that you are strong enough, until you learn to build one of your own."

Grace turned to look at Mary, the motion pulling strands of hair out of the plait. "Why would he do that?"

"He must," Mary replied simply, collecting the loosened hair again and starting over with the braid. "He has brought you here, against Warknife's judgment."

"Warknife?"

"His brother, who wanted to take you to your people on the mainland."

Grace sighed, "Aiyesonk."

"Yes, very good."

Grace's shoulders slumped. So Ishkodhonck had won that argument to her detriment. Had Aiyesonk won, she might be home by now, at the hands of Dr. Mercer, with medicines not made of flowers and peat moss. Hart oil for pain. Perhaps she'd have kept her leg and could marry without disgrace. Perhaps she would already be running down new brick stairs to the cartway. Or, equally as possibly, she might not have made it to the mainland at all. The island had been much closer, and she'd lost a lot of blood. The canoe might have been her final resting place.

A moment of silence passed as Mary finished the braid of blond hair that swung against Grace's left shoulder and breast. As the younger woman sat, Mary lifted a necklace of wampum shells and sea pearls over Grace's neck and tied it at the back, beneath the braid.

Grace fingered the necklace, feeling as if it were some kind of rite of passage or initiation process. "If Aiyesonk wanted to take me back to my people, why did Ishkodhonck not take me to the mainland, then? Why did he bring me here?"

Mary moved away from Grace and stood, staring toward the square of light coming from the doorway. "You impressed him. You survived. The others in your mishoon were killed, but not you. Survival is very important to the Wampanoag. He said your first word to him was to call his name that you had already learned—that you were wise, that you fought against him and drew blood. And then you did not take his powder when you met his fire-knife. He said you were 'strong with fear,' that he could burn your blood but not your strength. This is a value to him. He values your will. And now, he is bound to you."

"Bound to me?" Grace tried to keep her retort from sounding insulting. "What do you mean?"

"He has been coated in your blood. He wears it on him like a marking and will not wash it from his hogkooonk. He cut himself and took your blood into him and put his blood into you to give strength to live. He says he feels you now, and you are in his blood."

"I have his blood inside me?" Grace snapped, scratching at her skin.

"You do. You had lost much of your own."

She remembered the cuts on his hands. "Mary, I cannot be bound to him."

Mary turned to Grace and placed her hands on the young woman's cheeks. "You are not bound to him. He is bound to you. He understands the choice is yours to make. You will make your own choice."

"But I am betrothed to a man in Bost—Shawmut. I cannot—"

"I see." The elder kept the disappointment from her face, but Grace could sense it. "Fire Goose will build you a wetu, and he will teach you to plant the three sisters. He is a tooquinny enin, and will bring you fishes to prepare." Mary talked right on as if the man in Boston were of no consequence.

"Tooquinny enin? A fisherman?"

"Yes, a fisher. You are free as you'd like, but if you should choose him, then he is the one you've chosen, and this Shawmut man must find another, for you will prepare fishes for Fire Goose only. He is bound to you, and he will try for you." Mary attempted to make Grace smile but could see the young woman felt no joy in this prospect. "He is wise. He is literate. He will teach you language and ask for your language in return, and this knowledge will raise his status in the clan. If you choose him—"

"I won't," Grace cut in. "I want to go home, please."

"You will have to find someone to take you, for I fear Fire Goose will do anything for you but that. He does not feel the Ahcoonayog will admire you now." Mary glanced down at Grace's amputated leg.

"He cannot possibly know that. I won't stay here with him." Grace fought back tears that threatened to give her fear away. She had already wondered if Thomas Baltreaux would still admire her with only one leg. Hearing it come from someone else, a stranger, did not ease the doubt. "Please, I don't mean to be rude, but this is not my place."

"It is all right. The mainland is not Fire Goose's place. He understands meaning of home. But no one will take you there. You will have to find your own way."

Grace looked down at her thigh, cursing its immobility and throbbing pain. She wished she could run. "So I am a prisoner."

"No, you will be a Wampanoag."

Grace allowed an uncomfortable silence to pass before she said, "He calls me Wompsooksy."

"He does."

"What does that mean?"

"Whitebird," the elder said with fondness. "He said when he found you, at first he thought you were a trapped bird, for your white hair flew in the wind like feathers."

Despite Grace's sullen outlook on her fate, she smiled at this. "When I get back to Shawmut, I will ask them to reach out to you in peace here. Perhaps our people can help each other. I will ask Ishkodhonck if he would take me back to the mainland."

"He will say no."

Grace did not like the certainty of Mary's answer, nor the way the elder closed herself off after she'd said it. It seemed the two women abruptly had nothing else to say. Grace refused to mourn the loss of her leg, but the thought of its inconvenience—and the physical pain it still brought her—was always there.

She shrugged sadly. "I've not carried my crutch with me, and I'm not strong enough to get back on my own. Did Ishkodhonck say how I should get to the wetu?"

For the first time since the elder had closed her features, she smiled at Grace. "Just call for him."

Call for him? Her eyes went to the door of the nush wetu, and she sighed. *Was he out there?* "Ishkodhonck!"

Within seconds, he was standing before her, not speaking in the presence of the sonks, but bending to lift Grace against his chest to carry her back.

☙

Ishkodhonck whistled like a sailor as he laid the matasquas over the bent frame of the wetu he made for Grace. He had set her in her garden again—her ahteock, as he called it—and had shown her how to plant pumpkin, squash, beans, and maize. She was now proficient at it, and scooted along her rows of vegetables on a sledlike woven mat that he had made and kept oiled for her with animal fat. It rolled easily through the garden grooves and kept her from having to sit in the dirt to plant. He expected her to work, to harvest the food she would eat, and it was refreshing. Where some might have treated her as an invalid—she was certain Mr. Baltreaux would have insisted on nursemaids and inactivity! —Ishkodhonck treated her as a partner. As a survivor. A smile tugged at her lips, but drooped when she remembered the Boston Saltbox. She'd laid the plans with an architect. Mr. Baltreaux had already ordered the wood for the pantryway. She'd have painted it red so it could be spotted by the ships from the bay.

"Ishkodhonck!" she called, and he came, dropping to his knees in front of her, chattering words she couldn't follow. She reached into the pocket of her breechclout and pulled out a leather cord she'd tied together full of bits and pieces of nutshells and forest pods she'd dug from the garden as she worked. She'd pounded a hole into each piece with a sharpened awl until there were enough to make a necklace of nutshells. She placed the shells around his neck. "There! My gift for you." She pointed at it. "Gift."

"Giffft," he repeated, amused by the 'ft' sound, but he lifted the strand in his hands and smiled. "Magquonk. Gift."

Before Grace knew what came out of her mouth, she said, "Please, take me home. Home, Ishkodhonck. Shawmut." She watched his features fade. He knew what she was asking. "Mishoon to Shawmut, the mainland. Take me?" She pointed to herself and to him, and his jaw clenched.

He shook his head and said only one word—in English: "No."

That was final. There would be no more reasoning or pleading. In her desperation to lift the dark veil she'd wrought and to see him smile again, she leaned forward and placed a quick, chaste kiss on his mouth. He pulled back, his brows tightly drawn. His fingers shot to his lips to see what she'd done, what she'd left on his mouth, but there was nothing. A quizzical expression replaced the anger that had been there, and she kissed his mouth again. He pulled back a second time, but his puzzlement only made her laugh until he realized she was teasing him. He finally smiled at this and fingered the necklace again before standing.

He looked down at her quietly now, then bent at the waist and put his lips to hers. Quickly and impatiently, like a chicken pecking for seed, his jaw and mouth unmoving, his lips tightly pressed together, merely bumping hers, stiff and unaware of any meaning in the action, other than that he'd never seen her do it to any other man on Canopache, so it must mean something personal with him.

And so the days passed like this. Ishkodhonck would bring fish to her wetu at sunrise, they would have their Rising Meal—the only meal of the day—together, and then he would help her to her garden. He would go off to fish, but always he would bend to kiss her, never opening or moving his lips, just bumping his mouth against hers in his approximation of intimacy between them. Grace came quickly to adore this, the budding innocence of it all. She could almost swear it was better than the real thing.

She learned to walk with a crutch despite how Ishkodhonck enjoyed carrying her. Her dreams of the saltbox, tall ferns around kept hedges, turned to rows of maize that she planted in her sleep. She partook in meetings, activities, food preparation, and community gatherings. She pretended not to notice Ishkodhonck constantly displaying for her, but she could see the confliction in him. If he gained her, he gained status. A white woman who spoke English was a valuable asset in their trade with the mainland. It gained him a higher, fairer trade price, increased his worth, and would increase his wealth, his land plots, and his influence in the tribe, as a result. But there was something more. He was protective and careful of her in a way a man is not with something that is merely a possession or an asset. He nurtured her and listened to her talk, learned from her and never treated her as incapable, despite her unfortunate circumstance.

Flopping fish were thrown into an overflowing basket in the center of the table where Grace stood with the other women. The women were the only ones who approached her, and she learned through what Wôpanâak or Massautchuseog she had gleaned, that there was a reason the men didn't speak to her. They did not wish to challenge Ishkodhonck.

Mary had said there was a choice. That the choice was Grace's. Mary said Ishkodhonck knew this. It was more than Thomas Baltreaux would have given her. Her father had been friends with the Boston lawyer for years, and it was simply understood that Grace would marry the man. She'd been resigned to it, but now her father was dead and the mainland seemed another world away. She could see it sometimes from the shore, but unless a mainlander came to find her, she would never be able to set foot there without someone taking her. But still there lingered the thought of a countryside, running through fields of rhododendrons and saucer magnolias, and racing the ships to the windmill with the lantern in its cupola. The smell of molasses and horse sweat and stale oak as the rigs anchored. Wax and Lumberstock for the letterboy, and Shodder Lane for hot bricks in the winter. But there would be no running now. She could hop with crutches maybe a hundred feet before her arms felt weak and her thighs would throb. The windmill was invisible from the island.

Clatter interrupted Grace's thoughts. More fish were dumped into the basket by the fishers who had joined Ishkodhonck, and this time, he returned with the crew, hefting mussels and seaweed, and smiling broadly when he saw her scaling fish with a flat, sharp rock. There was to be a celebration that night, a mishodtappuonk. Pootop, a great gray whale, had washed up on the shore, and there would be oil, salt-cured blubber, and fresh whale meat to trade with the settlers on the mainland that would secure enough goods to last into the winter. This meant the people of the islands, organized under the petty-sachems, would all come together for a light feast of fish and seafood, and there would be races and games for the men while the women cheered. The prizes were substantial, and the men bet heavily with anything they possessed. All around Grace, an air of excitement reigned among the women. They chattered about the feast and prepared the meal as a community for all the men and regional sachems who'd arrive that night to partake in it.

Ishkodhonck came beside Grace, puffing his chest like a rooster. His games had already begun. He'd caught the most fish, and he was proud. The women congratulated him with flushed cheeks, but he'd come to claim the only praise he sought, and when Grace turned to face him, he dipped his head and bumped his lips against hers. She blushed and absently parted her lips when he kissed her this time. The custom was old to the people now, the change imperceptible. But Ishkodhonck's brows drew together, and he tried it again, leaning his mouth forward with his lips slightly parted, then pulling his lips together when they met hers. She laughed, and it was his turn to blush. Before he left again for his mishoon, a soft chuckle came from his throat.

"Nut assookish," he whispered, and just as he'd arrived, he left.

She felt his departure like a widening canyon, uncertain why its vast expanse should spread so inside her. *Yes.* She smiled. *You are foolish.* She knew the word; he'd taken to saying it so many times. *So very foolish.*

The festivities were merry, and the next round of games still to come was much anticipated. All the islanders joined together to cut up and salt-pack the whale as part of the activities, and they chewed pieces of the blubber as tokens for such a magnificent bounty. There were delicacies of raw muskrat and wild swan. Ishkodhonck followed Grace where she hobbled, acting as prop when she needed a rest, and feeding her so many bits of raw blubber that she was certain she'd expanded past her dress. Yet, when she refused, he kissed her instead. But with the hesitation that his kisses filled a space for something else he didn't want to discuss. She thought he'd be more cheerful in the light of the festivities, but he seemed shrouded in heaviness, severity, as if he'd sensed some foreboding in the evening to come.

"The games. Popooonk? Nervous?" she asked.

"Yes," he replied simply, but didn't convey more, and wouldn't meet her eyes.

The games were important to the men, she knew, and many of them carried themselves around the festivities with hooded expressions, but Ishkodhonck's was ominous in comparison, and it made her stomach flutter. *Was he afraid to lose? What happened if he lost?* She opened her mouth to ask, but was quieted by a whoop that turned heads from every direction. The fifth and final round of games had begun.

A wooden wunnonk bowl was thrust into Ishkodhonck's hand, and he took his place in the line of men, sitting crosslegged on the ground between his brother, Aiyesonk, and a man from another clan. Grace was ushered to sit next to the sachem's wife, Mary, facing across from Ishkodhonck, and Grace was relieved to have someone explain what was happening with the game. Another man of a clan she didn't recognize came by the line of men and handed out five plum stones to each participant. One side of each plum stone had been burned black.

"It's a game of chance," Mary said. "After all of their games of skill, the one to determine the true winner is a game of chance."

"I imagine that is irksome to Ishkodhonck?" Grace said.

"I imagine it is. Fire Goose is a thinker and rewards skill and strategy. But he is ahead and does not need many markers to stay that way."

"I hope he wins," Grace added, although she was certain she didn't need to say it.

Mary smiled naughtily. "He may acquire a gift to give you."

Grace watched the points tallied and caught on to the game. There were two hundred wampum-shell markers. The men banged the bowls of plum stones once on the ground. As the five stones leaped and resettled in the bowl, markers were awarded for the amount of like-colored sides that landed face-up in the dish: All five of the same color meant two wampum markers and the chance to go again. Three of a kind meant one marker and the chance to go again. All other combinations were unrewarded, and the turn went to the next player in line. When the caller doling out the markers finally ran out, the person with the most wampum was declared the winner of this round of games. The count of the wampum would be added to the point tally from all the previous games of the evening festivities, of which Ishkodhonck had remained in the lead. This was the final game, and it truly was a game of chance. Yet, he still seemed to be good at it, garnering groans from the other men when he went turn after turn getting three and five like-colors in a row.

"He takes it so seriously," Grace whispered to Mary.

"There is much at stake. Those who do not win get to keep their wampum markers, but he who wins will take great prizes away from the others. He will take his choosing of what the others have to offer."

It was no surprise when Ishkodhonck won. Grace cheered, but the gnawing question kept reoccurring of why Ishkodhonck did not seem content. *Restless*, Grace thought. *Restless and nervous.* He collected his shells, and stood as the other men brought him their soft hides, sharp knives, carved bows, arrows, clothing, tobacco, firewater, axes, feathers, dishes, beads, and more. Grace was impressed by what he was able to keep, but even more so at Mary's next words.

"Those are all nice things, it's true, but now is his grandest prize," the elder said. "He gets to name one thing of any man's that he wants to keep. He has always been wise in this decision, and it will bring him great wealth."

"Always?" Grace asked. "You mean to say he's won before?"

"Oh, yes. Many times. He will probably take one of Choganatchu's horses. Fire Goose has four of them already back on the mainland. They are worth much in trade."

"Four of them?" Grace was impressed.

Mary nodded. "Or the large flatboat that Pocametpeonk has purchased from the Ahcoonayog. That will bring Fire Goose much luck with his fishes."

That will take me home, Grace thought. She wanted him to choose that.

The two women waited with the rest of the onlookers for Ishkodhonck to gather his goods and claim his ultimate prize. Instead, commotion arose from the line of men. Aiyesonk stood toe to toe with his brother, and Ishkodhonck was bickering with him, both men grumbling too low for Grace to understand any of it.

"Oh, dear," Mary whispered to herself, but Grace caught it. "Oh, no."

"What, Mary!" Grace said. "What is happening?"

"He has made his claim, and he is being told it cannot be so."

"Why can it not? What—"

Grace's words stilled as Ishkodhonck whirled away from his brother's grasp and flung his pointer finger through the air at ... *her*. His voice thundered behind his finger, "N'pitchinnumup!" followed by a slew of words Grace couldn't comprehend.

"What did he say, Mary?" Grace said frantically. "What's he doing?"

"He said he has claimed you," Mary replied, far calmer than Grace felt. "He is being told he cannot lay claim to people. That is not how the game goes."

"But he is persisting."

"He is, yes. And he is," Mary took a deep breath, "offering for you."

"Offering? You mean he's ..."

"He's gathering together all his goods to make you an offer." Over the top of Ishkodhonck's hasty words, Mary translated, "He says because your father is dead, he will make the offer to you instead, and you will get all he has."

Grace paled, and the combination of nerves and whale blubber made her sick to her stomach. "Oh, Mary, why here? Why now?"

"He is making his desires public, in hopes you will not refuse him."

"I need more time."

Mary's voice grew grave. "If you refuse him, Whitebird, he will not live down the humiliation. But if you agree, he wins much, and all the clans know the prize he's won. He has made it known, he says, because he is proud of what he feels."

Ishkodhonck's finger shot out at Grace again, but his restless demeanor changed. He grew softer, almost pleading, and he sounded as if he were making new promises. "K'wommonsh, Wompsooksy. N'wommonsh." His breathing turned ragged. "K'wekontam n'weewo?"

Mary gasped audibly, followed by the immediate hushing of the crowd, and Grace had the feeling the elder wasn't going to repeat what he said. There was something strange in Mary's expression and a set to her jaw that looked defiant. Ishkodhonck's eyes met Mary's, knowing his fate rested in her hands, in her translation of his sentiments and requests, but when Mary finally spoke, she said only one thing: "He is asking you to marry him."

"Oh, no," Grace whispered. "Please, no. Not now, not here, not like this. I need more time. This is not ... my home, my people. He is not my ..." Her words trailed as he fell to his knees before her, his arms full of all that he had won, the furs, the wampum, handfuls of English coins —his voice desperate and tender.

"N'mog abbona pawgutash," he pleaded, pushing the piles of luxurious items toward her, "teagoash ... wuttamauog ..."

Mary kept pace with him, repeating his words over the top of his as he flew through a speech he'd obviously been preparing for most of the evening. "'I pay you five wampum belts of the rarest purple and black shells.'" His voice overlapped Mary's, but she continued, "'The coins of the coaters, wool cloth, tobacco, my wetu and all of my lands, my mish-oon, my four ponies, my furs …'"

Ishkodhonck's eyes dragged back and forth between the two wom-en, desperate for Mary's translation and for Grace to see the worth and sincerity in him.

"'… my tools, my dishes …'" Mary said.

"… Kah nammossuog. Mamussy."

"'And a lifetime of fishes.'" Mary's voice halted, and she looked at Grace, whose eyes were glued to the man in fear. The elder's final words came out every bit as pleadingly as had Ishkodhonck's: *"Take it all.'"*

Grace's mind reeled. He laid materials at her feet as if she could be bought and sold. *Is that what he thought of her?* That he could buy her, like Mr. Baltreaux? In front of all these people? Certainty and pride had cloaked him when he'd first stood to claim her, but as her hesitation prevailed, he visibly weakened.

"N'onketteam, ahquompsiny. N'menmenneky. …"

"'I'm well, healthy, able,'" Mary translated. "'I'm very strong. I will provide for you. …'"

"N'mog wuneechônuwôah menneky. …"

"'I will give you strong babies.'"

His brows creased together at Grace's reticence. "Mat k'wottooos?" Mary's whisper was as soft as his, "'Don't you understand?'"

He pointed to himself. "Wossuck."

"'Husband.'"

Then he pointed to Grace. "Kah weewo."

"'And wife,'" Mary sighed unevenly.

Ishkodhonck searched Grace's eyes, and she was sure the scowl he found on her face was disheartening. The warm night had turned cold, and she felt lost in it, a million miles from the home that she could still see from the beach. So far from all she'd always known. The candle-lamps of the mainland, perhaps lamps of Barnstable, glowed with be-witching welcome, taunting her to think of what a primitive future would hold in this place. Grace snapped out of the thought to find Mary and Ishkodhonck both staring.

"He is offering you all he has," Mary said. "Everything."

"Things," Grace said sadly, waving her hand in dismissal, a flicker crossing her mind of how Thomas Baltreaux had also taken to shower-ing her with *things*. What disappointment that Ishkodhonck had proved no different than Mr. Baltreaux in that regard. Perhaps there was not much difference in men after all. Yet, how different they were.

There was contempt in Mary's voice when she asked, "Do you understand what he is offering?"

"They are all just things."

"But they are *his* things. He is offering you everything. It is all he has."

"No, it's not," Grace replied sharply.

"Be very careful here, Whitebird," Mary said. "Search your heart, not just your mind. You will never be offered more than you are being offered right now."

A stubborn tilt jutted Grace's jaw upward. "Yes, I will." *I need more,* she reasoned. *More time. How can he be so sure?* She looked at Ishkodhonck and shook her head.

The note of warning had not left Mary's voice. "This decision will not go easy."

"You said the choice was mine."

"Aquy!" Ishkodhonck suddenly yelled amidst the arguing women, and then the proud man dropped his head in defeat. "Nooantam k'wadto coony."

"What is he saying?" Grace asked quietly.

Mary replied, "'I understand your coat-talk.'"

A shaky hand waved over all the goods at Ishkodhonck's knees, and he whispered, "Noona."

"'It's not enough,'" Mary translated.

Grace's eyes raced to his. "No, Ishkodhonck, you don't understand. What you are asking is—"

He cut her off, "Quot onch, k'wommonsh." Then he gathered his goods in his arms and stood, shoulders hunched, and walked off into the darkness.

"What did he say?" Grace turned to Mary, but Mary stayed silent. Tears burned behind Grace's eyes, and anger flourished through her. Even with its buildup inside her, it came out in a whimper, "You said it was my choice, and that he knew it was my choice."

"I said it was your choice to make, and you've made it. I didn't say there would not be consequences for making it."

The festivities and merriment had turned to quiet, and within minutes, the crowds were gone, slinking back to their lives, as Grace's life came to a standstill. Mary left abruptly with the sachem. The women scowled at Grace, and it seemed that the celebration was over, and she'd been the one to ruin it. No one remembered the whale, the great reason for gathering. They would all leave from this night remembering only

Ishkodhonck's impassioned plea for her, and her cold refusal of him. His humiliation, and her self-righteousness that she deserved more than beads and furs. *What had she done?* She'd listened to the offer and thought it through, and she'd done the logical thing, *hadn't she?* But then her heart rebelled. He'd offered everything he had. *Every material thing,* Grace corrected. *And he didn't offer—he demanded; he claimed.* Yet, a feeling sat tight in her chest that didn't go away. Disappointment.

The night was dark. No moon peeked through the fog that shrouded the island in dreariness. The fires had gone out, and the beach lay deserted where Grace still sat, recounting the events. She didn't know where her crutch was. It had gotten misplaced somewhere among the crowds when she'd been escorted to sit by Mary, and now it was gone. If she'd agreed to marry Ishkodhonck, he would have wrapped her in the furs to shield her from the cold, then carried her home—to their shared home—in his embrace. But now, she'd sit on the beach numbed and replaying the evening in her mind, until she grew cold enough to crawl or hop home. *Home,* she repeated. It wasn't home. It was a wetu Ishkodhonck had built for her that wouldn't even have a fire going when she got there. It would be as dark as the beach and lonelier inside than it ever was before.

In that moment, footsteps sounded along the beach. Their light patter would have been inaudible to Grace just a few months ago, but the sounds once too quiet to notice had become ingrained in her on this island, just one more indication that the place had taken over more of her than she cared to admit. She turned her head toward the approaching person until the shadow of Ishkodhonck loomed before her. The darkness covered his face, but he carried something in his hands. Without an utterance spoken between the two, he dropped what he'd been holding into the sand in front of her, and turned back toward his wetu. As quietly as his footsteps had come, the patter departed, and in the sand in front of Grace lay her crutch.

And so the days passed like this. Not a word was exchanged between Ishkodhonck and Grace. He stayed away, fishing and hunting, making trips to the mainland as if to add insult, even farming in his small field where Grace could see him plainly, but never once did he turn to her or speak to her. There'd been no fishes. She hadn't realized how much she had come to rely on the fish he'd once given her, but now that she'd picked her garden clean—his garden—she was hungry, and there was nothing more to eat. She'd have to learn to hunt and fish for herself, and it was doubtful any of the island people would help her learn.

She'd just gotten her morning fire going, when Mary appeared at the door with a rawhide cord full of flopping fish. The initial smile Grace wore vanished when she saw none in return.

"You have stayed away long," Grace said. "You are angry with me."

"No," Mary returned. "I am disappointed, not angered. The women of the elders council will be meeting tonight. You will be expected. They want to see what you can offer in exchange for a land plot of your own."

Grace looked down at her underwhelming fire. "Then Ishkodhonck wants me off his land."

"That is for him to tell you, not me." Mary went to the door.

"I am worth more than a few beads," Grace murmured, her face reddening as she said it.

But Mary turned to face the young woman with narrowed eyes. "Is that all you heard in his offer?"

"Well, I'll tell you what I didn't hear."

Mary scoffed. "You were not listening." She walked out the door, taking the fishes with her.

The rumble in Grace's stomach prompted her to grab her crutch and drag herself to her feet. Though not as swift as Mary, Grace had learned to move fast enough when the need arose.

"I listened!" she cried out after her. "I listened, and I saw! Wampum, animal hides! Things spread out before me like I can be bought!"

Mary called over her shoulder, "It is our way."

"Well, it's not mine."

"Isn't it?" The sachem's wife came to a halt and turned to face Grace, insult darkening the older woman's features. "Your white men do not buy you? With jewels and furs, fine houses of wood, promises … handshakes to fathers?"

Grace didn't dare answer.

"K'wommonsh." Mary hung her head, just as Ishkodhonck had done when he'd said it. "It is *I love you*. Wommon is *love*. It doesn't get any plainer than that, Whitebird, if you must have the words. But remember they are only words, and any man can say them. There are some things, though, that speak plainer than those words."

A patch of dirt on the ground became all Grace could focus on. If she looked into Mary's eyes, Grace would crumble. "You didn't tell me he said that."

"No, I did not."

"That's not fair. I relied on you to—"

"One does not need to know language to hear it. If you couldn't see it in his face, you did not deserve to be told. If all you saw were," Mary made the same throwaway gesture Grace had made on the beach, "beads and horses, and not that he was laying his heart at your feet, then ..." Her words stopped short. A faraway look replaced the frustration that had been there, and her tone changed as if a wind had rushed through it and shifted its course. She stepped toward Grace. "You have a white man in Shawmut. He has told you he loves you?"

"Yes, many times."

Mary nodded and turned away.

Grace didn't want to think of that, of Thomas Baltreaux, the careless way he said words. They never meant anything to anyone but businessmen who clung on them. Clients being sentenced. Someone brushed aside. "Ishkodhonck will not speak to me."

"No," Mary answered bluntly. "We cannot undo the choices we make, Whitebird. He risked all he had and was publicly refused. That mistake will not be made again."

"You think I'm a fool."

Mary sighed. "I cannot say. I do not know your white man in Shawmut." She tilted Grace's chin from the ground. "But I know this, Whitebird: If your mishoon had crashed against another shore, Fire Goose would have crossed all of the ocean to find you, alive or dead. So where is your white man from Shawmut, hm?"

Grace's eyes glassed with unshed tears.

"We can see the mainland from here. They can see us just as well. They can hear our drums." She pointed in the direction of Lewis Bay. "So where is your white man with his words of love and all they are worth to you?"

Grace couldn't answer that. Thomas Baltreaux had not come looking for her, not even to see if she were dead or alive. Ishkodhonck had found her, and he'd saved her, taking off her leg before it could kill her and nursing her to health with a gentle hand. Thomas Baltreaux had probably been filing land parchments or overseeing committee meetings about trade agreements. While she had lain thirsting, dying, unable to move beneath the heavy timbers of a crushed boat, Thomas Baltreaux had surely been dining on beef and oysters, drinking aged rum with his fellows, or taking a warm hipbath. She wondered how long it had even been before he noticed she was gone.

"Here are your fishes," Mary cut into Grace's thoughts, handing the girl the rawhide cord of strung fish. "Fire Goose was worried you'd hunger and insisted I bring you his largest lot."

☙

"You are punishing me," Grace spoke to the ring of elder men and women who lined the hides along the wall of the nush wetu. Three dancing fires came between the rows of elders on either side of the room, and Grace stared blankly into the flames in front of her.

"No, it is the way of it," the sachem, Pookettymis, spoke to her in the same strangely accented English his wife used. When he spoke in what he referred to as coat-talk, he addressed only Mary and Grace, for the rest of the elders didn't speak English. "You do not own land here. You're on Fire Goose's land, in the wetu he built for you, and you must pay him for it to remain. You don't have anything of value to pay. Where he asked marriage, bearing of children in trade for his offerings, he was refused. We talked among us, and he'll accept one thing from you needed that will benefit us all: that you should accompany him to the mainland on trade days, help him know the value of the white man's word."

"The mainland?" Grace asked. "He would take me there?"

"Yes," Pookettymis replied, "and you may stay there if you wish, marry your white man." The sachem spoke the words with such disdain that Grace had to swallow a lump in her throat.

"Ishkodhonck knows about Mr. Baltreaux?"

"Fire Goose knows only that a white man owns you."

Her jaw tightened. "But that's not true—"

"He asks the promise that you be present for his trading with the Ahcoonayog, so he understands terms of fair trade. Your men are ..."

"Sneaky," Grace finished for him. "Yes, I know."

Mary added, "If you do this, you will have the option of being an elder in this clan, if you wish to stay. Fire Goose has drawn a deed to give you the wetu, for you to keep it or sell the land as you choose, if you should help keep him from being cheated in trade."

"I would of course help," Grace mumbled. "I'm not so selfish as you imagine me to be."

Mary sighed. "Fire Goose will bring you no more fishes."

Grace's heart thumped. "I understand."

☙

A spear was a hard way to catch a fish. It required an immense amount of patience—mention nothing of balance, practice, and aim. To further aid in the impossibility of the task, Grace had to make her own spear, and she hadn't been any good at that, either. She spent hours sharpening her first bone fragment into a point, only to lose the daggered tip into the ocean the minute the water loosened the grip of the sinew bindings. Balance was not her strong suit, and aim proved the hardest task of all. Her looming shadow and careless splashing scared off every fish she encountered before she could get within a spear's throw.

And so the days passed like this. She perched on the edge of an outstretched rock, holding perfectly still, dangling her spear above the water, waiting for a fish to come into range. She imagined there must be an easier way to fish, but she didn't know it, and no one would offer help. The men on the mainland trawled enormous nets through the water, catching fish by the schools, but she had no such net. She was called one of the howanigus now—a stranger—just as the English were called, and this label didn't bode well for seeking help. But she persisted. She'd once been called a survivor, and she would survive. One tiny sunfish, not even big enough to cook, would be her reward today, if nothing else.

When snickers came from behind her, Grace turned. The men had come in from the ocean with their arms and nets full of fish. Ishkodhonck and his brother, Aiyesonk, both had multiple rawhide cords dangling with numerous fish: plump haddock, pink salmon, and glistening trout. Grace's stomach growled, and she realized the men had seen her woven mat containing one subpar fish and were laughing at her. All except Ishkodhonck. Across his back, a spear was strapped at the shoulder and rolls of handmade fishing lines were wrapped around his arms, mingling with the cords of fish. For the briefest moment, she held a glimmer of hope that he might help her. From where the men stood, they could plainly see her red, sunburned hands and the blood that came from her palms where the rough tree bark of a poorly crafted spear had scraped them raw. But when she waved Ishkodhonck down, he frowned, and the men fell silent. Aiyesonk shook his spear at her as if to scare her off, then put his arm around his brother's shoulder, pulling Ishkodhonck away.

"Please, speak to me!" Grace called out meekly, followed by, "I'm sorry," but her plea was unanswered.

Embarrassment overcame her. It turned to sadness when he looked back to her, his face expressionless, and tore from his throat the necklace of nutshells she'd made for him. It sailed to the sand, the pieces scattering, and he didn't glance back at it. Grace thought she might cry, just outwardly wail and moan and empty her eyes into the glistering sand. She prayed the display had been only for his friends' benefit, to save face in front of them, but she couldn't help but think that something more sacred than a nutshell magquonk had been shattered. When the men walked away, she didn't turn to watch.

Grace didn't give up until after the sun went down. Her cramps felt as if her stomach had flipped over on itself. She hadn't yet eaten, and her pathetic sunfish was well past dead, already half baked from a day spent on a bark mat in the sun. But it was all she'd caught: not even enough to stretch for breakfast in the morning. With her limp fish in one hand, she hobbled back to her wetu on her crutch, feeling a bitter chill in the air and the pangs of hunger tearing at her insides. If she thought her wetu had been lonely before, she was not looking forward to its cold lifelessness now.

But as she approached, an unexpected glow came from her doorway, and she moved numbly toward it. There, in the middle of her wetu, a lit fire warmed the room. Above it, suspended on sticks, an impressive trout had been cleaned and beheaded and was roasting over the flames. Just beyond that, three more trout were sprawled on a bed of fresh seaweed. Grace let out a long breath. Over her shoulder, she heard a soft padding sound outside, and she turned in time to see a shadow disappear around the corner of Ishkodhonck's wetu. But the smell of fish pulled her away from the door and toward the food, and she was so relieved at the feast before her eyes, that she fell to the ground beside her fire and cried.

And so the days passed like this. Grace spent each dawn learning to fish and collecting mussels and clams from the beach. Some days, she would catch a fish for her Rising Meal; some days, she would not. On the days that she did not, there would be a grand-enough fish to supply a whole family waiting for her at her wetu. *Family*, she thought, miserably. She had none left, but perhaps if she'd been wiser, she'd be working on having one of her own right now. This couldn't go on indefinitely. Eventually, he'd marry another. Where would she be then? She'd have to get better with her spear.

The grand fish that awaited her flopped on its deathbed, but it was only another fish. She never saw the man who brought it, and he never spoke to her. Pookettymis had told her that convention deemed she couldn't go to Ishkodhonck now, couldn't approach him unless he approached her, for Grace learned it a great offense to refuse to marry a man who'd openly courted a woman when that woman had not refused the courting. But she'd made the choice. It had been her mistake alone to make, and she'd made it. Mary had warned her to be careful in his handling, and she hadn't listened to those words. Now, there were no words at all.

Reckoning day dawned clear and bright. Grace caught two fish and felt empowered enough to make it at least through breakfast. The elders would be meeting again that evening, and there would be discussion of when she'd go to the mainland in what she only imagined would be a terribly uncomfortable canoe ride with a sour Ishkodhonck. She hadn't thought of the mainland as a tangible thing for so long that it still seemed unreal. This thought was rolling back and forth through her mind when a glint reflected off the water and caught her eye. Cupping her hand over her brow in the early morning sun, she spotted, way out on the horizon, a boat slowly moving closer to the island. It didn't move like the mishoons of cedar frames, birch bark coverings, and spruce root ties. Instead, it had the fluid motion of a flat-bottomed rowboat, and her eyes fixed on it. The closer it came, the more her heart raced. One of the fish flopped from where she'd collected it between two rocks, and it disappeared back into the Atlantic. She cursed it for only a moment, then fixated again on the boat as it cut through the water. She stared until she could make out individual people: Five of them. Men. White. Then the faint, recognized outline of Mr. Trainaird, assistant to Thomas Baltreaux, came into focus, and she broke into a smile. *He'd come for her!* She was found. She hadn't been forgotten after all. She waved frantically at the little boat until it made its way onto the shore.

Mr. Trainaird stepped over the edge, perturbed to get his buckled shoes wet. Grace wondered why he had found it necessary to travel in his best buckles, but she picked up her crutch and approached. Mr. Trainaird's eyes traced Grace's amputated leg, and she felt him visibly shudder from where he stood.

"Miss Hewitt," he bowed regally. "We heard from the tradesmen savages that you were here. We came as soon as we could."

"Not soon at all," Grace said. "It's been months. Where's Thomas?"

Mr. Trainaird appeared nervous at this question, wringing his hands like a scolded child. "Mr. Baltreaux had ..." the pause spoke for him, "business to tend to. He's quite busy of late with land grievances and horse-trading deeds."

Grace raised a brow. "So he couldn't be bothered to come for me." The other four men in the boat looked just as uncomfortable as Mr. Trainaird, and Grace wondered if she could really look that shocking to them. True, they could see her thigh through the breechclout she wore, and it was probably more skin of a white female who was not their wives than they had ever seen in their lives.

"He gives his regards," Mr. Trainaird said, "but he hopes you will understand that he simply could not get away. Duty calls."

"I see."

His eyes raked her body again, stopping at her stump with rudeness. "He heard you were ..." his hand gestured in the direction of her leg, "uh ... injured. And we thought it best that we clean you up before you should appear before him. Get you out of these savage knots," his lip sneered at her braids, "and skins." His hand kept gesturing up and down, toward her clothes, her leg, her hair, her crutch, her sunburned face. Apparently nothing about her was up to snuff.

"Of course," Grace answered coldly. What would Thomas Baltreaux think of her if he could see her in these revealing deerskins? If she knew that she ate raw meat and relieved herself in the ocean? And that she didn't really mind most of it anymore? "I wouldn't want to appear *savagely* before him."

Mr. Trainaird met her eyes, and some kind of unspoken battle waged between them. "You must know that he is anxious to ..." the hand waved again and muttered low, "know what rights the savages have taken from him."

Grace stiffened against her crutch and set her jaw. "You mean have I *lain* with any of these *savages*?" She'd once, too, called them savages, but no more. They were more civil to her now than any of the slips of men in the boat. "Do I possess still an ounce of virtue that Thomas could claim as his for the taking—that is it, is it not?"

"You make it sound so cold."

"It is cold."

He waved the harsh reality away with another gesture. These gestures! "Come now, we'll take you home, get you cleaned up."

Mr. Trainaird reached for her arm to help her over the side of the boat, and she almost went blindly, but something inside her held back.

Hadn't she waited months for this rescue? Yet, reason eluded her. *Was it rescue?* Her foot refused to leave its contact with the soft sand that warmed her through her moccasin. And then, she heard the sound. A *wa-oh, wa-oh, wa-oh* of male voices that came from the rocky mounds just beyond the beach. Her gut twisted, and she wrestled her arm away.

"You must go now!" she said to Mr. Trainaird.

"What is that awful sound?" he replied.

"That is the warwhoop! The men are coming to this beach, and they will think that you are harming me! Go!"

But her warning came too late, for within seconds, the cry became alarmingly loud and shrill, then stopped brusquely, as ten arrows lay nocked across sturdy bows that were trained on the unwelcome strangers. The warriors rose from nowhere, all around the rocky mounds surrounding the beach, and to Grace's surprise, the Indians were met with four flintlock muskets aimed back at them from the boat. Her heart fell through her chest.

"Kut askwy, Ishkodhonck!" Grace called in desperation. "Aquy!"

"You speak their tongue?" Mr. Trainaird asked, disgusted.

With hands shaking, Grace made sweeping motions for both sides to lower their weapons, as she struggled to maintain her balance. There was nothing here to fight about. Certainly not she. No one even wanted her anymore. "You must be peaceful! Lower your guns."

"This is an outrage!" he hissed, but he did as she asked, commanding his men to lower their weapons. "When Thomas hears of this—"

"Teaqua, Wompsooksy?" Ishkodhonck cut the man off.

"What did he say?" Mr. Trainaird barked at Grace.

"I ... think ... he asked what was happening," she said cautiously. She knew Fire Goose didn't know what words were being exchanged, but it was plainly on his face that he knew the white men would take Grace away.

The look in his eyes had gone from fury to confusion to unease and now to utter loss, as he motioned for the Indians to lower their bows. He drew himself up to his full intimidating height and faced Mr. Trainaird. "Tounuckquaque, howanigus wussoy?"

This one Grace knew without guessing—*greedy English strangers.* Oh, how many times she'd heard that one. She knew with all her heart that it applied to her, too, but she wouldn't let it anymore. Never again. Ishkodhonck had seen more in her than that, and she would prove to him that he had not been wrong, for the question that accompanied this slander held other words that spoke volumes, words she'd learned for trading: *How much?* He was asking how much he could offer the white man not to take her away. He was still offering for her. He had not given up hope entirely, despite his humiliation. *But must she always be bartered for?*

Mr. Trainaird growled again, "Now what did the savage say?"

"Please, you must hold your peace," she said. "He thinks that you own me, and he is asking how much he can give you to go away and leave me here with him." As she spoke this, she gradually stepped closer to Ishkodhonck and away from the men in the rowboat.

"With him?" Mr. Trainaird snapped. "Why would you stay with him?"

"And why should I not stay with him?" She stepped as close to Ishkodhonck as she dared and took interest in watching Mr. Trainaird squirm at the proximity. "He saved me. You did not."

"This is under duress, I pray!"

For once, she thanked her stars that Ishkodhonck knew not enough of the language to follow the conversation. "No, not under duress." Even Thomas Baltreaux, who would no doubt find it relieving that he didn't have to uphold a promise he surely wished to withdraw from a crippled invalid, wouldn't separate her from this inadmissible bond. "So, you see precisely what rights have been taken from Mr. Baltreaux. All of them."

The tubby man stepped back in shock at her boldness, and he stared. Simply stared—his mouth open like a guppy, his fingers jittery at his side. Without another word, he shoved a foot against the boat to set it adrift, climbed back over the side, and paddled away with all of the men in unsettling silence. Grace watched them until they were only the same glinting speck they'd been when she first saw them. They were gone. Her 'rescuers' were gone. She had made up her mind where she would call home.

With the boat vanished, she faced Ishkodhonck, her eyes bright and hopeful and a smile playing on her lips. "I did not go," she said. "He does not own me. I am staying with you. Weewo?" *Wife.* It was all she knew of what she'd wanted to say, but she knew he understood.

Yet, his face curved into a scowl, and his answer rang out with finality: "No." He turned, and as he did, so all of the men turned with him. Then they were gone. Just as the boat was gone, so, too, was Ishkodhonck.

No. The little word echoed in Grace's head. *He said no.* When she looked back to the rocks where her last fish had been trapped, the flopping thing had escaped just as had the first. Breakfast that once seemed a success was now also gone, and she didn't have the strength to hunt for more. *He said no.* She dropped her crutch and landed hard on her butt in the sand, spreading out her thighs and lying back into the warm grains of the beach. She'd wanted a Boston Saltbox to be home, but it wasn't ever going to be. She had wanted this to be home, but it didn't feel like one, either. She'd turned down Ishkodhonck's offering of a warm home, and now she had turned down Mr. Baltreaux's offering of a colder one. She held a deed to a wetu in exchange for making sure the Wampanoag were not cheated in their trades, but it wasn't home.

As the tide crept up the beach to her toes and ankle, she thought of how safe Ishkodhonck's large wetu had seemed when she'd opened her eyes that first morning on Canopache—when he'd been bent over her carefully, tending to her needs without complaint, a fire rising from his firepit, nasaump and fish sizzling over the heat, the smells now tantalizing her and making her think of her hunger. But she didn't stir. *What did she want?* Her eyes followed the trail of the sun across the sky as it burned and burned her. Still, she didn't stir, and, if she were honest with herself, she didn't even care if she died there. It was selfish, she knew, but she'd gambled and lost, just as Ishkodhonck had that fateful night of the feast. *I didn't say there would not be consequences for making it,* Mary had said of Grace's decision. She'd have to face those consequences.

But not today. Today the sun would scorch her as she lay on the beach, some approximation of a sacrifice her wounded mind was making, offering herself to the island if no one else would have her. She didn't sleep, didn't eat, didn't move, but as the sun sat lower in the sky, she knew the elders were congregating without her, that they were discussing her fate in their trade business. Perhaps they would wonder where she was. Perhaps they would search for her. Perhaps not. She was a tiny speck of sand, only noticed if among the other grains of a beach. Invisible on her own. They would continue with her fate in their hands, and Ishkodhonck would dump her back on the mainland where he might leave her, in the hands of others who also no longer wanted her. Someday she might find her way, but today she was lost at sea.

When the sun finally sank off in the west, the darkness was cold. The cool water no longer felt soothing against her ankle and knee and thighs as the tide rose with the moon and grew fiercer. Lapping water licked her waist, then torso, then breasts, then hair, and she watched it carry her crutch out to sea when it receded, only to rush back again without the piece of wood. Still, she did not stir. *Would it drown her? Would she fear it? Would she welcome it, only to fight it when it became too late?* Ishkodhonck had called her a survivor, had called her 'strong with fear.' But her fear of his fire-knife had been nothing then, compared to her fear now that she was truly alone, unwanted, a greedy English stranger —howanigus wussoy—lying on a beach that didn't want her, either, that was working viciously now to spit her out to sea. It pulled her, and she felt it physically move her down, the sand melting away beneath her, and then it was gone, and she floated outward in the strong current.

It drew her under, her head dragging along the beach bottom and then the ocean bottom, then rising to meet a reef that scraped her cheek and stung. The salt filled her nose, and she breathed out. A ghost limb kicked of its own accord at the base of her stump, and she felt it part nothing, give no path upward. The beach blurred away in bubbles of white when she opened her eyes underwater, and she floated for an instant, then sank down, down beneath a wave. In a fit of panic, she breathed in, and the water filled her throat and lungs, and she stopped sharply, propelling, flailing against the ocean bottom before the dropoff took her.

She wanted to live. She wanted the air. It didn't matter that no one wanted her; she wanted herself. She didn't need to run along the harbor lane, just needed to breathe. One breath at a time. She kicked her good leg fiercely, and her stump caught purchase on a jutting rock, and she launched up from it, gripping it and raising herself and thrusting her head above the foam to swallow the air as if it were more water.

There was the land. The beach rose like a great whale belly, and she shoved from the rock out of the current and into the next tide toward the beach. She crashed into it with her chest, her head driving over it, and she clawed and clawed, and she was on it, panting, climbing forward with her arms and one good leg, one foot that worked for two. The very breath of her was alive and it poured from her, pushed each previous breath aside to flood in and out too rapidly, to expel water in a cough, another following another. And when she looked up, Ishkodhonck sat in the dark on a short bluff, his legs crossed, calmly watching her climb through the sand. She laid her head down in it, defeated, and didn't hear his feet on the beach for the roar in her ears. Then, two arms were there, curling beneath her and lifting her against a familiar mantle of deerskin, still unwashed of its dark bloodstain trophies, a heartbeat finding her ear in the dark.

"Ken assookish, Wompsooksy."

Foolish. He called her foolish, but it wasn't heavy. Wasn't harsh. The tone was light as air, as if laughter might come on the heels of it. She wrapped her arms around Ishkodhonck's neck and lay her head in that space that had once been safe. She'd been here before. When he first had taken her from the mishoon to go under his fire-knife, she'd been in this exact place, and it had felt safe.

"I know what it means now," she whispered against his ear, "k'wommonsh."

She felt his smile against her cheek, as he replied quietly, "I know."

Of course he knew. Why hadn't she known? He carried her back to her wetu, and he laid her on the mat of hides next to a new fire. The heat mixed with the warmth of Ishkodhonck's body cut through her cold, wet clothes. She believed then that this was home. That he was the home, not the wetu. Not a place, but a moment. A time, a space in air between two objects. A man who would cross the ocean to find her, alive or dead. A man who would give her strong babies and a lifetime of fishes. But then, with the precipitous sounds of the warwhoop, he was gone.

The rowboats filled the Atlantic between Canopache and the mainland, their lanterns in the dark dotting the shallow bay, first like tiny fireflies, then like red torches of war. Grace heard Ishkodhonck's whoop among the others as she hopped to the northern shore, catching her balance on saltrocks and large mounds of peat moss and stunted cypress branches rotted and twisted from salty wind. Among the whoops, the men of the rowboats shouted, and shots sounded from muskets too far off. She guessed they couldn't quite make out the outline of the island mass. But they were there. English-yelling and French-cursing settlers rowing forth. They'd been met with hostility. A white woman was held captive. There was no more room in Boston for two worlds of men. Their guns rattled yet off too far, pluming smoke into the air. The acrid stench of wet wood and smoky rust filled the space between them. The slapping of the water sounded like scythes against wheatstalks. Their lanterns made them easy targets; at the butt of each light was a length of men, as obvious as map marks, though they were out of bow range. The muskets and waves unsettled the boats, and she watched the standing men slip in the faint light, sputtering madly to hold the sides, some swimming for shore, some about-facing. A cry bellowed from a Wampanoag who'd taken a ball, and her heart seized. Men swam back to the mainland, and still others reloaded, undeterred. More would come. *God.* As long as she remained, more would come. She'd done this, she feared. By not getting into the boat with Mr. Trainaird, she'd brought this on them all. And if these men died, more and more would come. At the moment she no longer wished to be found, they'd come because of her. These men who didn't want her would kill other men simply to claim her anyway. Her breaths grew ragged. Her eyes misted. *Why must she always be bartered for?*

Farther to the southwest, an empty dinghy listed toward shore, its lantern still dangling sadly by twine. Grace ducked from her cover and hopped to the boat, ignoring the aches her body still felt from jarring movement, the inconvenience. When she reached it, she extinguished the lantern and balanced against the boat as she lugged it to shore. A shot penetrated another Indian, and she heard the scream, though she saw nothing except the lanterns, fewer in number now. Most were drifting away, either empty of captains or retreating. The ones that remained were pelted with what arrows could reach, and she heard wood thunking wood, occasional groans, though thankfully no cries, and she tugged her boat behind the bluff, down somewhat into the dry canyon butted against the bog. *Later. In daylight.* There was nothing more she could do in the darkness. *In daylight, she'd tell him.*

But when she emerged, clutching a vine to pull herself forward, the lanterns were gone, and the Wampanoag were wading out to the shoals to collect any priceless items that drifted there. Then Ishkodhonck was in her path, blood coming from a wound in his side. He held out his hand to her and it was sticky, and he pulled her into him. She laid her hand against his wound, and he winced, but looked away and nodded toward the boat, frowning.

"I know." She looked down at their hands, entwined. "It's me they came for. And if I don't go, they will return. The more who come, the more who will continue to come. It will not end." Tears came to her eyes, and she said what she knew of it in Wôpanâak and hoped he understood the rest. "I must tell them that I wasn't a captive, that you are peaceful and good. I must help your trade and bonds thrive, or it will be severed forever. Because of me. Because of us."

Ishkodhonck's frown deepened. "No."

"As I promised you, I will accompany you in trade, on the mainland. When you come. I'll make it safe for you. And fair. Fairer than I've been to you. This is still my promise."

He let go of her hand, stood motionless for a moment, then pointed again at the boat. "I help," he said in English, and removed the boat from where she'd stored it, pulling it out to the now-quiet beach. "I took you Shawmut."

"You'll take me?"

He nodded, staring into the boat as if it were a foreign object, then touching the sand like he might never see it again. "Nut assookish."

When he turned back around to her, she had climbed into the boat herself, sliding along the bench, so much stronger and more agile than she'd previously been. She did find him a bit foolish, as he'd said, bleeding from the side and wading out into the water with a boat, but tears streaked through the dirt on her cheeks, stinging the cuts that the reef had left there. They'd both been foolish. He stepped into the boat and sat across from her, leaving his wound untended, and lit the lantern with a powderstone from his pouch. In the light, she saw her magquonk of nutshells around his neck, repaired. She tried to smile at it, but more tears fell. He studied her quietly, and she let him.

To find home is an endless search. To call a place thus is to give up another place that once was. To find the new, one must loose the old to the oceans of time and let it sink down, down into the sediment. To straddle two worlds is to lose something from each, never to gain the best of both; and home cannot be found within the heart of another if it is yet unrecognized in the heart of the self. But in knowing something that must be released, the return is itself a creature of its own time, its own ocean—one that must last the lifetime, yet take the lifetime to cross. Grace knew this now, all of this. She was strong with fear.

"Return," Ishkodhonck whispered, softly rowing in the darkness, halfway between Canopache and Lewis Bay. "I find you wherever your boat breaks."

"I know that you will."

"Home."

"It is right here," she said, nodding to the Sound, "between both worlds."

IN THE BLOOD

"*F*or heaven's sake, Dr. Rower," Antoine's prepubescent shrill rang out. "You picked a mighty day upon which to be late." The wiggling worm of a farmer's bastard tugged Dr. Leofric Rower down the hall toward a room filled with loud cries juxtaposed with whispers.

"On the contrary, boy," Leofric said, consciously toeing the tear his splintered wooden shoe had gnawed through his linen hose. "Seems good a day as any to be late." He eyed the hourglass on the hallway table. "Not that I'm late at all. It appears our patient is early."

"A man doesn't choose what time his cousin runs him through, sir."

"Nor does a man choose the time his body fancies slumber." Leofric fiddled with his demi-worsted kirtle and pulled his jacket over it, wishing for buttons that aligned enough to fasten. "His cousin, you say?"

"Yes, see—"

"I do see." He could ponder only briefly, when a meaty arm separated him from Antoine's. He turned to the man at his heels who'd followed from the foyer. A twisty, hostile sot of a man with a mustache fresh from the carnival of commedia all'improvviso.

"I must request," a meaty voice that matched the arm insisted, "that cause of death—"

"Has the fellow died, then?"

"Well, not yet," the meaty man said. "But I pray it held discreet. For you see—"

"Yes, I do see," Leofric said. "You are the cousin."

"But he didn't deserve the lady!"

"And I suppose she had no sword of her own?"

Leofric peeled the cousin's fingers from around his arm and turned toward the hallway into the operating room. The whispers fell silent; the cries remained, though growing weaker. A woman scurried to the ewer, and two men took abrupt leave, Antoine turning with them. The meaty cousin followed Leofric into the room, but the doctor pushed the unwanted culprit back out and yanked Antoine back in.

"I wish only for my assistant," Leofric said. "The rest of you, out. You, too, woman. Out." All protests laid to waste, Leofric turned to the young, eager Antoine, then to the patient, now unconscious. "My, this fellow has lost a lot of blood."

The doctor pursed his lips into a pucker, then twitched them from side to side, simultaneously twisting a jacket button in rhythm. A cluck of his tongue preceded a dash to the storage cupboard, where Leofric extracted two needles attached to the ends of metal tubes, rusted and pedestrian in construction, jointed together by the same clay cement that lined housing stones, and attached in the middle with an ineffectual tin cup and a pig bladder that was still crusted with the dried blood of previous patients.

"Antoine," Leofric said, "that dog behind Mr. Snivel's backhouse— have you seen it? Fetch that beast for me, will you?"

"The dog?"

"The dog, yes, yes, the dog." He wagged a finger at creased eye-brows. "Aht-aht, no buts." Then he clapped his hands together twice. "The dog."

Within minutes, the boy returned with the procured dog, sneaking in through the rear door, and depositing the yapping thing into the doc-tor's arms. A wave of ether found the cur's nose and knocked it uncon-scious. Antoine's jaw fell.

"The man needs blood," Leofric supplied in response. "Dogs are like humans in mannerism. Both run warm with blood, walk on land, and whimper when hungry. Both long for naps in the afternoon and chase with lolling tongues the tails of unaffected ladies. A man may have once walked on all-fours, but even if not, he certainly knows how to do it when begging. Their blood, therefore, must be similar enough."

"Is that a medical fact, sir?"

"Of course. Write it down." He pricked the dog's hind end with one of the needles, stuck the other needle into the patient's arm, and suctioned the tin cup over the latter needle hole. "So, let's give the man some blood, shall we?" A hint of a smile played across the doctor's lips when he squeezed the pig bladder, drawing forth blood from the beast and injecting it into the man, while Antoine worked to suture the sword wound at the man's ribs.

In moments, the patient was convulsing. His heart beat rapidly, and red splotches broke out around the needle in his arm. He shook without gaining consciousness, his eyes rolling back in his head, his tongue sagging out of his mouth. Strange wet gurgles left his throat, and his blood-receiving arm clenched into a curl from fingertip to wrist to elbow to shoulder. Then, everything stopped. After a pause, Leofric leaned his ear to the man's chest, but all was still.

"That was fascinating!" he said.

"Fascinating?" Antoine squeaked. "You killed him!"

"Oh, blather, I didn't kill him; his cousin killed him." The doctor waved his hand in dismissal. "I can't be held responsible for every sorry praddlebum who swings a sword around and sticks his cousin in the belly fat. Besides, I hear tell he didn't deserve the lady."

On inconvenient cue, the coroner's heels clicked down the hall. Leofric, annoyed but astute, plucked the needles from the dog's butt and the dead man's arm, and dragged the unconscious animal over to the storage closet, forcing the cur into a space entirely too small for its furry bulk. He had gotten the storage hasp mostly latched when the door to the room opened, and the coroner entered. Leofric stepped in front of his patient.

"Dead, I presume," the coroner said without looking up. "The family alerted me. This is my third stop here this week, Dr. Rower."

Leofric draped a corner of the bedding over the gaping sword wound at the patient's side in the time it took the coroner to remove the parchment and charcoal nubbin from a well-fitted linsey-woolsey pocket.

The coroner asked, "And how did this one die?"

"The Dyspepsia," Leofric replied. "Seems it took him early, the poor fellow. You know how it is this time of year." A scratching and whimpering came from the storage closet, and Leofric coughed loudly, clearing his throat to cover the sound.

The coroner looked at the storage closet, squinted, then added, "Best see you don't come down with the Dyspepsia yourself, Doctor," before he quit the room with a curt nod.

"Well, that was easy enough," Leofric said, dusting his hands together.

"The Dyspepsia?" Antoine asked disbelievingly.

"Sure, why not?"

"Is that a medical fact, sir?"

"Of course. Write it down."

"What if his family finds out?"

The doctor unlatched the storage closet, and the simpering cur leaped out, cowering in the corner and licking its rump. "I'm sure this poor chap's meaty cousin would heartily agree that the Dyspepsia is a fast killer of fine men. Faster, on occasion, than murder." The doctor looked at the dog.

"But—"

"Take this down." He waved a hand at Antoine until the boy lifted a feather and a parchment. "Dog blood not compatible. Next time, use a sheep. A lamb is calm. That might run in the blood to gentle a thrashing man."

New Mexico Farmhouse, Hard to Find after All Those Years

A series of raps sounded at the farmhouse door, matching the burden of the desert wind against bound shutters.

"Pinkerton, Mr. Westgate. I need you to come on and open up for me." The Pinkerton detective scanned his eyes across the dusty, dying ranch and back to the two men standing at either side of the closed door, guns drawn, still and silent as trained sentries. Nothing stirred, and the man galvanized himself for what he would do next. *Westgate—* eh, he could rot in hell. The woman, however, would be innocent, but she'd be standing by the man she'd married, probably right that moment on the other side of the door.

The cranky drawl of rusted hinges split the heat, and the detective wiped his brow, taking in the lanky cowpoke glowering through the tiniest crack in the door. *Homemade door,* the Pinkerton observed, *lopsided,* sagging where the foundation had shifted, scraping a line of resistance into the floor beneath the rancher's spurs. Westgate wore his dirty spurs indoors: showed what kind of woman he'd married and eased the

Pinkerton's guilt—but not the twitchy finger that itched at the Union-issued Colt Navy that had outlived its glory days.

Westgate cocked a brow. The years hadn't changed him. He still arrogantly set his jaw like a cold-blooded murderer and spoke through a particularly cool snarl, "Hell, Carson, it's been a while. Guess they don't pay you to leave jobs unfinished, huh?"

Detective Carson heard the click behind the door and could picture that LeMat Grapeshot, the way it had once glinted in the Texas sun as its barrel aimed at the base of a pretty woman's throat. Carson's wife had never let him wear his spurs in the house. *"Hang 'em up at the door,"* she'd say, so sultry, so husky. He'd always hung them up at the door, but no one asked him to, anymore.

In that second, one of the hidden Pinkertons scuffed a shoe, and a surprised Westgate moved swiftly to slam the door, foiled by Carson's much-swifter boot. A string of oaths left both men's mouths, but Carson wedged his way inside, the Navy drawn, facing Westgate's LeMat. A woman shrieked and froze in the corner, and the two men narrowed eyes at each other, circling like feral cats.

"Make your move, Detective," Westgate hissed, spit flying from his mouth. "You've waited a long time for this."

"Yes, I have," Carson nearly whispered. "My God, yes, I have."

Faster than an eye could blink, Carson drew his bead from Westgate and pulled the trigger, the detective's bullet whizzing through the air with a deafening report and an accompanying whir. A heartbeat later, the woman slumped to the floor, a halo of red on the wall behind her, a hole clear through her throat.

SMALL SACRIFICES

*T*he winter leading up to the Battle of Thompson's Station was the coldest on record, and Theodore decided he could lose the two fingers. Their blackened color had frightened him at first, but now he'd become used to their ugly familiarity. Like an old, drunk friend who showed up unannounced, his war scars were ugly and boastful and not going anywhere.

"My wife ain't writ for three weeks, Ted. Suppose she's dead?" Henry's voice split the silence. *Speaking of old, drunk friends.*

"Naw, Hank, but I suppose she supposes you are," Theodore replied.

The thought crossed his mind that his own wife might suppose both of the men were dead—heck, the whole bloody lot of them, as starved and frozen as they all were, sitting just outside Spring Hill. *Spring Hill*—that was a laugh. Nothing springlike about it. The snow had killed as many men as had the last battle. He looked again at his fingers and could feel their searing death through his gloves. Merrily—his blessed wife and salvation for seven years—wouldn't find him as handsome with two fingers gone. He was sure of it. But he'd been looking for a way to get back home to her ever since the dreaded War Between the States began, and the loss of fingers to frostbite might provide the panacea he'd needed.

"Why don't you just write to Ann, then, Hank?" Theodore asked. "I'll transcribe it, if you tell me what you want writ."

A long silence passed between the men, and Theodore was well aware that Henry was concocting something. They'd known each other since childhood and enlisted together on a couple of straw feet when their family farms, sitting side by side in the lush fields of Tennessee, had come under attack by advancing soldiers. It was maybe the only decision Theodore had ever truly regretted in his young life, but Henry had a bigger regret.

"Suppose instead," Henry stammered, nearly afraid of the words that would leave his mouth, "you just write to Ann and tell her I've died?"

Another moment passed, and Henry was certain Theodore would hit him, maybe snatch away the bottle of oh-be-joyful, but instead an understanding reverberated between the two old friends.

"I could do that, Hank," Theodore replied, "but you'd lose the farm and—"

"—I'd happily lose the farm if it meant losing her—"

"—and she's gonna need proof that you're dead. That ain't gonna be so easy as pennin' a letter."

"You could send her my ring."

"Yeah, but I mean dead." Theodore looked down at the ring Henry was sliding on and off his finger. So easily. There wasn't even a white line underneath the thing. Theodore hadn't been able to get his own ring off for years. Not that he wanted to. He wiggled the black, numb fingers of his left hand, and a thought throttled him. *It'd be coming off now.* "I got me an idea, Hank, to get rid of that woman'a yours who ain't worth shucks."

"Always appreciated your little black heart, Ted. Whatchya got?"

"Ain't my black heart, it's these black fingers." Theodore slid off his glove and braced himself for the smell that always followed. The moist lining of the leather glove had worn away to nothing, and from it spilled the stench of rotting flesh.

"Perdition, Ted! Why didn't you tell me?" The bottle slipped from Henry's grasp and spilled over his cavalry boots before he regained control of it. He couldn't stomach the rotgut with the new rot that filled the air. "You're gonna lose that whole hand if you ain't caref— Oh. Oh,

I see!" A smile lit Henry's drunken face. "Those black fingers look just about like they could fit this ring. Bloody shame about your fingers, though."

"Eh, small sacrifices I can muster. You do this for me, and I do that for you."

"And what am I doing for you, exactly?" Henry asked.

Theodore shrugged. "You take the fingers, you send me home."

"Home to your Merrily. That's all you've ever wanted. A way out of this war."

"And all you've wanted is a way out of your marriage," Theodore chuckled. "So we both win."

"But you lose your fingers."

Theodore reached into his haversack for his razor and his leather shaving strop. "I was gonna lose 'em anyway. Might as well lose 'em for a real cause." He eyed their two rings again. They looked so similar, two matching bands of tin, crudely cut, plain and undecorated. "You got a inscription on that thing?"

Henry looked down. "Naw. Couldn't afford one. You?"

Theodore shook his head and handed the razor to Henry. "You're gonna have to do this; I ain't got the stomach for it. Cut up high. Get the whole thing, and don't leave no stumps."

Henry twisted the straight razor in his hand. "I ... don't think I—"

"Tight lips, and do it. No Sunday soldierin', y'hear? I just sharpened that thing last night. Ain't gonna get no sharper. What you drinkin'?"

Henry grimaced. "Some slush."

"Give it here."

Theodore splayed his left hand over the rock he'd been occupying. He looked one last time at his full left hand, chugged most of the remaining slush, and finished off the rusty, spoiled-citrus taste by inserting his strop between his teeth. "Make it quick, damn you," he muttered over the piece of leather, and he closed his eyes and bit down, allowing the stale alcohol to run through his mind in thoughts of Merrily. *Oh, how he loved her. He'd be home to her soon. He'd be ho—*. Darkness consumed him before he had finished the thought.

Theodore woke to war nurses making a fuss over him, bandaging up his fingers, and Henry looming above him with pity, in between glances at the ladies. Theodore's whole arm throbbed, and he pined for whiskey and opium. He patted his pocket, but they'd taken his vial. He laid his head back and groaned. When the nurses left, Henry extracted from his own pocket a bloody linen handkerchief embroidered with his own initials, and carefully unwrapped Theodore's fingers. Encircling the blackened knuckle of the bloody ring finger, Henry had slipped his own wedding band in place of Theodore's.

"Perfect as can be, pal, except for your poor fingers," Henry said with a wry smirk, and he held them outstretched.

As he did so, a nurse came into the room and drew in a breath, grabbing the handkerchief from Henry, fingers and all. "This is unclean," she huffed. "You can't have this in here." He reached to take it back, but she held it away from him. "Are you injured somewhere?"

"N–No, ma'am."

"Then I'll ask you to return to your post, or I'll call in the captain." She rolled up the hanky and walked out of the room with it.

"Perdition!" Henry cried and paced.

"Go after it!" Theodore said.

Henry turned and walked down the narrow hallway, hiding behind rolling carts on wooden wheels, their tools scattered and blood-covered, large ceramic bowls of pink water, a mound of shrapnel and miniés retrieved from bodies, set to be melted down for reuse, and another pile of teeth, set aside for future dentures. He padded behind the nurse, then ducked to watch her throw the fingers into a tall wicker basket. Blood pooled at the bottom of the basket, and maroon rivulets escaped between weft and weave intermittently down the sides. He stepped toward the basket, but another nurse came around the corner, and he swung back. The nurse lifted the lid and dumped a large tin bowl of body parts into the basket, on top of the fingers. Henry cursed, and the woman looked his way, but he turned and fiddled with the scalpels on a cart, cringing at the blood that wetted his fingertips.

When she'd gone, he went to the basket and lifted the lid. A rush of stench poured out that, for some reason, he hadn't thought to expect. The back of his throat opened, and his mouth soured, but he held it down, and reached into the basket. He pushed aside two indistinguishable organs and a bevy of fingers, toes, and ears, bits of undetermined black flesh, until he came to his wadded handkerchief. He snatched it and slammed the lid and exhaled long and steadily.

When Henry'd made it back to Theodore, the injured soldier flapped the kerchief open, the parts of him still intact needing to see the parts of him now gone.

"Where's your ring?" Theodore said.

Henry's eyes went wide, and he peered over Theodore's shoulder. "Sakes alive." Henry's ring was gone. *The shrapnel scrap pile.*

☙

Much to Henry's dismay, the little metal mound contained dozens of rings, each looking the same as the next. He couldn't tell which one was his own, so he decided some manufacturer had had a heyday with the same tin mold, and meant simply to pick one from the bunch. Wiping his bloody hand on his wool coat pocket, however, he remembered what the pocket contained, and he pulled out Theodore's wedding ring that he'd yanked off the severed finger but hadn't yet returned to its owner. The rings looked so close. Maybe not identical, but Ann didn't have an eye for detail. She'd never know. And Theodore wouldn't really miss it, wouldn't even figure where it had gone. Henry brought the ring back to Theodore's bedside, slipped it on the severed ring finger quickly, and placed the fingers in the hanky in a small, wooden box with four greenback commissary notes that might have been worthless in Tennessee for all he knew, but it was all he had on him.

"Ain't much to leave her," Theodore said, eying the notes in the box. He took out his last payroll stub, curled into a tight tube and burned on one side where he'd rolled it around a tobacco leaf and had taken a few puffs, just to get some warmth into his lungs. Much good the paper did him anyway; there was no value behind it when the banks were empty or printing their own bills at random. But maybe it would be something for Ann, a few extra dollars for the trouble.

"But it got your name on it," Henry said.

"Won't matter. If she can cash yours, she can cash mine. Might look realer for her to know I's here with you, at the last, and thought of passing it on to her for some comfort."

"I s'pose they're writing up a Big Ticket discharge for that red badge of courage you got," Henry chuckled, "but first, you gotta write to Ann for me and send this box along." He smiled, and, despite the obvious pain, Theodore smiled back.

"Find me a pencil." By the time Ann would discover the coincidence between the box containing two fingers and the fact that Theodore was missing those exact same two fingers, Henry would be long gone. Theodore only prayed his blessed Merrily would be so happy to have him home that she'd forgive him the same coincidence. "And then, find me some more goddamn moonshine, so I don't look healthy enough to beat this letter home. I didn't just give you my ring finger for nothin'. I expect you to bring me some damn slush like a happy wife."

Henry grinned and left, and that was the last Theodore saw of him.

☙

The swelling in his hand had gone down by the end of the week, and the nurses kept telling him he had to wait for the surgeon as if reading from a script. When the doctor finally arrived, the man pulled a yellow paper from his pocket. Theodore expected a Big Ticket, but it was a parcel receipt.

"For that wooden box," the surgeon said, nodding. "I've been carrying the receipt around for days while I was in the other sick tent. Mailboys are scarce, but we had a driver headed off to the Tennessee tents, so we got the box sent off to your wife."

"To *my* wife?" Theodore said quickly. "You sent it to *mine*?"

"One of the nurses said it was to be sent off to a wife."

"But not just any wife! To *Henry's* wife!"

The surgeon picked at his teeth with the end of a sickle probe. "Who's Henry?"

"Didn't you read the inscription on the letter?"

"I didn't get a letter. Just a box. If there's a letter, it's thrown in that pile that fills the whole front walkboard. Haven't had a letter carrier in months, and it's not likely high priority now. Half of 'em turned to mold and mush after that last snow soaked the canvas. I was lucky to get that parcel out, you know, and only because I didn't want its bulk laid about. It smelled unholy; thought you mighta tucked food in it, and what a swath of flies that'd bring in. Sent it on Muller's pony, so it'll get there fast as anything ever does."

"But ... to *my* wife?"

"I reckon so, boy." The doctor took hold of Theodore's hand and held it into the light. He pulled a magnifier over the uneven stumps and studied them. "You ought to've let me have at those. I wouldn't have made such a mess of it. Could've saved most of this with a little rod wax and bismuth."

But *to Merrily*? It wasn't too late, though, surely. Not yet. It couldn't be. He'd be there soon, and he could surprise her, and she'd laugh it off and cling to him. Maybe he could even beat the box home. "When do I get my discharge, Doc?"

The doctor laughed. "Discharge? For some fingers?" He laughed again. "Toes, maybe, but hell, it's not even your trigger hand. I'll write you a prescrip for some laudanum and sulfur paste to keep it clean. Can be got at the commissary. Another set of clean patches, and you can rejoin your company in two days."

"Rejoin my company?"

If the new mail wasn't going out for months, he couldn't reach her. He could be in the company for years, traveling further on, north or south, no direction where, but further and further on. The farm was on its last legs, already gone to seed when he'd left. She'd sell it, he knew, and right quick; get what she could and leave the rest behind and go— where? He thought of her opening that box. Receiving no letter, no notice. A paystub with his name on it that looked like it'd been burned. Black fingers and a ring that looked like his. She'd imagine him blown apart in an explosion. The fingers all that were fit to send home.

He took a small solace in that she would know an imposter wedding ring when she saw it. Merrily had an eye for detail, and that one detail would make her wait. She'd know that ring wasn't his.

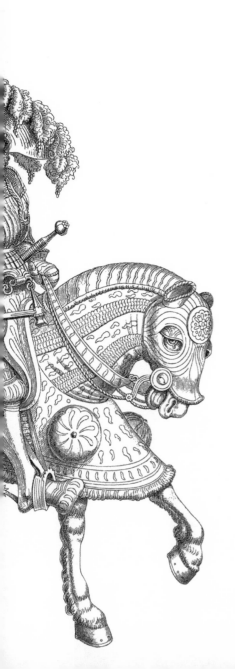

THE DESERT JEWEL

*A*llison Mulvayle spun toward the opening door. In the space between Mitchell Castor's proud stance and Allison's surprise,
there passed only the wail of a distant Atlantic & Pacific Railroad freight lumbering through the outskirts of town, and the creak and
moan of overburdened hinges. Her eyes darted to the new scuffmark
marring the peeling fleur-de-lys wallpaper.

"I did not mean for it to slip out, Mr. Castor," she said, shifting her
gaze to the rowdy townspeople beneath the window where she stood.
"Mr. Blenk shouldn't have repeated it."

"Well, he did. He repeats everything."

A sound from Allison's throat was drowned out by the Main Street
Friday night saloon-goers, some of whom would soon be opening her
door in much the same fashion as had Mitch, but with a different kind
of frustration. "I was drunk. He bought me darkshine and stood right
where you are now, coaxing me. It slipped. Surely you can understand
that, Mr. Castor?"

"We can skip formalities. You sure it's mine?"

"Mr. Castor—"

"Mitch."

"Everyone knows no man is responsible for the goings-on in this room. You don't have to stand there so heapin' mad. Ain't no one gonna pin it on you."

"Ain't what I asked," he said, watching her fidget with the folds of her skirt and her fabric-covered buttons, trying to smooth her petticoat and whalebone stays into place when they were already perfect. "I asked if you're sure it's mine." His voice was softer this time. Her hesitation frightened him, but finally she made a nearly imperceptible nod. "How?"

"What?"

He took off his hat and threw it on the bed, taking the room in a few strides. "How do you know it's mine?" He promised himself he was not going to crumble when he saw her eyes turn bright and misty—this woman he had gone out of his way to lay beside on every cattle drive down from the Idaho Territory.

"I asked Ricky if I could visit someone in Socorro, with a chaperone." She stopped prematurely, distracted by the voices in the saloon downstairs. "Must we speak of this now?"

"Yes." Mitch dug a finger through his vest pocket and pulled out a coin, inspecting it absently before he tossed it at the dish on her bureau. The clanking tintinnabulation of metal on metal struck her like a slap, and he felt disheartened when he saw her wince. "Don't worry about them drunks. I'm buyin' my time here. No one can say nothin'."

"While I was in Socorro, I ..." she demurred, "bloomed. When I returned here, I was stricken with a fever from the sudden exposure to the bar air, the unclean miners," she shuddered, "and I took ill for a time. You know how Ricky is if you've got the discomforts; he quarantined me in the basement for a spell. By then, I should've bloomed again, but I didn't. And in between this time—"

"I came through on my cattle drive, bought you for three nights."

"In between blooming in Socorro and taking discomforts, there was only you. For three nights from Idaho on a cattle drive, yes." The last sentence sounded wistful.

Slicing through the softness of her voice, the door burst open again. The stench of watered-down rotgut rushed the air on the heels of a drunken gambler, a shopworn Colt New Army revolver slung low across his hip, as he stumbled to catch his footing over the threshold. This man was exactly the kind of man who would wear his gunbelt inside an establishment, and when realization hit him that Allison wasn't alone, he measured Mitch with a leveling gaze.

"I just bought my token, cowpoke," the drunken gunslinger slurred. "I'm here for," he raised a finger, "that woman. That gorgeous woman. That ... yellow hair." He made a motion as if to run fingers through Allison's blond locks, a color so uncommon on the New Mexico border, but he met instead with Mitch's upheld palm.

"You'll wait your turn, slinger," Mitch said. "You don't burst into a lady's room without knockin', and I already paid up."

The gunslinger said desperately, "For how long?"

"For long as I'm here."

The man scowled but slinked slowly back out the door, and Mitch wrenched it shut on its squeaky hinges, sliding her makeshift vanity against it for good measure.

"Thank you for that," Allison whispered.

"Don't seem to me like there's nothin' to thank me for."

"It will be taken care of, you know."

"Hell's that mean? Taken care of?"

"I don't get to keep her, Mr. Castor."

"*Her?* Call me Mitch, for God's sake, and why don't you get to keep," he cleared his throat, "her?" A pang struck him when he said it. Allison couldn't possibly know the baby was a girl, but flashes came when he blinked: a chubby baby's face, a tiny girl's fingers wrapped around his own, a pink blanket suckled in the gurgling mouth of a content bundle staring back at him in wonder. *Her.* He named her: Violet, Lily, Iris, Rose —after flowers. He heard her voice—her first words: "Pa" and "No" and "Because why?" and "I don't want to." He watched her grow: knitting, cooking, learning to ride. An image of the first boy she brought home racked him suddenly, standing on the porch with a shotgun ready to kill the first sumbuck who made his daughter a—. The word hung in the air around him. *A whore.* Like her mother. *A bastard.* Like his daughter. The emptiness in Allison's voice jarred him back to reality.

"As soon as Ricky finds out about it, he'll send the girls with that awful root poison and some Bang-Me-Johnny, and I'll be cramped and ... and bleedin' her out, like all the other girls has done." A catch stuck in her throat. "It's just ... I ain't done it before. And she ain't just some drunkard's baby; she's yours. And you," her voice cracked, but she threw her head back, steeling herself for the derision she expected to follow, "you ain't just some dirty miner. You're—"

"I'm just a cowman is all, Alley Cat. I ain't nothin'."

Allison scoffed at his simplification. He was never drunk. If he went over his time, he paid for it without complaint. If a man was already occupying the room, Mitchell Castor dutifully waited. And he waited only for *her*. While she expected that he must have other women between the vast territorial wastelands of the Rio Grande Valley, New Mexico, and whatever town he called home, Idaho, when he came to the Desert Jewel, Mitchell Castor asked only for her and always by name. She'd never even heard him utter the name Sapphire, as the other men called her, except to remark on the color of her eyes. What better was there in a man out here? Allison's hand roamed across the expanse of her belly and sought against her fingertips the tiny truth it held. Mitchell Castor was not 'just a cowman.' She'd been in love with the man for three years.

"It'll be taken care of," she spoke evenly. "I swear."

A gunshot rang out in the street, pulling them from their temporary world, and Mitch walked to the window and let the shutter slam. His fingers were shaking. He dropped his hands quickly to his sides, fiddling in one pocket for his watch fob, and in another pocket for a second coin.

"My time's up," he said grimly, and sent the coin rattling into the brass dish just to cut the silence left by the gunshot. The two-bit ricocheted off a disarrayed stack of pasteboards, then the side of a cut-glass carafe of brown liquid, before landing in a spinning spiral in the bottom of the dish. He approached her slowly. "Come to me, Alley Cat. Ain't no harm in it now." As easily as he ever had, he pulled her against him and buried his nose in her fragrant, clean hair. The thought crossed his mind that he must smell like months of cattle stink and horseflesh and sweaty flannel bedrolls, but her sapphire eyes broke the spell.

"Not for that coin, Mitch. I won't take it."

A corner of his lip curled into a smile. "You wanna marry a cattle-man?"

Her eyes fired. "I told you it'd be taken care of."

"Yeah, all right. So you did."

His smile faded, and he released her so suddenly that she fell against the small sideboard, grasping at the window casement to hold herself upright. She clutched the wobbling oil lamp and porcelain ewer before they could rock to the floor. When she turned around, Mitch had lifted his hat from the bed and was screwing it down on his head. He kicked aside the makeshift vanity blocking the door—toppling trays of burnt-out matchstalks, wax color sticks, and pads of crushed powders and flowers—and sent the rickety piece of furniture sliding into the laughably small hope chest and brass hipbath that had butted against it. The door flung open before he even realized he had his hand on the knob, and he wished there'd been a key in the lock for her to turn behind his exit when he saw the drunken gunslinger standing in the hallway.

Mitch couldn't shake the anger. The anger that this gunslinger would get to touch her, that she wouldn't even bend enough to ask Mitch to take her away from here, beg him to marry her, to be responsible for something besides cattle counts and stock prices. Before he could think about his actions, his finger struck out at the chest of the gunslinger.

"Rough her up, and I swear to God, I'll brand your fuckin' face," Mitch seethed. What had come over him? Never in his life had he threatened a man wearing a gun, and more foolishly still, never before had he turned his back on one. But the look of something deadly must have rung out from Mitch's eyes like a warning tocsin, and the perplexed gunslinger simply touched the brim of his hat and nodded, and Mitch strode down the staircase into the saloon without so much as a glance back.

"Bang-Me-Johnny," a voice spoke that Mitch didn't recognize as his own.

"Hard stuff for you tonight, Castor?" Ricky said, taking a cut-glass decanter from a line of them, each with various amounts of clear and brown liquors and each with a leather rawhide strip around the neck with identifiers etched in sloppy charcoal. "You don't look like you usually look after you seen Sapphire. She leave you unsatisfied?"

"Naw, she satisfied me," Mitch said, then looked down at the drink Ricky placed on the bar between them.

Ricky knew it wasn't Mitch's usual look. As the cowboy eyed the drink—much harder liquor than he usually took—he noticed Ricky's hand come into view, slowly snaking out along the bar top. When the bartender pulled his hand back, two shiny entertainment tokens sat at Mitch's spot on the bar.

"I told you she satisfied me," Mitch said.

"And I'm tellin' you she didn't. Not with that look." Ricky poured more of the brown liquid into Mitch's glass before the disheveled man had even taken a sip of the first round. "Slug it. It's on me. Just like she is next time." The bartender nodded again at the tokens.

Mitch laid his limp hand over the well-worn glass, scarred with nicks from years of drunken abuse, and the room whirred with drunkards, swaying close, bumping by, talking with mouths full of marbles.

Someone stood too fast and a stack of shellacked chips scattered to the floor like clay hailstones. Before Mitch could change his cloudy mind, he gripped the glass so hard he thought he'd break it and chugged the shine down in one swallow. Fire followed. Mitch sputtered and nearly vomited as the heady drink singed his mouth and throat and belly—and he swore his lungs and thighs and feet, too.

"A man could get used to that, eh?" Ricky chided, filling Mitch's glass again. "On me."

The cowboy tilted it back as before, and this time the burn was welcomed. The glass hit the bar with a smack, and Mitch's eyes turned as fiery as the liquid felt going down. "What's her contract stand at?"

"'scuse me?"

"You heard me. How much for her?"

"She's two-bits for ten minutes, Castor."

"Ain't what I mean, and you know it."

Ricky's face that had been jocund, now split into unsettled fragments. "She ain't for sale no other way, Castor. She makes more damn money for this saloon than any other whore I've acquired, and more than the gambling tables and rotgut combined. Everyone wants the Sapphire, ain't just you. She's into me near six thousand in debt, and it'll be years 'fore that contract wears out. By then, hell, she'll be more worn than the contract, and you can have her, with my blessing."

"Six thousand, huh," Mitch let out on a low whistle. "And suppose I can rustle up six thousand to buy out that contract?"

"Even a cattle baron like yourself would be hard up to raise six thousand. And you'd put me out all those incidentals that I ain't interested in losing: the men who come in here just for her, and end up spending their whole pay on booze and blackjack just waiting their turn. She ain't for sale." Ricky poured more of the rotgut in Mitch's glass and pushed it toward the cowboy. "Peace offering." He watched Mitch drink it. "If you just need a woman to wife who won't put up no fight, I can sell you Ruby, Jade, or Pearl. The Desert Jewel can make up for them just fine."

"I only want Allison."

Ricky grunted. "Jesus, Castor, why? You fancy she's going to give you what she gives you in that room? You get her to where you ain't payin' her, and she'll turn into the ice queen. You'll be beggin' me to take her back when she don't please you in your own bed like she pleases you in hers."

"I don't care how she pleases me." The whiskey didn't even burn when it traveled down Mitch's throat this time.

"That so." Ricky leaned back against the counter and crossed his arms, fixing a glower on Mitch, trying to figure the cowboy out.

The room was filled with shouting and laughter all around them—other gamblers and ranchers, miners, and even low-key comancheros, trying to get the bartender's attention for another drink—but the two men leveled each other with glares as if nothing else existed.

A vicious gleam entered Ricky's eyes, and a snarl twitched his lips like a flickering rattler tail. "Well, well. Turnin' noble on me, Castor?" He pulled a leather bag of chaw, stained and moldy, from the drawer at his hip, without rending his eyes from Mitch's. "She's got a little problem I'm gonna have to take care of, don't she. And the fool girl told you 'fore she told me. Tsk-tsk." One pointer finger wagged at Mitch, while the other shoved a wad of Indian chaw along tobacco-tinted gums. "Don't be noble, Castor. No one likes that trait in a fella; makes hypocrites of otherwise decent men. The bun ain't yours, just 'cause she says it is. It could just as easy be mine."

Mitch's eyes sparked, and he impulsively chucked his whiskey glass at Ricky's face, the connection of flesh and glass leaving a budding welt and tiny cut across the bartender's cheek.

Ricky touched the spot of blood, and his snarl grew. "Feel better now?" He leaned both palms against the bar and loomed over Mitch. "How else you think she pays off that debt? Six thousand is a lot of money, even for a busy girl."

The bar stool seemed to leap from underneath Mitch. He raked his spurs along the dowels before picking the wooden thing up with two hands and swinging it over the bar. Ricky ducked, but the stool clamored against the line of decanters and the pyramid of bar glasses, bouncing off the chalkboard, cracking against the mirror, raining shards of glass and booze over the bartender. Ricky bled from his arms, face, and neck. All the merry commotion in the bar stopped, and eyes turned to Mitch. Patrons instinctively reached for their gunbelts—some drew; some just waited—but every man seemed to know this wasn't his fight to finish.

As dribbles of liquor waterfalled over the counter and sluiced into Ricky's Continental suit, Mitch sneered at him. "Slug it. It's on me."

But before Ricky could get to his feet, all that was left of the fight was the violent swinging of two batwing doors, creaking angrily on hinges that needed oiling.

Mitch didn't go back to the Desert Jewel. There was no reason to. He'd never be welcomed there after the way he left, and the tales had gotten to him through the months and the miles that the girls had made a potion of roots and flowers that cured Allison of her little inconvenience. Well over four years had passed since then, and he'd never again made the trip that way into the Valley. It only crossed his mind on the occasional sleepless night when the wind cut through him just right, tallying every grief he'd ever given himself.

"Who's gonna be on watch tonight, Boss?" Bunker's voice split through Mitch's thoughts of how uncomfortably hot the weather had lately been, how hard that was on the cattle.

"I suppose you ain't volunteerin', huh, Bunk?" Mitch smiled.

"I came over here to say, 'No way, not me, sir,' but, hell, you know I'll volunteer to ride the lead bull if you ask it of me."

Mitch chuckled. "Tell Lazy he's on first watch tonight. I'll take second."

"You sure, Boss? You know you ain't got to."

"What kind of man am I if I ask other men to do the things I won't do myself? We'll be back home tomorrow, and I'll have time to sleep then."

Bunker looked away from Mitch and out over the grazing cattle. "The boys've got a bottle passin'; you want I should bring you a swig?"

"I s'pose I could use that."

The interlude was interrupted by the clattering of horse hooves approaching the campsite, and a careless rider shouting out, "Boss! Boss!"

"Easy, Stoke!" Mitch hissed. "You tryin' to start a stampede?"

"Sorry." Stoke's face reddened.

"This ain't your first day out here. Hell's worth all the racket?"

"There's a wagon." Stoke was out of breath from his breakneck pace. "Out … over that way. Southeast of here, Boss. Broke a axle. Women in it … been there starvin' for days in this heat, looks like."

"Jesus," Mitch said, followed by a slew of colorful, indiscernible oaths. "Round up the remuda, Bunk. Stoke, you fill some canteens from the crick and rustle up some jerky from anyone who can spare it. Juan! Sam! Get your saddles on! Lazy, you mind the cattle; you're on first watch, starting early, I'm afraid."

No further explanations were required, although Lazy whined a good deal. The rest of the men could sense the urgency. Mitch headed to the strawberry roan he'd acquired in an Apache trade, strapped down bedrolls and blankets across the cow pony's spavined flanks, rolled a calming palm over the upward-facing C on Gusano's rump, and saddled the old boy. Gusano meant 'You worm!' in Apache, Mitch had found out after receiving the insult and finding it, in turn, a fitting sobriquet for tough old Gus. The Indian had lost a good cow pony for a few cans of coffee, canteens of firewater, and an old Henry repeater that wasn't worth its weight in tin—that last thought preceded the sliding of a Winchester repeater into Mitch's saddleboot. Out here in Shoshone country, a man couldn't be too careful guarding his cattle. A woman, however, was a whole other commodity rarer and more valuable than the entire Castor herd.

Mitch, Bunker, Stoke, Juan, and Sam—all weathered, bowlegged cowmen who might well have been born on horseback—were saddled and riding within heartbeats. The broken-down wagon in question was some twenty miles out from where the men had camped, but Stoke found it through his field glasses and by tracking his own backtrail. Mitch couldn't imagine what a lone wagon carrying women was doing out in the middle of this unforgiving land, but the men didn't hesitate to ride forward and find out. They were met with a startling welcoming committee, however, when a sunburned, bedraggled woman stepped from around the edge of the wagon with a Spencer carbine butted against her shoulder, her eye along the barrel. One look at her shaking fingers told the men she didn't know how to use it—not that that would be any consolation if she suddenly took it upon herself to learn.

Mitch reined Gus in sharply when the barrel sighted on him. "Mind pointin' that at the ground?" he barked. "You hit my horse, and you're gonna face one feisty man who could disarm you of that Spencer 'fore you even found the trigger."

The woman lowered the carbine quickly. So it was as Mitch suspected: she didn't know how to fire it. At least she had the good sense not to prolong the agony of an ill introduction over the barrel of a gun she couldn't shoot.

Her eyes met Mitch's, and she tossed her head in the direction of the wagon. "Axle's broke."

"I can see that," Mitch responded, more coldly than he would've had he not been met with a rifle on his own land. He was sure that she didn't know it was his land, but then, his land went on for thousands of acres. She'd already been riding on his land for days without knowing it.

"Can you fix it?"

"No, ma'am," he smirked, fingering his hat brim, deciding whether he needed to take it off in her presence. Something seemed familiar about her, but he was certain they'd never met. "No way to fix nothin' out here. You're a hundred miles from a town with supplies." He decided to leave his hat on. The sun was scorching, and this woman had gone without a bath for at least as long as he had. No point in trying to impress her. "What're you doin' out here?"

"Headin' to Idaho." She fingered the barrel of the carbine as nervously as he'd fingered his hat.

"For?"

"A man."

Mitch snorted. "Any man, or one in particular?"

"One in particular."

"Who might that be? Maybe I heard of him?"

"Mitchell Castor," the woman replied, and she felt Mitch's eyes grow heavier on her. "My sister said—"

"Never heard of him."

The men expected his reply. A man never revealed his hand until he knew what game was being played. The men were quiet, waiting for the woman to say more, when something broke the tension.

"There's no Mr. Castor?" a tiny, wispy voice came from the other side of the wagon, and five sets of male eyes followed the dainty, childish sound. A little girl, maybe going on four years old, stood huddled near the far end of the wagon. Her oversized calico dress was worn and dirtied beyond any hope of salvaging, and a strip of red bridged her nose from cheek to cheek, the burned skin peeling where she'd rubbed it. Guarded, questioning eyes looked first in awe at Gusano and then found the gaze of the man who rode the beautiful horse.

Without any prompting or notion as to why he was doing so, Mitch slid from the horse and walked toward the child as if a rope connected his center to her, and she had tugged it. Something in his gut twisted, and an instinctual feeling came over him, an uneasiness met alarmingly with a violent, sudden peace. A blanket of calm tossed over a riptide of restlessness that he hadn't even known existed in him for so long. He didn't speak a word; there was nothing to be said. As a father knows, he knew.

The child looked up at him, and without conscious thought, he put his palms beneath the girl's armpits and lifted her into his arms. The curve of her jaw, the tightness at the corners of her mouth, and the straight line of her nose left not a doubt that this was Mitch's daughter. The blinding, sapphire eyes and the blond, soft hair said the girl was, too, Allison Mulvayle's. He buried his nose in the girl's hair and smelled his daughter, taking in deep breaths of her. She smelled of child sweat and range dust and skin oil and sunburned flesh, and she was real. She was a thing he could smell and touch and see, so vividly, colorfully real. He crushed her against his neck almost violently, absently, feeling her tiny breaths against his skin, running his palm up the back of her head to pull her closer, far closer than was even possible, kissing her temple, as she wrapped her tightened fists into his bandana and held him in return.

The men had alighted, each in turn, standing in a semicircle, not needing to be told what was happening. The woman behind the Spencer didn't need to be told, either.

"Her name's Elizabeth. And I take it you're Mitchell Castor."

"Elizabeth," he repeated, daring not to set the child down, for fear she'd vanish like a desert oasis mirage to a thirsting man. "Elizabeth." His mouth found her baby-soft ear, and he whispered, "My Lily, my flower."

"Elizabeth Jewel Castor," the woman replied. "My sister gave her your name. Said it was only right."

"Where is Allison?"

"She's … she's gone." The woman's eyes glassed over, and she shook her head. "I'll tell you, but this ain't a tale for my niece."

"Campfire tonight, then."

The reality of the situation snapped the men into place, pulling the canteens from their saddlehorns and the jerky from their rucksacks, and going about packing up what belongings and necessities they could harvest from the wagon. There'd be no way to fix it out here. It would have to be abandoned. Two other young women, Mexican señoritas, came out of the dilapidated wagon to be greeted with water and a surprised smile by the Mexican ranch hand, Juan. Giggles followed the fumbling of his hat and ridiculous, sweeping bow, but Mitch knew the women would find an easy ally in the vaquero.

Mitch slung little Lily around to one hip, and she clung to him like an urchin, her tiny hands so tight around his neck that she choked him, but he didn't say a word against the stranglehold. Her sweet, tight grip was a welcome noose after his years of desolation and loneliness.

"Boss," Bunker said, extending his canteen out to the little girl. "She's probably thirsty."

Lily put her mouth to the canteen and lapped from it greedily while Bunker tilted the metal container. Never once did she let go of Mitch's neck.

"By God, she's a pretty thing, ain't she? Who'da thought you'd spawn somethin' so pretty?"

Mitch smirked. "Lily, meet Bunk. He's gonna be real good to you, little flower. You need anythin' and can't find your ol' man, you holler at Bunk, okay?" Mitch pulled the canteen away from his daughter's mouth. "Not too much at once, or it'll make you sick."

A gleam brightened Bunker's face. "This kid might just be a good cure for them frown lines."

☙

Christina Mulvayle raised the jug of stale, watery whiskey to her lips, thankful for it. She hadn't tasted anything so sweet since leaving the Rio Grande Valley, and she sipped sparingly, savoring the treat as she eyed her Mexican househelp, Rosa and Lucinda, batting their fickle eyelashes at Juan. Mitch followed her gaze, but he wasn't as alarmed as she was. They were ladies; Juan would take one or the other to wife before he'd take either to bed. Mitch ran his palm lovingly over the head of the child who lay curled in his lap, her grip tight around his belt loop, as if somehow in the night she might lose him while she slept. Her smooth breathing fascinated him, and even as Christina spoke, he could not keep his eyes on the woman for too long without them trailing back to his sleeping daughter.

"Allison ran from that place, and she came to stay with me out past Socorro," Christina said, between chugs. "She gave birth to your baby in the middle of my kitchen. I helped her what I could, but she got it in her fool head that she was goin' to get to you. Come on up to Idaho Territory and bring you your daughter."

Mitch shrugged. "I don't know what I woulda done with Allison. She'd never'a lasted a minute out here, fragile as she was. Not seein' a town for months on end. Eatin' out of cans."

"She was coming on a stage from New Mexico up to Idaho, as far as she could go. She packed a bag and took Lily and left to find you, but it's guessed some Apaches found Allison first. They slaughtered the men, and everyone supposes they took the women for wives or to sell over the border, but they ain't been heard from since. How it goes. No woman can survive out here—if it ain't one man, it's another. Lily was found hiding in the coach by the fellas who came upon the scene, and they brought her home to me, but hell, ain't no saints in this. They coulda just as well taken her, too, for all the good there is in these parts.

"Jesus," Mitch cursed through clenched teeth and took the whiskey jug she passed him.

"By some stroke of luck, Lily come back. But no Allison."

"No body, though."

"No body. I had a little funeral for her, pegged in a stick cross, all that. Raised Lily for years, but I can't do it no more. I got nothin' to give her. Figured my sister was on her way to bring you Lily, then I oughta at least follow out her wishes and bring you your daughter."

"It was a fool thing to do." The set of Mitch's jaw showed he meant it. "If Stoke hadn't been ridin' guard out farther'n he shoulda been, no one woulda ever found you."

The whiskey bottle brushed her lips again and still tasted like heaven. "I ain't sorry I did it." She gazed at the little girl curled in his lap. It looked to Christina like he'd needed the company desperately.

Mitch ran his hand across Lily's shoulder, feeling her grip tighten at his belt as she squirmed against his thigh and made the murmuring noises of a child in dreamstate. "I ain't sorry you did it, neither. No woman wants to hear a man say he didn't love her sister, I know, but that's the way of it. I'll love this little girl she gave me, though. Probably be the only family I'll ever get, way out here." He took the jug, swigged, and passed it back. "You comin' on to my place, or you got some reason to head back to Socorro? You didn't have much in that wagon."

"I don't have much at all. I have an adobe in the Rio Grande Valley, but I can't say as I'll miss it."

"You'll probably miss it when winter comes to this place," he chuckled. "I got little line cabins, plenty of meat chops, and a whole array of men who would gladly marry you or protect you, whichever you ask of 'em. You're welcome to stay. If you wanna head on back Socorro way, I'll have some armed riders escort you through Shoshone country down to Salt Lake City to catch the stage, and I'll buy your ticket out. Either way, Lily stays with me. She ain't goin' nowhere."

The Paso del Norte sun was hotter than anything Mitchell Castor had felt in years, and he soberly vowed he wouldn't bring his cattle down to Mexico in the thick of summer again. Despite how Bunker and Stoke had argued with Mitch not to take Lily on the long drive, she had come, refusing to be left behind for fear her father would never return. How many times he'd had to promise he would never leave her before she had truly believed him, he could no longer count. Bunker said Lily ought to have been left in Idaho with Juan and the Mexican woman Juan'd quickly snatched for his wife—Lucinda—and Sam, who'd taken pretty Rosa just as swiftly. But for all the men complained of inconvenience, they longed to see the author of it: constantly doting on the little girl, showering her with trinkets from the nearby towns, teaching her to throw ropes at rocks and horseshoes at posts, listening to her campfire songs of cowgirl princesses riding tame bulls through jungles to meet with serpents and elephants and fairies. They'd even taken to drinking sarsaparilla, simply so they could pass the jug to her and listen to her bubbly laughter when she drank with the men as they oiled their guns and sharpened their knives on old leather strops. The men utterly loved her. Mitch knew this was a pattern he should probably curtail if he wanted to raise a fine, upstanding lady, but it was inevitable: Lily was destined to be a child of the range.

The little girl clung to her father's leg as they shuffled through the Mexican marketplace. The cattle sale had gone better than expected, and Mitch told Lily she could have whatever she could fit in one rucksack, including the gifts she had promised to get for Lucinda and Rosa, and another she should pick out for Aunt Christina. A day trip through Socorro and the Rio Grande Valley to see her aunt would do Lily well, and Mitch had planned it for the following morning.

Christina Mulvayle had come back to the Upward C with intentions to live in a line cabin and take a husband after her wagon had broken down, but her first winter in Idaho turned out to be her last winter in Idaho, and when the snow finally thawed, she was on the first stage back to the warmth of the Rio Grande, taking one of Mitch's cowhands with her. Mitch let his mind float wistfully back to the Rio Grande Valley. What would come over him when he stood before the Desert Jewel? What would he feel? Anything? Instinctually, he hugged his daughter against his knee, and she squirmed with happiness to break away.

She was lost in bright, colorful Native baskets and blankets, strings of beads, and egret-feather headwear, her eyes wide with adoration for all things excessive and extraordinary. He leaned his arms around her on the table, and she held up a handful of beads the color of sapphires.

"Like your eyes," Mitch said, and he heard the hollowness of the words come back to him. He'd said them before, in a different life, as a different man. There was a sadness here, in this part of the country, a sadness that clung to him closer than his daughter did, a feeling of never knowing what he could have changed or might have been.

"And these are like your eyes, Pa," she exclaimed, holding greenish-copper beads up to his flecked hazel eyes. "Like a lizard's. You have lizard eyes!" She squealed with delight and clutched them both to her chest. "They fit in my rucksack, Pa, both of them."

"¿Cuánto?" Mitch asked the merchant. She held up two fingers, and he held out two coins. "Gracias, señora."

"Gracias, señora," Lily echoed and patted the older woman's hand, both of them smiling.

Mitch placed his palm on Lily's head and bent to kiss the top of it, as a wave of blond hair that matched hers moved past the table like an apparition. Blond hair in a market of Mexican and Indian women stood out like a cardinal in an Idaho snowstorm. The hairs on Mitch's neck stood on end, and a cold jolt of unease shot through his body in the moment just before he turned to stare at the cascade of blond strands that fell straight down the mysterious woman's back. But the woman wasn't a mystery. Mitch felt it all through him: the answer to the riddle, the questions. A smile curved onto his face before realization sank in and wiped it away.

The woman's blond hair was loosely encased in a leather band that went about her forehead. An elkskin blouse came up to her neck, covered her shoulders and arms completely, and came down her torso in a boxlike, unfitting square, cinched only at the waist, and then hanging into a skirt below the cinch. Cords of tiny leather medicine bags hung around her neck, and thick moccasin boot leggings came up over her knees, but there was nothing else. No trace of the jewels that had once graced pale fingers, now bronzed, as worn and callused as a laborer's. Her lashes and eyelids held no sign of the matchstalk charcoal that had once been traced there in delicate lines, the indigo powder made of crushed violets that had enhanced eyes of nearly the same color. The thin blouse let Mitch know she wore nothing beneath it, but as his eyes traveled up to hers, the sapphire eyes that had once sparkled vibrantly were dull and blank. And then the picture filled in: the raven-haired Indian at her side, clutching her around the waist as she swayed listlessly against his bare chest, the child strapped to the board across her back, silent as Indian babies always seemed to be, and the protruding abdomen of a belly rife with new life.

Mitch led Lily deeper into the marketplace, away from the woman, this ghost of their past. He let his daughter's attention linger on some feathered pouches, and he turned and watched from afar as the blond hair moved among the rows. He instinctively put a hand on Lily's shoulder, and cupped it harder than necessary. The Apache's arm snaked tighter around the woman's pregnant middle, and this figure who had once been Allison Mulvayle responded to it in kind. When the man spoke, she turned her head to his voice and lifted her brows.

The bartender of the Desert Jewel had once accused Mitch of being noble, but he hadn't been noble then, and he wasn't going to be noble now. Her ghostly face terrified him, as he hid his child from her view, praying for the distance to remain between them, for the man not to notice Lily's blond hair. His heart raced, and he stood immobile, unable to think of anything but Lily in his grasp. He tugged his child to him, then slowly drew the butt of the Lindsay Twin-Shot pistol tucked in his utility belt, and held it in his hand, feeling its weight. He saw before his eyes everything that his daughter might have become, and though perhaps no worse than what he could offer, it didn't include him in the picture.

The marketplace was crowded, but Lily finally saw the blond hair and pointed frantically. Mitch quickly lifted her into his arms, stepping backward, away, nearing the marketplace crowd in hopes of blending in. When he holstered the Lindsay and looked back, the Apache and his wife, her eyes unchanging, were wending their way along the merchant tables as if the world hadn't suddenly shifted, yet Mitch clutched Lily to his chest, unable to draw breath without her at his lungs, breathing for him, into him. He trembled. Violently, he trembled. What did he feel?— He didn't know. Was it pain? Was it heartbreak? No, it wasn't quite. It was somewhere between that and something else. *Relief*. Utter relief.

He had wondered what he would do if he ever saw Allison Mulvayle again, alive and breathing. Now he knew. And he wasn't noble. He could not save everyone. He couldn't save Allison. But he had saved Lily.

"Pa, that woman had hair yellow as mine," she said, her arms tightening around his collar while she grappled with the rucksack.

"Yes, she did, little flower," he whispered in her ear and took the rucksack from her hand, easing her burden as she lay lovingly against his shoulder, his heartbeats finally slowing in time with hers when he saw the stable that held his horse. "Yes, she did."

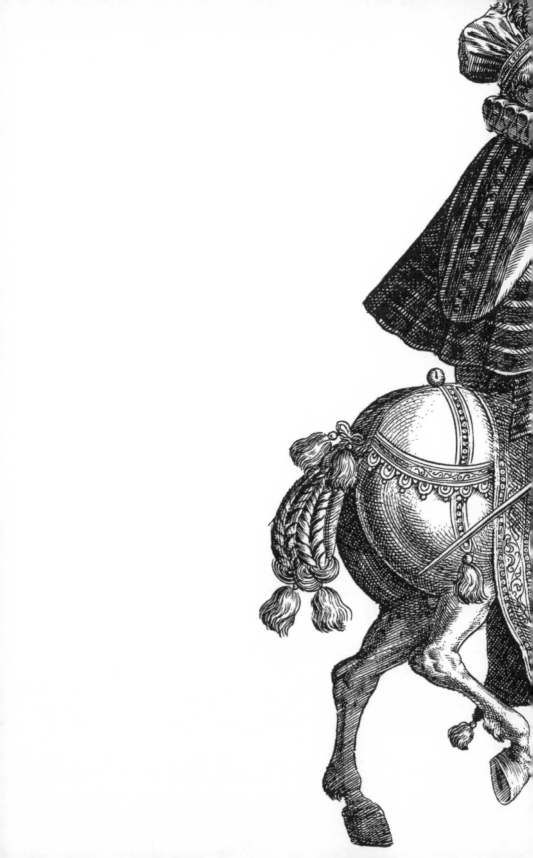

A CLEANING TO THE STOVEPIPE

*P*erceval Béquignol doesn't notice me and never has. He brushed the tip of his saber scabbard against my shin outside the egg coop and followed it brusquely with, "Watch where your hoofs land, boy," before trotting off to mind his whiny old painthorse. I puffed up my chest, batted my lashes, and damn near curtsied, but with the amount of creosote powdering my face from his father's abhorrent maintenance of the wood stove, I might as well have spit on the ground and cupped my widdlies. Percy Béquignol may be a soldier of the National Guard, but it's no reason at all not to know the difference between a boy and a girl.

I try to pardon his inattention to the flat-chested plain thing that I am. I make excuses that the way my maman docks my hair, the breeches that I must don to scale a chimney, and my indelicate features make it hard for someone to notice, if he's never looking. And not that I want Percy to look, either. My maman always says that you can tell everything about a man from the way he treats those beneath him—she says this as she shoves me out the door to collect pay so's her decanter never dries, mind—and if this is my criterion, then Percy Béquignol is a despicable man. Still, he could notice that I'm a girl, just once—and I wouldn't say no if he asked me to the theater after noticing. I've never been to the theater, see. To go with a man like Percy would raise a curtain on a new life.

As far as occupations go, I do the jobs that no one else wants. There's not much competition, see, if I don't mind breathing in soot, burning myself with lye, and shoveling horse chips into the fire. And it's not that I *don't mind* these things, mind; it's just that a young woman born to my station has no other prospects to speak of. My maman often slurs that I'll be a spinster if I don't go make myself useful, and I haven't the heart to tell her that I'd rather be a spinster than in the employ of a man who hasn't looked my way long enough to discern that I'm not a boy.

Of course, I'm not really in his employ. It's Percy's father, Jacques-Joseph, whom I must tip my cap to. If I ever thought Percy a despicable man, the thought vanishes when I am met with his father. Jacques-Joseph is a man of no mercy. He could crush the spirit out of a ghost. I give Percy all the benefit of the doubt in the world because he was fighting iron to turn out half as well as he did, under the arrogance and ignorance of his father's rearing. I, on the other hand, am not so lucky to escape Jacques' wrath, and as Percy is now old enough to go off to the Revolution, my giving Percy's own poor manners the worn-out pass gets harder to justify by the week. Endurance and silence for a pocketful of deniers has become my sullen burden.

This particular morning, I have been partaking in the unpleasant task of cleaning the pipes and chimney of Jacques' wood-burning stove. He is most careless with this contraption, never correctly operating the flue nor emptying the ash pans beneath the wood grate. That's how Mr. Lembeau's roof caught fire, and I had warned him; I truly had. Instead of thanking me for the advice and taking the needed care with the stove, I was fired from Mr. Lembeau's employ, thus ending up in the clutches of Jacques-Joseph Béquignol and his militaristic son, Percy. There is always work to do on this homestead; I doubt I'll have the relief of being fired from here.

I have traveled back and forth from the cast-iron parlor stove to the horse stable near a dozen times today, carrying buckets of ash to the soap pot. Making lye soap is a messy, painstaking, and smelly process, so Jacques prefers it done in the stable, while Percy—more a man of his whiny old painthorse than of the indoor parlor—would prefer that I take the boiling pot back into the house. Either way, I can't win this. To anger one is to anger the other; to anger neither is to leave a job undone. There will be no gratitude, only indifference, and all I can do is get back to the boiling pot in time to stir it. Surely, both men would notice the inconvenience more if they ended up with lumpy, ugly soap.

The pipe and chimney cleaning have left me in a state of disrepair, covered in black like those traveling minstrels we've heard of in the New World. I've heard lots of stories from there. Seems everyone's intrigued with it lately. We may be headed into a rebellion such as theirs, I hear, but up here in the northern Pas-de-Calais countryside, I only get that impression from Percy. He'll soon be gone permanently, I also hear, to serve in Paris. I wonder if his whites and blues will stay so sharp in the dirty city. I wonder if he'll miss my cleaning them for him—*that boy* who cleaned a nobleman's uniform.

Stories will come back to me, then, of how the ladies swoon over him and how he treats their kind with syrupy charm. When he doffs his tricorne, they'll see his thick mop of matted, sweaty hair, and they'll think it roguishly handsome; their first thoughts will not be of how stubborn that sweat is to get out of the lining of his hat, or how, where a head sweats, so, too, does the back of a neck. That sweat around his collar is an impossible chore, but the women he'll charm are the type who only notice these things once they've married into them. *Oh, the poor, unfortunate creature that woman turns out to be!* Yet—though I've never been privy to his syrupy charm or thought fondly of his sweaty mop—I wouldn't say no if he were to ask that very thing of me. What woman would have the willpower of negation against a thing like Perceval Béquignol? I doubt the boy—and he is a true boy, not but seventeen—has ever heard a woman negate him.

These are my silly thoughts as I return to the parlor to find Jacques —better known to me as *Lord Béquignol, sir*—quibbling on about something or other with the fourth Lady Béquignol, something involving his prat of an only son and a woman Percy's took an unpopular fancy to. I've no way to put this delicately, but it's not a fancy at all, merely a flight of fancy, something rather more unpopular, and Jacques does not even see fit to hush his voice with me in the room. I'm wondering if, perchance, *he's* forgotten that I'm female, too—deemed me too unladylike in my breeches to bother with manners or social etiquette. Colorful language pours from his mouth, until the Lady exits the room to save her bleeding ears, and Jacques' sharp tongue turns to me as a dupe. My place is merely to take it if it's served to me, even as a cold dish, but I try to act disinterested while I diffidently shovel around the remaining ashes in the stove. I've turned into a quiet pip of a thing in this man's daunting presence. No wonder Percy was of such vile mood this morning en route to the stables; no doubt his father had already pegged him full of holes.

Then, as if I'd spoken of the devil, the devil walks in. Fresh back from a jaunt, Percy is splashed with mud up the front of his knee-high boots and white fallfronts (*Bless it, who thought of a uniform with white fallfronts?*) and along the tips of his royal-blue longcoat. He holds his tricorne in his hand as if asking a girl to marry him, but in this case, the stance serves for apology just as well. My face scarlets when his eyes fall to me, knowing I'd heard well enough already about his indiscretions. As a boy, however, I am dismissed quickly. It does not matter if boys know of indiscretions.

"I had a most unpleasant visitor today, Perceval," Jacques starts.

My eyes narrow. *He did? I saw no visitor. I'm the first to see visitors, and—*

"A little birdie," Jacques continues, "told me some news."

Ah, metaphorical visitors are not so easy to spot. I stand and wait for this news as eagerly as Percy, but I can see that Percy plainly knows already what is going to be said. He allows his father to say it anyway.

"Matilda Brackenridge is not a plaything," Jacques says. "She is an English maiden—"

"*Was,*" Percy boldly corrects.

His father and I freeze into place, and Jacques' nostrils flare in and out like Percy's whiny old painthorse. Percy throws me a get-back-to-work glance, and I pretend to dust some of the ashes back into my dustpan. Instead, I dust them out of it so that I may linger longer, dusting them in again.

"And have you intention to marry her, then?" Jacques asks.

"Certainly not. She is English! She is disdainful, flighty in the head, inelegant of manner, foolish, clammy as a fish, and unable even to sew a proper sampler. You should have seen the pathetic attempt she showed me—"

Poor girl, thinks I.

But it is Jacques who answers: "Matilda's father has come forth, hearing of your ..." Jacques can't find a word. He steals a glance at me. *Murder! Don't look at me! I am of no use in this!* "... your ... your ..."

"... indelicacies," Percy adds, smirking.

I fear I'll need to sweep up the pieces of Lord Béquignol's burst face, but instead, he remains eerily quiet in his manner. It is almost more frightening than when he explodes.

"Yes, *those*," Jacques replies. "Lord Brackenridge says that you have soiled his daughter and that you will have to marry her."

"I'll not marry her. She is painted."

"Perceval! There is a lady present!"

Percy flashes his eyes at me quickly, and then his glance chases after the path his stepmother took up the stairwell. "No, there isn't. Unless you're insulting *me* by that. In which case I'll remind you that I wield more than one saber."

He only carries a smallsword, thinks I at this, but then, well, it's fitting.

"Hush your vulgarity!" Jacques says. "The only way you'll get out of this bed you've made is if you marry another, and make quick step of it. Else you're stuck with Miss Brackenridge, and I dare say I'll do nothing to stop her father from making right on his daughter's honor. Would that I had daughters, I'd do the same. And Lord help them if they ever suffered the likes of you, you blackguard."

Oh, bravo! This is quite the first time I've been in line with Lord Béquignol, and I dearly want to shout it. Not that he could ever keep those hypothetical daughters from suffering a Percy, mind, but what a thought to say it aloud! I pretend to be sweeping some more of the ashes, when Jacques' eyes meet mine again, and something unreadable plays across his face.

Then, he abruptly states, "You'll have to marry Isabelle."

I choke audibly. Something is stuck in my flue. *Merde! Did I just say I was in line with Lord Béquignol?*

Jacques repeats, as if calling, "Isabelle!"

"Who's Isabelle?" Percy asks.

I drop the dustpan, and the awful clatter is rivaled in comedy only by the cloud of ash that puffs around me, coating me from foot to face. "I am Isabelle," I supply, coughing and waving my hands wildly.

"That boy?" Percy asks.

"What boy?" Jacques returns.

"The chimney-sweep boy?"

"That's not a boy, for heaven's sake, lad. Did I raise you that dense?"

I say, "Yes, you did, sir."

"Don't agree with him, boy!" Percy yells.

Percy's eyes crease to slits. I drop the dustpan again. *When did the blasted thing become so slippery? Am I sweating?* He takes a man-sized step toward me, and I swear that I am shrinking. The rest of the showdown, I see now, is to be between me and this young man who wears fainted women draped around his neck as ascots.

I manage, sharper than I should, "I'm a girl."

"How long have you been a girl?"

"As long as you've been a cad, sir, so all my life, I suppose."

"Clever," he murmurs—not for me to hear, but I hear it—then louder, "And how long have you been clever?"

"A mite longer than you, I'd wager."

Percy's hand goes to his sword, an action I'm sure is so instinctual that it doesn't register. All his words are under his breath, "A smart-mouthed little thing—"

"Been smart longer than you, too." *How bold am I, so all of a sudden!*

And then, there comes a face that defies all description, something like realization. "… And I'm … I'm to … to marry you?"

The patches on my shoes become the most interesting thing in the room. I can't look up, can't meet his fiery eyes. There's disappointment in his tone that makes me feel ashamed, though I've not reason to, and my voice turns unnaturally apologetic. "I'd make a good wife for any man, sir. You don't have to say it like you're spitting poison. I can sew and cook and launder and keep a house clean. I can clear up a sooted stovepipe, muck out a stall, empty chamber pots, and right a broken axle. You name me one other wife who could do all that with nary a complaint!" When I finish my laundry list, I am shaking. I turn on my heels and run—out of the parlor, out of the kitchen, out of the house, off the porch, and past the egg coop, before I hear Percy yelling after me.

"No!" he calls.

I cannot block him out, cannot outrun him; his legs are longer.

"No, wait! Don't run off! You would." He catches my arm and spins me around to face him, both of us breathless. I'd never known before how tall he was, how swift his strides, how iron his grip. "You would. Make a good wife for any man. It's just …" he loosens his grip, "not for me, see."

"No, sir, I'm afraid I don't see."

For a moment, he fidgets with the fingers he's just unlatched from my arms; then, he takes on the charming air that must have swept a hundred women off their feet. "Oh, bother, if it gets me out of marrying Matilda, then … well … at least you're French."

"I am that, sir." *Poor Matilda! What she's missing! The girl really ought to learn to sew a sampler.*

Percy leans in. "Isabelle, *girl*, will you clean up and go to the theater with me tonight?" A devil pulls Percy's mouth up at one corner. "You'd be a fool not to."

The words fly around in my head like magic carpets. *Oh, how many times I have wished for him to ask me, wished for just this very thing! How lovely and sincere the words sound as they tumble from his mouth, and how I had yearned for him to notice me.* He is noticing me now, his eyes roaming up and down me like there is some spot he's missed. *Yes, yes! I'll go to the theater! Yes, yes! I'd be a fool not to!* I'd be a fool not to marry him! *A fool!* If his father wills it so, then Percy will follow through—knowing he'll hardly have to be bothered with me when he's called off to Paris—and in this one chance of fate, I have at my fingertips the unobtainable man. I nod my head, but inside, my maman's words come back to me: *you can tell everything about a man by the way he treats those beneath him.* In this moment of my nodding head—right when his eyes light up with the realization that he's captured me for good and for true and that I am a better prospect than Matilda—my mouth betrays me.

I swear it is somebody much stronger speaking, when I somehow reply, "No, thank you, sir. I shall remain the fool today, but all the happier for it tomorrow."

THE LIGHT AGES;
OR, HOLES IN THE HEART

*For my Aunt Julie, whom I never met but for family photos and
the parts of my dear father's stories he could never speak aloud,
through the hole her absence left in his heart.*

eriwether Capp meeting Julie Fischer was one of those rare
accidents as likely as a repeat of the Carrington Flare, so
the announcers on the field radio promised of the solar di-
saster fluke thirty-seven years later, on its anniversary day. With one
lucky swing of his cracked Spalding, he'd sent the baseball too high,
over the wooden board, past the village oak, and into a second-story
window of the Fischer house. It could have bounced off the Greek Revival pilasters or the pedimented gable. It could have thunked against the
heavy cornice, nicked the moldings, or rolled down the colonnaded back
entryway. It could have been any window. But it was Julie's, far up at
the back of the old mansion on Mallard Street, near the lake that punctu-
ated the cul-de-sac of the upper class.

Meriwether chased after its arc, heard the glass shatter, and paused
at the end of the block to watch what unfolded, half hoping no one saw
it, but knowing more so that his scholarship depended on him doing the
right thing about it. He hoped picking up the graveyard shift at the all-
night depot stables for a couple months would earn him enough in tips

to afford a pane of lead glass—they had to have lead glass, of course. He didn't want to have to sell his phonograph; it was his only sanity against studying. He could maybe part with his C piccolo, for it was his D♭ piccolo he used most frequently these days. He wouldn't part with his treble flute, though, not for a window. His father would be angry if he asked for a loan upfront. But he was only two years into his medical degree at the university, and had to rely on honesty and accountability to get him through the last three years of it without being let go. He'd have to tell his father. This was his desperate thought as he picked through some mulberry bushes and crouched across a deep thicket of Winged Elm branches and maple saplings—trying not to snag his team uniform —to approach the backside of the mansion and survey the damage before walking around to the front of it facing the lake. He saw a shadow move within the room, behind the broken glass, and he stood under it to catch the attention of the person inside. When no one visited the sill, he called to it.

"Hello, there! I'm sorry about your window!" He looked up hopefully, but no one came into view. The shadow, however, hovered there. The obvious outline of a woman. He scrunched his lips together. "It were I who broke it, but I will pay for it," he tried again.

As he kept looking, a single hand came from the side of the pane and pulled a lace curtain shut over the opening. A feminine hand, gloved like a young lady. The shadow then moved freely behind it, and he could make out the shape of his baseball in the hand, silhouetted behind the lace.

He scowled and muttered, "Blasted, I'll come up for it then."

The front columned porch was too oversized to be welcoming, but that was to be expected of the houses in these parts. Old money. They'd been rooted here since the first settlements, and they came from railroad stock, mercantile enterprises, shipping industries, patents, steamboating, and blatant conning. Some of the founding men conned still, and the county protected them because their hush donations paid for the scholarships that allowed Meriwether to become a surgeon. He would be one of the first doctors to specialize exclusively in the liver, spleen, gallbladder, and surrounding lymphatic system. Someday, he, too, could make a donation to the institution, but he swore it would come from honesty and hard work, not legal scamming that would be illicit were anyone brave enough to cease looking the other way. He knocked on the excessive door, wondering if the sound could even penetrate to the other side of the thick mahogany.

After a long moment, a maid answered. "Yes?" she asked brusquely.

Meriwether presumed the maid wasn't supposed to answer the door in this manner, and he took it to mean that the man of the house wasn't home. The woman of the house, however, clearly was. A singsong voice curled through the high rafters of the large, open foyer behind the maid.

The brusque woman straightened and painted on a weak smile. "I mean," she started in a whisper, "how may I help you, sir?" and ended in a near shout.

Meriwether bowed formally. "I have by accident sent a baseball from our practice over the fence and into your window." He indicated behind the house and watched the maid take in his sweaty uniform, a patch of dirt on his right hip and buttcheek. He blushed at his appearance and ran a palm through his black hair, which was usually neatly parted to one side and waved upward on the other, unmatching a trim mustache that grew in too light. He usually wore a sacksuit with fabric buttons, a plaited coronation stock-tie with matching waistcoat and pleated trousers. "Forgive me," he said apologetically. "I do not permittedly call in such a state, but I came straight away from practice to claim responsibility and give my utmost in regrets."

The singsong of the house's matron rang. She approached the door, shooed the maid away so imperceptibly it almost passed for polite. "We shall retrieve the ball for you, my son." She nodded toward the stairs, and the maid went without a further word. "You may step inside."

"Oh, no, ma'am. I'm far too unkempt to—"

"I insist," the woman said, drawing on his arm. "I never leave my door open to the perturbations of this town. It is safer inside than out."

"Although not safer to admit a stranger, I should say," Meriwether laughed to ease her, but she only twitched her lip. He cleared his throat. "A woman upstairs has captured my baseball. I should very much like to thank her for the return of it, and to apologize in person for my upsetting of her toilet."

"You are mistaken, my son," the woman said, smiling. "There is no one upstairs. But Matty will fetch your ball. Matty!" she called up the stairs after her.

The maid came to the landing with her fingers wrapped around his baseball, and she called down, "I'm here, Mrs. Fischer!"

"No," Meriwether said, "there was a woman. I saw her."

"This woman came to the window?" Mrs. Fischer said, curiously, glancing at Matty when the maid returned. She held out her hand for the ball.

"Well, no," he replied. "But I saw—"

"Then it was only your imagination, boy. My daughters are at boarding school. Perhaps it was Matty?"

He looked to the dark, overworked, ungloved fingers of the plump, middle-aged maid as she stayed silent. It wasn't Matty. "Perhaps, it was," he said softly, taking the ball from Mrs. Fischer. "Please tell me what I owe you for the window. I do rightly apologize for the inconvenience of all this."

"You must have quite a swing," she replied, the song back in her voice.

He shrugged sheepishly. "It gets me by."

Mrs. Fischer smiled at him and ushered him toward the door. A sound came from upstairs, and Meriwether looked toward it, then Matty disappeared after it like a hot poker had spurred her rump into motion. He opened his mouth to say something, then closed it. It wasn't his concern. He had what he came for.

"I can pay in installments if you're obliging, or if that's not desirable, I can take a loan from my father to pay it in full. I will—"

"Fear not about the window. It is only glass. Sometimes it breaks." She waved it off indifferently. "My husband will fix it. You just run along to your practice before it ends without your mighty swing."

"But I—"

"And be careful of this town," she added, closing the door between them while she said it, lowly, as if it were a secret. "It will chew up nice boys like you and spit you in the gutter."

For a few moments, Meriwether stood on the porch, bewildered. The ball popped up and down in his palm without him knowing he was tossing it. He felt he might be listening for something, then thought perhaps the whole thing had been his imagination, from ball to woman to window to porch to maid to Mrs. Fischer. He studied his ball. No, he reasoned. There was a young woman.

He walked back around the house, through the thickets that kept the backside from view or access, and he reveled in the quietude of the nearing dusk, its thickness like a laurel he could wear, a fog coming in from the lake. He stood there, in the thicket, for minutes and minutes, the sun dimming in the distance, until her lamps were lit. She was real, he knew. He'd stayed long enough to satisfy his curiosity, but she wasn't his business. He turned to go, and then the night filled with an exotic music. Like a violin, but heavier, huskier. The throat of a humming bison. The vibration of bees. Geese, wings scything, migrating south into a glass jar. He turned and looked back, and it came from her room, the glass she'd broken out the rest of the way. Some ancient instrument known only to time, a hollow sound like a wooden tub, with strings of fine horsehair that stretched and suspended like lifelines for Clotho, Lachesis, and Atropos to sever. He really should go, he decided, but he walked from the thicket toward the house, unashamed to be still standing in his sweaty, dirty uniform, ungentlemanly and wild, her horsehair threading into him and pulling him inward, then forward. He dropped his baseball in the grass.

"Psssst," he stage-whispered outside her window. "Hey! Hey, you making that music!"

It stopped. He felt an airy vacancy fill in like dirt in a pit, leaving him suddenly heavy of a burden he didn't wish to possess. But her hand came to the curtain, and she pulled it back, and it seemed to take her a moment to get situated before the sill.

"Hi," he said stupidly. "You found my ball. I broke your window." He felt like his words were as heavy as his gut once she'd stopped playing. "I'm Meriwether. Meri. You can call me Meri."

"Hello, Meri," she said sweetly. "I suppose this hole in my window does permit my song to travel." She laughed pleasantly, one side of her face lifting higher than the other.

Meriwether was confused. Why had anyone said she wasn't there? She was there. "Will you play it again?"

"Sure."

"What is it?"

"This old thing?" She held up a V-shaped wooden box with a hole cut through its heart and strings pulled taut across its middle. "It's a psalterion. It's what I play best, given the state of things." She held the box oddly in her left arm, bracing it against an elbow that hardly complied, and she drew a double-stringed bow across it with a swift right hand, seeming only to graze it as if the strings were insubstantial. The song was an uncommon rendition of "El Capitan March" followed by a bawdy, "My Gal Is a High-Born Lady."

Halfway through a Ragtime version of "A Hot Time in the Old Town," Meriwether found himself climbing up the trumpet vine trellis that scaled the nearest pilaster, his face nearly at her sill. She was laughing over the beat, and it was all he could hear.

She turned her face, stopped, laughed at him, and leaned one arm on the pane. "Why, hello, Meri. You may as well climb up." She smiled, and it was lopsided. "My mother might have told you that I'm Julie."

"No," he said, climbing one leg into the window and hauling himself in clumsily to avoid the broken glass. It had been swept from the floor. "She rather told me that you didn't even exist." He could smell himself through his soiled uniform. "I'm sorry to drop in on you like this."

She laughed heartily until she snorted, "Drop in on you like this!" then cupped one hand to her mouth in embarrassment that faded quickly under more laughter.

She was a merry creature, he surmised. The world came to her like a song. She set aside her psalterion with little grace, and it was then he saw that she held one arm up against her chest, its fingers curled in on themselves. When she caught him looking, she blushed, and her merriment ended.

"You ought not be in here for long," she said. "If Mother saw you, she'd have one of her conniptions that could last well into the dawn. She gets so full of hyperbole and swansong when my father is away." She looked down and plucked a single string with her right hand, which seemed to work as it should. Her left arm never moved. "Of course, I speak too fondly, Meri."

"You may, of course. I will repeat nothing of it. I only climbed up here because your mother, well." He paused. "May I speak fondly, too?" When she nodded, he said hurriedly, "Your mother insisted that you were only a figment of my mind."

Julie laughed. "Yes. You get used to it."

"Used to what?"

"Not existing. Being in a half-life where night is a companion, and music is a voice of the wilderness that proves a world beyond a broken window that doesn't exist, either."

He furrowed his brow and looked to the bed.

"You may sit," she offered, waving one hand at it. "I'm not really a poet, I swear."

He remembered the dirt on his uniform only after he sat, then stood again quickly.

She looked at the window, bemused. "I have never seen this window open. I have rarely even smelled this city, and here it is, like a marketplace rushing in." With this, she smiled with the right side of her face, the left side blank, trying to follow along.

He wanted to ask her about it. He knew the bodily signs from his classes, but the story was always different. Instead he looked about the room and noticed a whole row of instruments. He imagined everyone asked about her arm, her smile. A hammered dulcimer on a mount, rigged up with one hammer on a metal foot pedal. An mbira thumb piano, a concertina, and an even larger psalterion in one corner, standing like a harp. "You play all these?"

Julie smiled. "Do you like music?"

"I do. My father says it keeps me from my studies, but I insist to him that something must." The strings of the dulcimer were irresistible to him, and he dreamily plucked them. They were tuned beautifully, so he plucked another.

"Can you play it?" she asked.

He shook his head. "This is from the Dark Ages or something."

"Ha!" she said mockingly. "The Dark Ages were Dark because they had no art or music." She laughed and winked with the one eye that would move. "Shows what you university boys know." She pointed to the H on his uniform.

He didn't want to watch her when she moved, but he couldn't help himself. With the wrong leg forward from the bed, she shifted awkwardly where she sat, sliding one hip out from under her, the other only following as a shadow. She hoisted herself off the bed and onto her right leg, and he could see that the entire left side was dead. Her left arm crumpled against her chest like a wrinkled newborn's, as useful as a stick. The left side of her face stayed blank, and her left leg dangled lifeless at first, then dragged behind its sister leg with no contribution of its own. He glanced away, and the heaviness was back in his gut, a pit of dirt, sandbags stacked against the firebreak of his belly. This is why she didn't exist. He looked back at her, and she came toward the hammered dulcimer, a walk like an injured animal, a drag-lumber.

She laughed when she got to the instrument and lifted the hammer in her right hand, then placed it in her mouth and talked around it, "Prepare for the transcendent."

Her right foot slid over the custom-made pedal for the second hammer, and as she pressed her toes down on it, she plucked with her right hand, her fingers moving like tiny seizures across the strings. One hammer hit, and again, and the strings sounded out the introduction to the first movement of Chopin's nocturnes. She slid her good hip into the moveable pedal hammer to caress it forward and back and to side and to side across the wooden face, then shifted it with her hand in the fractions of seconds between notes, then back to the plucking as if she'd never left it. Her fingers danced, and then she reached for the hammer in her mouth, flicked it against three strings, and set it back in her mouth in time for her fingers to strike the next note.

Meriwether's jaw fell open. It sounded like a softly hammered, echoing harp, and even with one hand and one foot, she never botched a beat between hammer and pluck with the same fingers. "Incredible," he said genuinely, the pit in his gut replaced again by that airy lightness, as if the high, gauzy notes filled him like a hot-air balloon. "Why have you never played at the auditorium?"

She missed a beat, hit the wrong string. She laid the hammer down and looked at it as if it had suddenly grown foreign to her.

"Do you never leave this house?"

"Why would I leave this house?"

"Because there is a whole world out there." He gestured toward the window.

"A whole world for you, Meri." Her foot lifted off the pedal, and the hammer struck an ugly note that hung there. "Not a whole world for me."

"But look at this gift you've got."

She turned to him. "You can ask it."

"Ask what?"

"What would you like to ask?"

He sighed and looked down at his two working hands, twiddling into each other like a nervous child. "You mean, do I want to ask what happened?" He didn't look up at her, but he felt her half-smile. Heard a struggle for air that he hadn't noticed before. Did she only have one lung? Is that what he should ask? "No," he said, too high to sound convincing. "If you wanted me to know, you'd tell me. A gentleman doesn't ask."

"They breed you university boys to be gentlemen now?" she said playfully.

He looked her in the eyes, unafraid this time. "Let's talk about Chopin."

She laughed. "Do you know what a blue baby is?"

He shook his head and plucked a string.

"It is when a baby's skin and lips are blue at birth because of a heart malformation. Somehow the blood does not get the right amount of oxygen, or it mixes through the heart in a way it's not supposed to. Through a hole." Julie reached back to the dulcimer and picked up the hammer, struck a couple notes. "I have a hole in my heart."

"God," Meriwether muttered. "They can't fix it?"

She shook her head. "Some doctors have tried on other babies, but there have been no successful operations. The babies die. When I was only days old, I had a stroke." She shrugged one shoulder and laughed as if that were all there was to do about it. "Now we just count the days."

His lower lip came down as if to speak, but instead he picked up her mbira and thumbed some off-tune chords.

"It's all right if you don't know what to say. You don't have to say anything."

"I do have to say something," he spoke too quickly, too loud. "Why have you never played at the auditorium?"

She shushed him at footsteps on the stairs. "It's Matty! You have to go."

He thrust the mbira at her good hand, hurried to the window, and gingerly climbed out feet first over the broken glass. One piece caught him on the arm and tore a jagged cut. He cursed loudly and dropped to the roof of the columns, then shimmied down the iron trellis and out into the night. Behind him, Julie had taken up the psalterion again, and her double-bow rowed across the strings like a listing boat, the seas around it willing the calm to filter out in gentle waves. Meriwether slowed and listened and floated into the moon and the stars on an open ocean of placidity and consolation, reveling in two working hands and two working legs, but mourning the new hole in his heart.

He couldn't sleep that night. How could he ever sleep again? How could he go to Psychology 2 in the morning, to Art History and World Civilizations 1700 to Present after that, knowing that the world was wrong? That something in it was broken now? And it had always been broken, but now he knew it? And World Civilizations 1500 to 1700 had been spooned in a dint of victories, and no one had ever mentioned how broken it was, that there were broken things more beautiful than victories. He couldn't sleep. His arm throbbed from the cut, and it folded in against him like a newborn's. Would she hear his piccolo, and think it an instrument she could never play? He'd bring it anyway. He'd take it to her like an offering. For being complicit in all this. For being on this side of the window.

Then he shook his head of it. He couldn't go back there. She didn't exist. He couldn't go around creeping into windows like the boys who got expelled or arrested. And of course she'd like his piccolo. She didn't begrudge him his two working hands. Stop it, he told himself. He could not sleep. Stop it, stop it, stop it. You don't have to save her. She doesn't need to be saved. She just needs to be heard, to be seen, to know she exists. She exists. Just help her exist.

The next morning, he dragged himself to Psychology 2, and the morning after that, and the morning after that, evading John's study hall and extra baseball-tossing with Ira, and jogging the millrun with Levin, then off to Anatomy, and Anatomy again, and again, and Medical Biology, and skipping Cedrick's dissection study so he didn't have to explain his head in the clouds, until he found himself standing in the thicket of Winged Elms and maples in a following dusk, holding his Db piccolo. He lifted the neck joint to his mouth, took in a deep breath, and pressed down over the lip plate. Out came Sousa's "Semper Fidelis" march, surprising Meriwether. It seemed so patriotic, but that wasn't what he meant. But he'd committed, so he played it as loud as he could, and he watched as two lamps lit in outer rooms of the house. His care couldn't be bothered to stand witness. Julie's window was still broken, covered merely by the lace she drew back, and she stuck her head out, looking toward the edge of her property. He knew she couldn't see him, so he played louder, and he heard her laugh. A moment later, she joined him at the window on her psalterion, the medieval sound of it, Baroque and tinny, somehow blending with his shrill march. He smiled around his lip plate and played until the back door opened with a slam, until he sank back into the trees laughing, marching with his piccolo piping all the way back to his dormitory, to evade John and Ira, Levin and Cedrick, to sleep.

On a following Sunday, Meriwether stepped out of his apprenticeship at St. Mary's Hospital just after dawn, coming off his nighttime shift in the fresh-death ward, where he'd prodded newly dead livers and lymph nodes for the better part of twelve hours. His eyelids so heavy they felt attached to his cheeks, he hardly noticed that he'd turned onto the brick walk of Main, where people bunched in cliques near the newspaper stands and the biscuit vendors, the bacon wrappers and the carts of fine cigars just in off the Erie & Kalamazoo line of the New York Central Railroad, bought up by those fat Vanderbilt pockets some time back. Everything came in from New York now.

Just as he was pondering the cost of a biscuit, he stepped in front of Mrs. Fischer on the boardwalk and looked up sharply. She gasped with dramatic histrionics. The man on her arm must have been Mr. Fischer, and Meriwether stuck out his hand, glad not to be wearing his uniform this time. He wasn't exactly fresh, but he wasn't covered in sweat, either. He hoped the scent of livers and gallbladders didn't linger on him.

"Mr. Fischer." He shook the man's hand before Mr. Fischer knew what was happening. "Meriwether Capp. I'm the man who broke your window. I never intended to leave it broken, and I do still mean to make right on that."

Mrs. Fischer cut in between them. "Nonsense! It's already fixed. We are having a dinner party tonight and can't have the house draughty."

"Is that an invite?" Meriwether asked with a grin.

Mr. Fischer, purportedly confused about Meriwether's relation to the family by this sudden familiarity, said, "Of course!"

Mrs. Fischer elbowed him in the ribs. "My daughters are home from boarding school this afternoon. It's a feast with close friends and family. We don't let our family circle get too wide."

"I'd be delighted to meet your daughters," Meriwether said.

"Oh, my." She put a hand to her heart.

"All of them," he added cheerily.

"Yes, well …" Mrs. Fischer elbowed Mr. again, this time an obvious plea for interference.

He snapped-to, but his eyes were on rashers of bacon strung on lines across the street. "Well, dinner is at five of the evening, then. Dress nines." Mr. Fischer clapped Meriwether on the shoulder and slid him to the side in the same motion, walking past, dragging his wife behind.

"I'll be there," Meriwether called.

Mrs. Fischer turned and narrowed her eyes at him. "Son, do you by any chance play a fife?"

He laughed tightly. "No, ma'am, I do not."

She stuck up her nose and followed her husband, and Meriwether turned away, exhausted but newly reeling. A fife. What was this, Valley Forge? But he felt revived. He'd be having dinner with Julie Fischer. For one night, he'd be in the family circle. There'd be smiles and gravy boats and poached country ham and sausage links, and he'd hear her laugh, and perhaps she played in the parlor on occasions like these, with the sisters gathered, maybe one on the low keys of the family's grand piano, and Julie on the high keys. He could walk away from this night knowing she had a fine life, fine sisters and friends, and that even in the solitude of a room, perhaps she wasn't really lacking anything but someone to listen to her play. Her sisters were home now, and they would fill that void, at least for a spell. He smiled to himself before falling onto his mattress for blessed sleep.

Four p.m. came entirely too soon, but Meriwether prepared himself with his pressed scholar's suit, a gentlemanly ascot in a turnover style, and a pair of polished quarter-brogue Oxfords. He spread Atkinsons Bear's Grease through his hair and shaped it into a fine wave on one side, parted straight and trimly on the other. He shaved with a straight razor along his neck and cheeks, but left his sorry little mustache, and dabbed his neck with rosewater and tucked a sprig of mint into his boutonnière. Then he walked through the empty baseball practice field, past the village oak, and out to the upscale streets of the city's richest families.

He arrived too early. He'd meant to be fashionably late, but he was a fast walker, and that's something he never really remembered about himself. Matty let him in without a word, and he stood ignored in the foyer of an oddly quiet house for a dinner party. Voices chattered softly beyond the piano, and he instinctually followed them and came up behind Mrs. Fischer and another woman talking over a box of jewelry. In between whispers, he caught the word 'heirlooms,' and then Mrs. Fischer's voice fell out too loud.

"No, not for Julie. Don't give her any of the modern pieces." She thumbed through the drawer. "Here. Here's a junk piece from Mimi's side. Give that to her. But the pearls for Violet, and the rubies for Amanda. Don't caboodle them, now, Francine, for they are their respective favorite colors."

Meriwether didn't say a word, but he stared at the back of Mrs. Fischer's head and hoped she felt it like a hammer. She must have felt it like something, for she turned around right at that moment.

"Ah." That was all she said.

"Yes," he replied, and walked into the parlor and seated himself at the piano as if he'd been invited to do so. He began with what he could remember of the introduction to *La bohème*, and he was fixated on the fingers of his left hand, keenly aware of which keys they pressed as they skittered down the ivories, all that would be missing if he only had the righthand notes. He knew she could hear him play up in her room, where she dressed for the dinner party. He was announcing his arrival. Or sending a telegram. Or. Could he fashion a foot pedal to play the keys of the left hand? Something with soft felt tips that struck each key lightly. He could patent something like that. Or could he play her left, while she played his right, a duet come together over the notes of Bohemians living in the Latin Quarter of 1840s Paris? Had it been Mrs. Fischer's mention of the name Mimi that had brought *La bohème* to his fingers? He struck a wrong note when he thought of Mrs. Fischer, and he shook out his fingers, willed them to begin again, to caress again. Music was a language spoken between only two souls; Mrs. Fischer was not in this song.

He was playing when the guests arrived, and Matty nodded at him to continue playing as if it had been planned. He wrinkled his nose as two aunts and their husbands, three willful neighbors, one old friend of Mr. Fischer's from college, and two sisters of indiscriminate ages—close to his age, close to Julie's age and looking like her—came through the doors in pairs like a roll call for the Ark. His eyes went to the stairs. She would come down last like the belle of the ball. Could she come down those stairs? Would someone have to carry her? He'd volunteer when the task was called upon.

He stood from the bench, and the two sisters curtsied to him. Violet, who was getting the pearls, and Amanda of the rubies. He wasn't sure he liked knowing the family circle, but here it was. The tension was palpable. He had upset a precarious balance, so it seemed. An outsider in a circle of secrets, a hiccup to upend the manicured normalcy. Mr. Fischer clapped him on the shoulder—which seemed to be his way—and asked him his prospects.

"I'm studying to be a specialist surgeon, sir," Meriwether said. "I've got a job at St. Mary's Hospital, but I'm of a mind to have my own practice someday."

"What's the specialty?" Mr. Fischer asked with genuine interest.

"Currently the lymphatic systems. But I'm concerned with the secondary organs. Liver and gallbladder, primarily. Kidneys, spleen, and their toxins, secondarily."

Mr. Fischer's eyes lit up, and he looked at his two daughters, then back to Meriwether, to his daughters, then back to him again. Meriwether studied the stairs, and the two sisters blushed over him and argued about who'd take his side. He groaned.

"Just save one side for Julie," he said, surrendering.

The room went quiet. There was a long beat as neighbor and aunt and old college friend glanced at the tablecloth, then the cacophony resumed as if it had never stopped.

"Girls, set your places on either side of him," Mrs. Fischer said. "Stop arguing about it. Oh, husband!" she called after Mr. Fischer, "Husband, can you have Francine bring out the boiled fish? We ought to start while it's warm."

Meriwether made to protest, but Violet cut him off and seated him between the two sisters. He hoped for an empty spot for Julie across from him, but Mr. Fischer's college friend pulled the velvet-backed chair out for Mrs. Fischer, and she sat across from Meriwether instead. He sighed and hoped at least the hot meal would be good. Amanda flushed next to him, watching him through batted eyelashes, and when Mr. Fischer brushed by his wife on his way to the head of the table, he leaned in to her, one eye on Meriwether.

"He's going to be a surgeon," the man said too obviously.

Mrs. Fischer beamed and looked from Violet to Amanda, avoiding Meriwether's blank expression.

A simple chicken broth with chives came around in gilt-edged demitasse cups, placed before each guest, and Meriwether saw there were no more empty seats at the table. A lump hardened in his throat. Heads bent down around him, and Mr. Fischer began the words of a prayer.

"Ought we not wait for Julie?" Meriwether asked.

The father faltered.

Mrs. Fischer said in her best singsong, "I don't know whom you imply. Husband, continue."

"Dear Lord and Savior, our Father—"

"Your daughter," Meriwether said defiantly.

Mrs. Fischer looked hard at him but didn't miss a beat. "My daughters are both here. You must be mistaken, son."

Mr. Fischer picked up quickly, "Thank You for this food we are about to consume in Your name."

"You have another daughter. Julie," Meriwether said. "Upstairs. I've met her."

"May we use this food to do Your work," Mr. Fischer spoke over the top of Meriwether. "Amen." He stuck a large silver serving fork into a slab of boiled fish and cheerily said, "Who's hungry?"

Voices affirmed in unison, and Mr. Fischer's college friend was the first to ask about the stocks for business, how the economy had been improving. The women tittered on their own side of the table, husbands separated from wives, about a knitting circle newly formed at the old armory. Meriwether sat quiet, staring at the lukewarm strip of fish that was plopped on his plate unceremoniously. The men on one side, talking about fixing the walls around the floodplain. The women on the other side, gossiping about Harietta's new baby, which was unanimously ugly. Violet cleared her throat demurely and touched her foot against Meriwether's, and he moved his to the side. The men, the new taxes invoked on the contractors and insurers. The women, how Mrs. Nelson was failing to bring her daughters correctly into Society, unanimously. The men, the corruption involving the contractors. The women, quilting with a larger-eyed needle.

"Do we just not talk about her at all?" Meriwether finally said.

The table quieted and looked at him, then away.

"About whom?" Mrs. Fischer asked.

He looked dead at her. "Julie."

"Who is Julie?"

One of the neighbors repeated, "Yes, who is Julie?"

Meriwether snapped at her, "Oh, come on! You face her back window, Mrs. Parrish!"

"You will mind your conduct, young fellow," Mr. Fischer reprimanded.

An aunt said, "Who is this boy?"

"I don't know him," Mrs. Fischer said. "He's here with Violet. He's Violet's friend."

Meriwether stood from the table quickly, scraping his chair backward across the imported tiles. "So we never even acknowledge her? That's just how it goes? We wait for her to die, and when she does, it doesn't matter, because she was never here?"

Mrs. Fischer stood. "You are mistaken and delirious! I don't know whom you mean."

Meriwether went to the stairs, but Matty and Francine blocked his way with trays. He yelled up, "Julie!"

Mr. Fischer stood. "You need to leave, young man."

"Julie!"

Mrs. Fischer turned to Violet, "Your friend is precipitously rude."

"But he's going to be a surgeon," Violet whined.

"Young man!" Mr. Fischer said again and flailed toward Violet and Amanda. "Oh, what is his goddamn name?"

"I told you it was Meriwether," he answered for himself. "And don't trouble yourself. I'm leaving. Thank you for the hospitality." He dropped the napkin he'd been holding. "And the limp fish."

He was out the front door and down the street and at the lake before he even knew it, staring into its quiet lapping, constantly erasing his reflection, erasing him. What was it like to be erased? To be invisible? To be already dead before you were born? How could she laugh at darkness? How could the sound of music even reach her? It wasn't she who had a hole in her heart.

The lake was murky green from too much dredging, and fish flopped near the surface, overstocked. He imagined these were the fish he'd just been served, domesticated to the point of tastelessness, too countless, nothing unique in them anymore. He stood by the water, hands in both pockets, until well after dusk, unmindful of the muddy banks seeping into his polished leather Oxfords. When twilight began its slow recession like a thickening fog, Meriwether headed back to his dormitory, taking the roads of the rich folks this time, rather than the back woods through to the university fields. He thought he could hear music playing.

That night, again, he couldn't sleep. His distractions kept him tight as a marching wind-up toy. Psychology 2 felt trite, by comparison. What had it truly to do with life, if real life was hidden anyway? He wanted to know how her organs worked. If the left side was dead, how did that affect the nerves around the left kidney, the pancreas, the spleen? Were they working properly? Could he fix it? Why hadn't he studied nerves instead? He picked up his treble flute and piped into the mouthpiece at around three in the morning, despite the thin walls. Payback for the rhythmically thumping bed of the scholar in the next room, who wasn't supposed to admit girls on the campus after dark, nor in private at any time. What he really wanted was the grand piano—how slick it had felt under finger. By four in the morning, he was up and pacing, and placing a new brown wax cylinder on his Edison Home Phonograph. George Gaskin's "Down in Poverty Row" and "In the Baggage Coach Ahead." Ferruccio Giannini's version of "La Marseillaise," then Gaskin again with the old Civil War standard, "Tramp! Tramp! Tramp!" with the piccolos taking flight like thirsting hummingbirds.

Meriwether stared at the cylinders and in his sleepless delirium, something came to him. She doesn't need to be saved, he remembered anew; just help her exist. Like a snapping spring, he leaped across the room and dumped the lockbox from under his bed out onto his mattress. $32. It was a lot of money. He'd been saving for his own medical practice once he got out of college. To pay that first loan. But now he knew he needed it for something else, something bigger than loans and workaday savings.

He skipped Psychology 2, despite how his slipping marks gnawed at him, and took his valise and the electric trolley down to Marsh and into town, hopped off near Lansing Street, and stepped into Wind Brothers, & Co. Had livers, spleens, and gallbladders not been his father's calling for him, this store would have been Meriwether's own calling for himself: with its rows and rows of sheet music in rotation by popularity, hooks fastened to the wall boasting wind instruments of every stripe, and along the back, box lutes and fiddles, marching batons and replacement piano keys. He smiled. She'd love this place. He'd bring her here.

"Ah, Master Capp!" an old toothless grin met Meriwether at the counter. "How be you, lad, and how is the father?"

"He's well, Mr. Placer. I'll tell him you asked after him."

"You do that." The old, leathery man came around the counter with a small wicker basket full of white, tan, and brown cylinders. "I've kept the newest ones set aside for you. Afraid they're a tasteless lot—'All Coons Look Alike to Me' and 'Chin, Chin, Chinaman' and so on—but there's a gem or two." He lifted one of the brown wax pieces. "'Kentucky Babe!'" He wiggled two wiry eyebrows, untamed as a wizard's, and smiled.

"I wish I had enough for it, Place." Meriwether pulled the $32 out of his pocket. "This is my life savings right now."

"And you've come to spend it all in my sorry little shop?" Mr. Placer chuckled.

"I have. I need a Home Phonograph with an installed recorder."

"Your Edison break? Those damnable pieces is always breaking." Mr. Placer went back around the counter and pulled out a box of parts. "I can fix it here for you for 2¢ per part."

"Naw, mine is tip-top. I just need one more. And," he counted on his fingers, "four blank cylinders."

"Well." Mr. Placer looked at the money.

"I know," Meriwether said. "It's not enough. But if you'll take installments—"

"I was just about to say that this amount should come out to exact. So's you can pick from the small Home models and take the cylinders of your choice, and that should be exactly perfect."

Meriwether looked down, ashamed. By his quick math, it was at least $13 short. "Sir."

Mr. Placer patted his hand. "You just tell your father I said hello and not to be such a stranger to us old sorts down here in the dying part of town. I did near raise the man, lad."

"I—I will tell him, sir. Thank you."

Meriwether selected the best, hardest wax cylinders he could find in the bin, while Mr. Placer installed a recording box inside the cabinet of one of the smallest phonograph models. Meriwether unlocked his tweed valise and hefted the items into it. The insides smelled like old clothes and his mother's bread from the loaves she'd always tucked away for him, after his departure back to school from an extended weekend home. At the bottom of his bag were a wax brush, his two piccolos and his treble flute, and his matching phonograph from home. He placed the traveling phonographs carefully, stacking their sound horns, and adjusting them around his expensive treble flute. He wished for a moment he had a fife, just to be a pickle, but that would be too much fun. The valise hardly clasped, but it was packed, and heavy, and he figured he could manage it for a single trolley ride. He stepped on at Lansing and off near the cul-de-sac of Mallard. At the back of the thicket, however, he paused. How to get it to the second story? The idea was rather flawed if he couldn't get up to the second story.

He left the thicket, walked under her window, and called up, "Hey, Julie!" There was no answer, so he picked up a small pebble and lobbed it at her glass pane, hoping he wouldn't break this new one.

After another moment, the window slid open, and she answered behind the curtain, "Is that you, Meri?"

He laughed with the thrill of joy that coursed him. "It is! Yes, ma'am, it is."

She put her head out the window. "Well, climb up."

He started up the trellis and came nearer to her sill and said, "I have something for you. It's large and heavy."

She raised her brow, and laughed at him, and he blushed.

"It appears I'll never say the right thing, will I?"

She shook her head and laughed again, but she obviously knew what he meant because she pointed to the back entryway. "Is it covered?"

He nodded.

"My father gets his private deliveries at the back of the house, where Pullman answers. Tell Pullman that it's a business package for Vincent Fischer and to leave it for Mr. Fischer in his office." She patted his hand on the sill and whispered conspiratorially, "My father's office is right across the hall from me."

Meriwether perked and climbed down and did as she instructed and climbed back up seamlessly. He pulled himself into the open window— dressed this time in a clean scholar's suit, handsome despite the dark rings under his eyes from lost sleep.

Julie's lip twitched on one side. "You smell better."

He grinned.

"I never thought you'd come back. It's good to see you. You're looking ... tired?"

He laughed, and they quieted themselves and listened to Pullman's footsteps in the hallway. Once the butler had deposited the valise in Mr. Fischer's office, Julie and Meriwether opened the door and stepped out into the hallway together. He let her lead and marveled at how she got around, dragging one leg, but not lacking for speed or accuracy when she was determined. They entered the office, and Meriwether heaved up on the valise.

"I've always wanted a cannonball," Julie said, watching him heft the weight.

"Splendid. I've brought you a matching pair."

She laughed outright, and his face appled. He squeezed by her, embarrassed by her ease, befuddled by his own scissorbill awkwardness around her. How did she, of all people, make everything seem so easy and light? He set the bag on the bed in her room. Down the stairs, he heard the singsong of Mrs. Fischer rattling off a honey-do list to Francine or Matty, whichever unfortunate soul happened to be in her closest proximity. Julie held a finger to her lips, and one side quirked into a smile. Meriwether unlocked the valise.

Julie drew in a breath and looked at him. "Is—Is that …?"

"An Edison Home Phonograph." He tuned in to her reaction, and he heard her labored breathing again. A sound he wished he couldn't hear, but he knew that was selfish. He only didn't want to hear it so that it wasn't true, but he knew to wish her changed or different would be his own form of erasing her, too. Still, he knew what the hard breaths meant. She'd said they all counted the days. He didn't want to count the days.

He pulled the two desktop phonographs from the valise and placed them side by side. One was worn and well-loved; one was polished to a new shine. He unlatched each one and lifted the wooden lids, and inserted the horns into their slots. Their top surfaces held serial numbers and the words 2-MINUTE-4 with an arrow through it, meaning the play and recording time was two minutes or four minutes, but all Meriwether had were cylinders and a reproducer marked '2M.' Two minutes would have to do. 'EDISON • HOME • PHONOGRAPH' was entwined in a gold and black ribbon on the front of each cabinet.

"Oh, Meri." It came out as a strained whisper.

"The world ought to hear you."

She walked to the players and ran her fingers over the bright brass as gently as she'd touch a baby. When she looked up at him, her eyes were huge with glassiness. "Show me."

"I will show you." He closed the window tight, lifted the handcranks out of the cabinet bellies, and inserted the handles into each base, screwing them in place. He popped the top of a cardboard roll box and pulled out the cotton swathing, then a blank wax cylinder, and held the hollow tube with two fingers stuck through the middle inside it. He slid the record over the mandrel and lined it up on the leftmost side. "What shall we name your song?"

"My song?" she said, looking into his valise and lifting out his piccolo. "You mean *our* song." She handed it to him.

He smiled and took it. "Our song. Only if you desire the high notes."

"I desire them fiercely."

"Will we be left alone?" He glanced at the door.

"Yes." She looked away. "Yes, we always will."

Meriwether sighed.

"Name it: 'The Light Ages.'"

He nodded and felt a heavy sinking in him, but he had to make this right on the first try. He couldn't afford more clean cylinders or even to take them in to Wind Brothers to be shaved down. He wished he had a bigger horn to collect the nuance of every sound on the diaphragm, but this would have to suffice. At least the rubber hadn't dried out in the gasket, so the sound would be as crisp as it was ever going to be.

"Wind the mainsprings with the crank," Meriwether said. Thirty to fifty revolutions would provide enough power in the spring motor for a single record. He cranked the first one as he told her about the mainsprings and about the 2M gear positioning for a two-minute record and reproducer. "Now, you."

She turned the crank on the second machine, and she searched for the gear positioning, and nodded.

From his pocket, Meriwether extracted his chain watch and laid it on the bed between them. "We have two minutes. I want you to play whatever you want for two minutes. Something original of yours. Something straight from that hole in your heart."

Julie chuckled, and went to the psalterion. Tucking it against her unmoving left arm, she practiced a few slides of her double-bow across the strings and looked up at him hungrily. In her eyes shown pure desire for this miracle of music placed out before her, for this buffet of such luxury, such power. For the Light Ages.

"When you're ready, I'll introduce the piece. From the time that stylus drops to the time I pick it up, you must be silent, understand? It records everything."

She nodded and held her bow out, ready. The idea of music played across her eyes, and he read it there. He knew. He heard her song before she'd even begun it, and he nodded, flipped the switch, pulled the knurled button outward and lowered the carriage of the reproducer into playing position, and set the diamond stylus carefully down on the left-most side. His eyes jerked to the pocketwatch, and he wetted his lips to speak.

"'The Light Ages,'" Meriwether enunciated clearly. "An original composition by Julie Fischer."

"And Meriwether Capp," she added.

He glared at her and shook his head, but she smiled as if holding in a giggle and nodded. He pointed at her, and she breathed, fluttered one eye open and closed in a dreamstate, and pulled her bow across the strings. Echoic chords filled the small room like a choral canon in a vault, repeating back on themselves, and Meriwether stood perfectly still, not wanting even the rustle of his clothing fabric to register over her song. He watched the second hand count off their time together as she swelled and ebbed into verses of herself, and she watched him with every draw, as if she played each note just for him, for them, in that space that surrounded their harbor. He wanted to step toward her, but he stayed planted so his shoes were silent. Perhaps his heartbeats could have been heard, the enormous choir that sang in his chest. At the last five seconds, he held up his hand for five, four, three, then a conductor's finishing pinch, and he put his finger to his mouth, lifted the stylus quickly and carefully, and flipped the switch. He stood with his back to her, feeling the swells stirring through the room, staring at the tiny machine that had captured her.

After a moment, he said, "Dulcimer," and turned and pointed to it. "Play some harmony over it. You've got a few moments to practice." He carefully pulled the cylinder off the mandrel and held up the record, covered in wax chips, and Julie readied the dulcimer. The wax brush sat in his bag, and he lifted it out and brushed the cylinder gently over her wastebasket, collecting the wax chips in the bottom. He then slid it back on the mandrel and clicked down the button to set the phonograph to play mode, instead of record. He readied the neighboring phonograph to record a new blank cylinder that he pulled out of its package and slid over the mandrel, checking that the gears were set, the crank properly wound, and the reproducer steadied in place for the switch. "Piccolo or treble flute?" he asked.

"Piccolo," she said. "It sounds so patriotic."

He chuckled. "Only when it's playing Sousa." He lifted the C piccolo to his face. "But watch this." Quickly, he glanced at the pocketwatch, switched on the first phonograph and set its stylus, then moved to the second, switched it on, and set its stylus down on the new blank cylinder, as well. He put his finger to his lips, listened for the song's introduction and her addition, which made him smile, and then he pointed at her when the psalterion started.

At first, she only listened to her instrument, mesmerized at its playback, but he made a waving motion at her, and she came in slowly with the hammered dulcimer, plucking some light strings in harmony with the psalterion, then cascading in with rhythmic hammers like a waterfall.

Meriwether was swept into a current, and he put the lip plate to his mouth. His piccolo danced around the dulcimer like a streamer of wind, a high call to her low moan, and he harmonized in the rafters, giving the song an operalike quality to its new balance. He cut in and out with his piccolo, adding airy solos and playing with her notes in an improvised call and response, until he cut out completely and held up the seven, six, five, four, fadeout, and *fini*. He quickly lifted the stylus of the second phonograph and switched it off, then removed the stylus of the first. He slid off the second cylinder, now containing both layers of the song, and he brushed the wax into the wastebasket, then slid it onto the mandrel of the first player, and inserted a new blank cylinder onto the second player. All the while, he heard her labored breathing like it was part of the song. When he turned to Julie, she already stood with her mbiri in hand, a single tear running down one cheek. He smiled and ached, and smiled wider.

They recorded the next layer with the mbiri and treble flute over the top of it, and when Meriwether held the countdown, he had tears in his own eyes this time. He blinked them away, removed the stylus quickly, and stood there, his skull humming with vibrations, his lips still puckered tight with tension, but releasing, releasing. He brushed away the wax with tenderness.

"Thank you," Julie whispered.

"We're not done yet," he said too brusquely, unsure of this next step, but sure it must be done. Sure that it was only step one to getting her to Wind Brothers, & Co., to the lake she couldn't see from her window, to the vendors on Main Street that she didn't even know existed. Had she ever seen capillary waves on a lake's surface? Skittering water bugs? Smelled the rashers of bacon strung up on twine between the vendor carts in town? "There's something else to do."

Meriwether turned to her, looking so serious that she laughed at him, and he took her working hand and walked through the door. She limped behind him, and he followed the light through the hall toward the windows in the front part of the house, overlooking the street. They walked up a brief incline and past a room that looked deserted, then into another of the same abandoned folklore. Cobwebs strung across old furniture that was stacked as if forgotten. The sun poured in through large windows, and faded stripes into dusty chairs and a sagging settee in the French causeuse style, its wide seat meant to accommodate women's oversized bustles, the aging fabric left over from another place and time. Julie's room had been surrounded by things as forgotten and ignored as she was, their bodies bent and drooped, scratched and broken in the same way, the idea of reupholstering merely an axiom for a poorer family name. Meriwether frowned and led her to the window in the half-attic that overlooked the large pedimented gable above the Corinthian columns of the front entryway. He slid open the window.

"I'm not supposed to be in the front of the house," Julie whispered to him, looking over her shoulder.

"You're not a piece of furniture." Meriwether stepped out of the window onto the gently sloping gable, its front tip overlooking the brisk pacing of Mallard Street. He turned and held out his hand for her.

"Meri." She looked down and shook her head. "I can't."

"Of course you can." He flicked his hand with emphasis. "I won't let you fall."

The gable sloped imperceptibly beneath him, and it was sturdy. She leaned against the pane and balanced her unresponsive side against it, sat on the sill, and put her working leg through the hole and out into the wilderness. Meriwether took hold of her leg, then hip, then arm and waist and shoulder, and she was out, eased down to the roof and sitting with her good side on the shingles.

"Oh," she breathed out in wonder.

"See?" he said. "Trust me now?"

"I guess I trust you. You haven't yet tossed me over the edge," she laughed, but her tone was hushed.

"Forget her. She's not up here. She can't stop you. You aren't old furniture, Julie." He slid her nearer to the edge, but still safely away, and pointed to the lake at the end of the cul-de-sac. She marveled at it and watched the people rushing by, and he positioned her securely, then stood. "Don't move. I'll be right back." He saw her face go pale, but he turned toward the window, popped through it, and faced her again, shadowed by the pane. "Trust me."

He walked quietly through the neglected hallways, then into Julie's room, packed up the new phonograph and the final cylinder, and carried them back to the gable room. At the window, he paused, and he watched her out on the front roof, her hand around the ledge, her face enraptured by every briefcase and body and dog and red dress and ribboned hat passing below. His chest tightened, and he stepped through the window onto the roof, and walked out behind her.

"It's something, isn't it?" he said quietly, so as not to startle her if she hadn't heard him.

But she'd clearly heard him as if it were all part of their song. "It's something," she said without pause.

He set the phonograph on a flat part of the gable, unlatched it, pulled out its horn, and wound its crank. He inserted their record and reached one hand out for her as he dropped the stylus with the other. "If we can't bring you to the auditorium, then we'll bring the auditorium to you."

The stylus glided over the grooves, and the introduction began, and for the first time, he heard her giggle in the background of the recording. He smiled. She hadn't been able to help her laughter, and now it was recorded there, at the beginning of their song, forever. A static pop announced the tinny sound, and the swell of orchestration blared out of the horn, ignoring the warped higher notes that had been stretched across cheap wax.

"Oh, Meri," she said, by way of acknowledging everything, all the pieces falling together, and one by one, the people in the streets looked about them for the music. She laughed at their initial confusion, and then the eyes turned upward as the hammered dulcimer came in, a piccolo soaring overhead. She drew in a panicked breath, but Meriwether squeezed her hand.

"It's okay. It's supposed to be like this. They're supposed to hear you."

A crowd gathered beneath them as Meriwether set the stylus again and played the song a second and third time, and the people in the streets who weren't too late to catch the trolley stood in a wondrous circle, looking up at the horn that made it all possible. And then there was Matty, down in the street below, out from the entryway of the house to see the matter of it. And then Francine and Pullman and Mrs. Fischer, her tight mouth and wide eyes raging against it all.

Julie gasped.

"She can't do anything," Meriwether assured. "Look at all these people. She can't deny you this, not now."

Julie relaxed and laid her head back against his shoulder.

Meriwether dropped the stylus again for another two minutes. "This phonograph is yours. It is my gift to you. For whatever anniversary occasion you want to call today."

She sighed against him, and he felt her labored breaths. "Let's call it a birthday," she whispered, then laughed and waved to the people below with her one good arm.

They waved their handkerchiefs and gloved hands back at her, and one shouted "Again!" as the stylus came back down. The light glinted off the lake, and wind blew strands of Julie's hair across her face, and she'd never been more alive, birthed, her own song a part of the world beyond stone walls, her fingers entwined in his, her giggle forever stamped into the song's title, and even Mrs. Fischer below—her tight mouth softening into delicate lines, a hole closing in a heart.

EVERY STEP COUNTS

*R*ose Mercaida—*the* Rose Mercaida of the renowned Henningberg Estates—ran her thumb back and forth over the chipped piece of gilt porcelain until the flesh reddened, then tore, then bled. Absently, she moved her forefinger over the teacup's rim in the same fashion until that finger, too, bled. The dainty porcelain cup was from her mother Estabelle's set—*the* Estabelle Catherton of the renowned Henningberg Estates. As the drops of blood formed on Rose's fingers, she threw the teacup at the wall, shattering the fragile thing into pieces.

Within moments, she'd walked, counting each step aloud, to the hutch beside the parlor table, swung open its creaky doors, and pulled from its perfect place the rest of the tea set. Rose eyed the pieces, counting each cup once, then again, the matching creamer and sugar bowl, pitcher, tongs, and tiny spoons. And then, she released her hands from the tray. The porcelain shattered along the hardwood floor with such a racket that she heard her husband, Errol Mercaida—*the* Errol Mercaida of the renowned Blester Park and now of the renowned Henningberg Estates—stir in his study. As the shards flew and rolled and rested where they'd landed, she noted each piece.

Counting the steps back to the sink—twenty-three, always twenty-three—she lifted the bar of lye soap and pumped the water until the rusted, brown liquid fell into the basin below it. Eleven pumps—it always took eleven pumps. She scrubbed her hands until the blood stopped, then counted her way to the broom closet. The way the broom sat on the floor, pushing up one side of its cornhusk bristles into a permanent lump, annoyed her. That would have to be fixed. She'd remember to tell Errol to fix it right away. It could not wait. No, it simply could not, she decided. The thought was broken when she looked down at her fingers and realized the blood had reappeared. She couldn't touch the broom with blood on her fingers; that wouldn't be right. So, she stepped the fourteen steps back to the sink, pumped the eleven pumps on the waterspout crank, and scrubbed with lye soap until the blood was gone.

Back at the broom closet, she lifted the broom, then swept the mess in both the kitchen and in the parlor before the blood could form again on her fingers. The blood had helped her concentrate, given her focus. Twenty-three steps back to the sink, and she'd scrub with lye again, then carefully put the broom into the closet in the opposite direction, curving back the bent bristles. That would have to be remedied. And soon. It'd be all she could think on, until Errol fixed it. He'd have to fix it soon.

Weaving through the kitchen and parlor, she looked for stray pieces, evidence of her distress. Oh, how her mother had loved that set! How had one become chipped unbeknownst? Surely Errol was to blame. The lout had never been careful. On her trail through the now-invisible disarray, she noted the nicks in the wall where the culprit cup had slain the early-Victorian fleur-de-lys wallpaper—that would have to be fixed!—and she ran her toe over the hardwood where the beautiful hand-gilt pitcher and teapot had collided with it, noting that it was two strips of the hardwood that required immediate replacement. Before the blood could start pooling again, she wiped a fingerprint from the hutch glass with her handkerchief, then peered inside to right anything that might have moved from the departure of the tea service. Only a Wedgwood bowl had been bumped, and she stoically bumped it back. Something would have to fill this space. She pondered what could possibly fill it, pleased that this thought took her mind momentarily from the problem of the bent broom husks.

Rose stood over the sink basin again, at count seven of pumping, when Errol meandered into the kitchen. She raised her unoccupied hand, warding him from speaking.

"There will be four more," she spoke brusquely, and noted with respect how Errol calmly waited for four more thrusts before speaking.

"I heard crashing from the study. Is everything all right?"

"No. There is a nick here in the wallpaper. All of this wallpaper will need to be redone. There are two dented boards in the parlor that require replacement. The top hinge on the hutch needs to be oiled. It is creaking and moaning like an old biddy, but do be careful, Err, not to leave a smudge on the glass. And wipe the oil down so there is no trace of it dripping. I don't like the smell of it, either. Maybe spritz the air with that French cologne I like—"

"Do you have blood on your fingers?" he asked indifferently.

"—I wasn't finished. This one cannot wait. The broom, Err! I must have a hook installed in the broom closet so that its husks cannot be bent. Its husks are bent. You know we can't have that."

"No, no, we can't have that," he whispered, looking again over her shoulder. "Are you bleeding? Let me have a look."

"A little lye will do the trick. Something must fill a space in the hutch," she went on, staring out the window, noting the smudges along the sill. She counted them. There were four. Why had she not noticed them earlier? Errol must have put them there, the lout. He'd never been careful.

"Lye will only rip it open. Let me bandage it up." He placed his hands cautiously on her shoulders and turned her toward the wash closet.

She held her breath. *The smudges on the windowsill!* She had to clean them. There were four of them. It would be all she could think on, until she could return to blot them clean, tidy, right again.

MUSIC KNOWS NO COLOR

"Colored American Day," Joseph scoffed. "What a slap in the face, Grandpap. There oughta be—"

"We do what we can," Frederick silenced his grandson and prodded the twenty-two-year-old toward the Music Pavilion. "We keep talking until everyone hears."

All around them, the smells and sounds of the White City rose like a duststorm, felt like a leather glove left out in the rain, tight and constricting as it shrank. The August sun beat a path through the Midway Plaisance, and thousands of fairgoers streamed past the Electricity Building, the Machinery Building, the Woman's Building, and the sparkling, modern, polychrome Transportation Building—weaving their way as if lost in a maze that made them insignificant by comparison. Grandpap veered off at a crossroads of the maze, and Joseph kept walking toward the Music Pavilion. The reflective white stucco buildings at the end of the Court of Honor made the classical White City architecture luminescent. Joseph's fist squeezed around the handle of his violin case. He'd never felt so small. He'd never felt so out of place.

"Watch it, negro," a woman blurted as she bumped him.

He'd never felt so black.

"My apologies, ma'am." Joseph wished he had a hat to tip. Why hadn't he worn a hat? Every man there was tailored in sacksuits and Continentals and crisp gray waistcoats with one blaring, unifying accessory: there wasn't a man among men who wasn't wearing a bowler derby upon his fine groomed head. Joseph scowled. He hadn't owned a hat since the age of seven, and the flimsy thing had only been made of thinboard and homespun wool. His scowl deepened, and he squeezed his violin case in his fist when the offending woman bustled off in a huff, her own veiled and feathered fascinator cocked toward the Woman's Building.

"I suppose we all have our place," he muttered, and set his sights again on the Music Pavilion. He'd show them. He'd wait in the wings through Sidney Woodward and Deseria Plato, and The Black Patti, and then he'd show them. He'd listen through the buskers, the minstrels, and Abigail Christensen's lengthy dissertations on Colored Spirituals and Shouts, and then he'd show them all. Show them all what? What exactly would he show these privileged people who own more on one ring finger than he'd make in all his life?

At once, the air was filled with music, drowning out all other thought. The Stoughton Musical Society, America's oldest choral society, sent its renditions of early American music reverberating through the Plaisance, bouncing off the walls of the crudely structured Beaux-Arts-styled buildings, and ringing through Joseph's ears with the merriment of folksy eight-part harmony. White music, he mused, on Colored American Day. But what music it was. The onlookers who were gathered around the excessive stage couldn't tell the difference, he supposed. He was certain his grandpap, the instigator behind Colored American Day at the World's Columbian Exposition, had purposely staged this wholesome, downhome showing. To throw the white folks a bone. Joseph chuckled at the paradox.

He shuffled his way through the crowds and headed toward the Colored entrance. It had been three decades since the emancipation of the slaves, yet here he was, entering through a separate door at the back of the stage, a door that weaved through all the stage draperies and the cables needed to light up the fair with this new invention from Nikola Tesla called alternating current. The entire exposition was glowing with the invention, shining well into the night and keeping everything, even the two-hundred-sixty-four-foot Ferris Wheel, lit up as clear as day.

"You may use this entrance," a man's voice caught Joseph off guard.

"Pardon me, sir?" He wished again for a hat.

"It's Colored American Day," the man gestured. "You may use the white entrance for this day only."

Joseph smiled and took a few steps toward the indicated entrance. Then, he abruptly stopped, turned, and touched two fingers to his forehead where a hat brim should be. "No, thank you, sir," he replied proudly and headed for the Colored entrance.

The stage vibrations rattled through the makeshift walls of the neoclassical structure built to withstand only temporary use. Every pulse shot through him until his heart thundered with the beat. As he walked toward the stage, he tapped his feet from heel-to-toe, heel-to-toe, heel-to-toe with the rhythm of the Ragtime ensemble enlightening the parasoled and derbied audience. He knew they'd never heard anything like it. Imagining their faces paled in shock brought a twitch of satisfaction to his tight lips. He'd show them.

Through a wave of applause, he heard shuffling on the stage, though from the Colored wing, nothing was visible but a peek through the slats to see the Zoopraxographical Hall, where Eadweard Muybridge was giving lectures on the Science of Animal Locomotion using his moving-picture zoopraxiscope; the white cupola of the building where Frank Haven Hall was demonstrating printing plates for books in Braille; and a confection stand where F. W. Rueckheim was selling ungodly delicious chunks of sticky peanuts, popcorn, and molasses.

A sudden noise jarred him. The sound of his name being announced. His grip tightened around his violin case, and the murmuring of Southern spirituals passed through his lips. A silence like none he'd ever known rushed through the crowd. He knew now exactly what he'd show them. That classical music knew no color.

When he approached the edge of the stage, he felt the heat from the alternating current bulbs that surrounded him. With the violin tucked beneath his chin, he shut his eyes to the gawking, to the whispers of shock from frilly-laced women who had never dared imagine that a man such as he—a man without a hat—could be educated in the ways of this sophisticated instrument. He shut his ears to the rustle of naysayers' mutterings that buzzed through the crowd like the steady hissing of the lightbulbs beside him. And he raised his bow. He'd show them.

Within moments, the onlookers' tongues blazed with new mutterings. This skinny, scraggly man of twenty-two—his tan trousers mismatching his loosely fitted overcoat, his thick black hair high atop his head, his droopy hound-dog eyes too large for his face—surprised them with every note. He didn't kowtow to their whims with spirituals or Ragtime or Southern minstrels. No, it was classical music that billowed from his wooden muse. In his hands, a violin was a songbird, and he gave it wing. He could hear the whispers coming back to him now: Who was this boy? Where did he come from? He's Frederick Douglass' grandson—that boy? Well, it's no wonder! And to think, we judged him so! Listen to that music—not the music of a negro! But it was. It was the music of his very soul. Let them have their zoopraxiscopes and bowler derbies. Give him his violin.

He played until his fingers hurt, until a stiff muscle in his shoulder told him he was finished. When he laid his violin in its velvet-lined box, there was silence. Only silence. He thought they'd liked it, but ... Had they even enjoyed the music? Were they simply waiting for the next musician, getting their money's worth from the show? He lifted his case and walked off the stage in the quickening silence before his thoughts could travel to a darker place.

"Mr. Joseph Douglass?" a husky voice stopped Joseph before he could get too far from the Music Pavilion. "You're Mr. Joseph Douglass, grandson of abolitionist Frederick Douglass?"

Joseph slowly turned. "I am."

"I'm Eldridge Johnson. I make a player for discs of the United States Gramophone Company. Ever heard of it?"

"Never."

"They are discs with recordings. I want to record your violin. I have a proposition." Eldridge wrung his hands and looked a little too professional, too polished. "You'd be the first negro to record."

Joseph bristled. "Why don't you try the Stoughton Musical Society? Everyone seemed to like them. I didn't even get applause."

A group of regally dressed women paraded by, and once more, Joseph wished for a hat. My, wouldn't he be doffing it now.

"Did you hear that violinist?" one of the women gushed.

"Oh! I was stunned," another exclaimed. "I couldn't even catch my breath. I was so breathtaken, I didn't even clap for the poor boy. Imagine my manners."

Eldridge Johnson smirked. "Appears they liked you, too, Mr. Douglass. I don't think the Stoughton Musical Society stole anyone's breath. My offer still stands."

"No, thank you, sir," Joseph replied as politely as his grandpap had taught him. There was something about the well-dressed man that reeked of capitalism, opportunism. "Maybe some other day. But I'm planning a transcontinental tour." He puffed up his chest. Where had that come from? No black man had ever undertaken a transcontinental tour. Still, he made up his mind on the spot to do it.

Eldridge scoffed, and his demeanor turned visibly cold. "It won't be a success. You're a negro, in case you hadn't noticed. No one will come."

Another group of onlookers swarmed by, and Joseph recognized them from the Music Pavilion audience.

"Oh, that violin," a swooning woman sighed. "I could listen to that for days straight and never tire. I'd touch not food nor drink nor bed— just listen for days."

Another laughed, "Surely you'd faint dead away."

"I'd faint anyway," came the merry reply, as the women passed.

Joseph smiled and turned to Eldridge Johnson. "Oh, they'll come, Mr. Johnson." He met Eldridge's eyes without hesitation. "They'll be there. You'll see."

He'd show them. He'd show them all.

HISTORICAL NOTES

"The Orphan Train" became the springboard for my forthcoming third novel, *The Only Way to Cheat a Hangman*, which dissects further the problematic nature of the Orphan Trains as suppliers of child labor. The Orphan Trains were real-life nineteenth-century trains that brought New York orphans into the rural Midwest to be adopted by Midwestern farming families; the endeavor started what would later become our modern-day foster-care programs. Though there were many happy stories of homeless kids being adopted into loving families, there were also many stories of children being fostered only for their farm labor, being badly abused and underfed, and being used for sexual exploits.

"Every Time It Snows" is based on a real Civil War snowball fight that took place, the Great Snowball Battle of Rappahannock Academy, which began on the morning of February 25, 1863, between General Robert Hoke's North Carolina soldiers and Colonel William Henry Stiles' Georgia soldiers, when Hoke's camp instigated a march comprising infantry, cavalry, and skirmishers with the intent of capturing Stiles' camp using only snowballs. Stiles and Hoke are real-life historical individuals, but the rest of the mentioned characters in the story are fictional. There were many Civil War snowball fights, but this particular one is noted for its unique strategizing, its ample snow coverage (documented in soldiers' diaries to be between twelve and twenty inches), and its sheer number of participants. It's important for me to note, however, that despite the viewpoint of the story, I do not empathize with the Confederate "cause" in the slightest.

In "Casting Grand Titans," the landscape, setting, weather, architecture, and structures surrounding the [State] University of Iowa are all carefully researched, from the broken bell to mistimed class endings to the Legislature being held in the same buildings. Stores, streets, buildings, and neighborhoods of downtown Iowa City are historically accurate, and the town layout is based on cartographer J. H. Millar's map of Iowa City from 1854. Signage, spellings, and prices inside the store are from historical handwritten grocery lists. University president Amos Dean is an embellished real-life historical figure, Sylvanus Johnson was a real-life bricklayer of the town, and Charles Berryhill was a real-life printer. The mentioned names Judge Carlton, Strohm, Thomas Snyder, and Secretary of State McCleary are real-life individuals of the town from maps and the census. The mentioned "Cordelia" was the real-life daughter of a prominent town figure; the daughter died very young, and the whole town mourned, thus to "visit Cordelia" became synonymous with going to the cemetery. Dr. Jolliet's mentioned ancestor was the real-life seventeenth-century French-Canadian explorer Louis Jolliet (sometimes spelled Joliet), and the names of the enslaved girls came from a historical ledger of runaways. The rest of the characters are fictional, although Agatha Acton's life is based on a botanist of the time who was kept from getting a degree and higher wages because she was female.

"Yellow Flowers" makes reference to the yellow fever outbreak of 1793 in Philadelphia and how black men were sent into the city to help with the sick, volunteering for every position from nurses to gravediggers, because white men thought that African Americans were immune to the fever. When it turned out that black men died at the same rate as whites, about two hundred and forty black deaths altogether, the black population was vilified instead of being haled as heroic volunteers.

In "A Lifetime of Fishes," the lifestyle, clothing, and characteristics of the Wampanoag peoples come mainly from modern-day history resources, in order to depict the Wampanoag as accurately as possible. Older accounts are often skewed, biased, and not as reliable or respectful. The Wampanoag were one of the only Eastern Nations to have a written language, so it's thankfully preserved today. I have used mainly simple early spellings taken from original phonetic writings by early translators that do not necessarily reflect modern-day diacritical marks or spellings; the Wôpanâak language is being newly revived by the extraordinary Wôpanâak Language Reclamation Project as you read this. *An Easy Introduction to the Old Indian Language of the Atlantic Coast* by James Waldo Colby, though published in 1906 and a bit archaic, is an invaluable resource for definitions, structure, and phonetics, as is John Eliot's 1663 Wôpanâak Bible translation and *Wood's Vocabulary of Massachusett*, the earliest substantial vocabulary of Massautchuseog, recorded by William Wood and published in his *New England's Prospect* in 1634, representative of the North Shore dialect of the now-extinct language. The study guide "The Pilgrims and Plymouth Colony: 1620," by the late speech historian and Mayflower descendent Duane A. Cline is also beneficial, as is the incredible work of jessie "little doe" baird, a linguist from the Mashpee [Mâseepee] Tribe of the Wampanoag Nation, who founded the Wôpanâak Language Reclamation Project and is creating a dictionary of the once-lost Wôpanâak language. With their written language, the Wampanoag made land deeds, written agreements, letters, and trade charters, and had English books translated into their language, including the first Bible ever printed in North America. Women were treated as equals, could hold property and clan positions, and could make decisions at clan meetings. Depictions of the feast and games are based on both primary and secondary sources, including the observations of the Englishman Roger Williams. The Wampanoag are one of the only Native American tribes to remain still on their original land. All of the characters are fictional, and this is the first short story I ever wrote.

"In the Blood" is based on actual early European blood-transfusion experiments and procedures using animal blood, though the characters are fictional.

In "Small Sacrifices," Thompson's Station and Spring Hill, Tennessee, were two real-life Civil War locations, with a battle being fought at Thompson's Station on March 5, 1863, and a later battle being fought at Spring Hill on November 29, 1864, but my story and characters are fictional. The winter of 1862-63 was fantastically cold, however, so that part is true.

"A Cleaning to the Stovepipe" came of my dabbling with my second novel, *Falcon in the Dive* (Regal House Publishing, 2024), which takes place during the French Revolution. Names and places morphed from this story into my novel, though the stories are completely different. The locations and the French Revolution are obviously real, but the characters are fictional.

"The Light Ages; or Holes in the Heart" is dedicated to my aunt Julie Angstman, who died before I was born and who—I must say for my father's sake—did not have the type of life I depicted in her story, because she was not born in the 1800s. She came from a time and place (1940s-70s) where her family and friends cherished her and were proud of her, but through the spinning wheels of what-ifs that drive my fiction, I wanted to show how our lives are shaped beyond our control by the time and societies we're born into. The story location is liberally set in

Haslett, Michigan, where Julie and my father grew up, but it is an embellished amalgamation of generic Midwestern college cities in this time period. While Julie Fischer is based on my aunt Julie in that she was a blue baby with a hole in her heart who had a stroke in the hospital that left her paralyzed on one side of her body before she could receive a needed heart surgery, the rest of Julie Fischer's story, including the characters in it (with the exception of mentioned real-life song composers), is fictional. My aunt Julie did love music, however, and she loved to laugh—I kept those parts of her life.

"Music Knows No Color" is a fictionalized account of real-life historical individuals Joseph Douglass, Frederick Douglass, and Eldridge Johnson, depicting Joseph's groundbreaking debut at the 1893 World's Columbian Exposition (aka the Chicago World's Fair) on Colored American Day, an event organized by famed abolitionist Frederick Douglass to introduce black culture, poetry, and music to a mainstream white society. Joseph's extraordinary playing of the violin, largely (ignorantly) regarded as a white-person's instrument at the time, made him world famous, and he is credited with being the first black violinist to make transcontinental tours, haled as "the most talented violinist of his race" and the "Dean of Race Violinists." Eldridge Johnson would go on to found the Victor Talking Machine Company in 1901, and Joseph Douglass was the first violinist (of any race) to make recordings for them. All of the musicians and inventors mentioned in the story are real-life individuals. This story came from my research for a forthcoming novel, *A Guest in the House of Winter*, which takes place in Chicago in 1893.

All other characters are fictional, though many are sourced from the diaries, town records, and historical resources of their respective time periods, and their settings are mostly accurate to their time and place, even though fictionalized.

GLOSSARY OF WÔPANÂAK TERMS

[in order of appearance]

CANOPACHE: *place of peace* [Wampanoag name for Nantucket]

POONEAM, NETOP: *hello, friend*

NUTUSSAWES ISHKODHONCK: *I am called Fire Goose*

APPISH: *sit down, stay down*

WUTTATTAMWAITCH: *cup*

NIPPE: *water*

NEEMAT, HOWAN NO ESHQUAW: *my brother, who is that woman*

CHOHQUOG: *long knife or sword*

NOOT: *fire*

WIASECK: *knife*

WOMPSOOKSY: *Whitebird*

MATASQUAS: *a woven mat or wall covering made of bark, reeds, or bushes*

SHAWMUT: *Boston*

TEAG K'MEECH: *what'll you have to eat*

NASAUMP: *a dish of dried corn, berries, and nuts, boiled until it thickens like porridge*

SOBAHEG: *a stew made of seasonal ingredients*

NAMMOSSUOG: *fishes*

WANACHIKMUK: *a smoke hole in a wetu*

KUNNAM: *wooden spoon*

NAMMOS: *to fish*

ATCHANAM: *to hunt*

POOTOP: *whale*

MESQUASHCOO: *brook trout*

QUAHOG: *clams, oysters*

MEESHYOG: *eels*

ASHONTYOG: *lobsters*

WUNNYSU: *pretty*

ANACOOONK: *farmwork*

WETU: *house or wigwam*

AIYESONK: *Warknife*

TAUBUT: *thanks*

NUSH WETU: *longhouse*

WUNNIISH: *farewell*

SONKS: *the chief's wife*

SACHEM: *chief*

PNIESE: *leaders, war leaders, or advisors*

MISHOON: *canoe made of a cedar frame and covered with birch bark*

HOGKOOONK: *clothing*

THE THREE SISTERS: *maize, beans, squash*

TOOQUINNY ENIN: *a fisherman*

AHCOONAYOG: *the English settlers, literally "coaters"* [people who wore cloth coats]

AHTEOCK: *garden*

MAGQUONK: *gift*

WÔPANÂAK: *the spoken language of the Wampanoag*

MASSAUTCHUSEOG: *Massachusett* [the spoken Algic Algonquin languages of several southeastern Massachusetts tribes]

MISHODTAPPUONK: *feast*

NUT ASSOOKISH: *I am foolish*

POPOOONK: *game, ceremony*

WUNNONK: *bowl*

CHOGANATCHU: *Blackbird Mountain*

POCAMETPEONK: *Quill Feather*

N'PITCHINNUMUP: *I claimed*

K'WOMMONSH: *I love you*

N'WOMMONSH: *love me*

K'WEKONTAM N'WEEWO: *will you be my wife*

N'MOG: *I pay you; I give you*

ABBONA: *five*

PAWGUTASH: *literally "water-money"* [wampum shells that were high quality]

TEAGOASH: *English coins*

WUTTAMAUOG: *tobacco*

MAMUSSY: *take it all*

N'ONKETTEAM, AHQUOMPSINY: *I'm well, healthy, able, and will provide*

N'MENMENNEKY: *I'm strong*

N'MOG WUNEECHÔNUWÔAH MENNEKY: *I'll give you strong children*

MAT K'WOTTOOOS: *don't you understand*

WOSSUCK: *husband*

KAH WEEWO: *and wife*

AQUY: *don't; stop; enough*

NOOANTAM K'WADTO COONY: *I understand your coat-talk* [meaning English]

NOONA: *not enough*

QUOT ONCH, K'WOMMONSH: *all the same, I love you*

POOKETTYMIS: *White Oak*

HOWANIGUS: *a stranger* [usually English or French settlers]

KUT ASKWY: *wait*

TEAQUA: *what is this*

TOUNUCKQUAQUE: *how much*

WUSSOY: *greedy*

ACKNOWLEDGMENTS

This collection in its entirety was the first-place winner of the Shorts Award for Americana Fiction and was a top-50 finalist in the Launch Pad Prose Competition.

"Corner to Corner, End to End" won honorable mention (third place) in the Bevel Summers Prize for the Short Short Story and was published in *Shenandoah: The Washington and Lee University Review*, Vol 63, Iss 1.

"The Orphan Train" was published in *Tupelo Quarterly*, Vol 1, Iss 2.

"Every Time It Snows" was a fiction finalist in the Coalition of Texans with Disabilities Pen 2 Paper Writing Competition, and was later published in *Gulf Stream Literary Journal*, Iss 17.

"Casting Grand Titans" was excerpted in *Women Writers, Women's Books*.

"One Night, When the Breath of August Blew Hotter" appeared in a shorter version in *In Between Altered States*, Episode 34: Manipulation, and in its longer draft in *Poiesis Review*, Iss 6.

"Yellow Flowers" was excerpted in *Vol. 1 Brooklyn*.

"New Mexico Farmhouse, Hard to Find after All Those Years" appeared in a shorter version in *In Between Altered States*, Episode 33: Revenge, and in its longer draft in *Poiesis Review*, Iss 6.

"Small Sacrifices" appeared in an earlier draft in *Footnote: A Literary Journal of History*, Iss 1.

"Every Step Counts" was published in *Big Muddy: A Journal of the Mississippi Valley*, Iss 18.1.

"Music Knows No Color" was published in *Atticus Review*'s Music Issue, and was selected by *Atticus Review* editors for a Pushcart Prize nomination.

THE AUTHOR WISHES TO THANK

Michael Litos, Eric Shonkwiler, Hannah Keeton, and Paige M. Ferro for their early edits and beta reads. Ethan Rutherford, Matt Bell, Amber Sparks, Ryan Ridge, Kathy Fish, Schuler Benson, and Jennifer Wortman for being advance readers with kind words.

Thank you to the journals and publication outlets that published earlier versions of some of these stories; the world is richer for having your words in it. Thank you to the Bevel Summers Prize for Short Fiction for giving me the first award I ever won for my prose; I was so tickled to get paid for a short story that it still makes me tear up.

Thanks and love to my long-lost twin sister agent, Elizabeth Copps at Copps Literary Services; my exuberant publicist Lori Hettler at TNBBC Publicity; and Amy Bruno at Historical Fiction Virtual Book Tours.

So many hearts to Jesi Buell at Kernpunkt Press, for being such a cheer-leader for the indie press and all things literary. She's amazing to work with, and her heart is two sizes too big.

Love, love, love to my friends and family, especially Mom, Dad, Mike, and Bro, for all the support; Ted Scheinman, because hearts; and my German Shepherd, Torgo, whom the master approves. To C. H. Uties— *k'wommonsh*. All things love-of-history in my life can be traced back to my father; blame him.

"Casting Grand Titans" is dedicated to the wonderful Kathleen Grissom, whose love and portrayal of botany in her books got me to thinking, then researching, then outlining, then writing, one of my favorite stories I've ever written.

ABOUT THE AUTHOR

LEAH ANGSTMAN is also the author of the historical novel of seventeenth-century New England, *Out Front the Following Sea*, available from Regal House (tinyurl.com/regalsea), and the novel of the French Revolution, *Falcon in the Dive*, forthcoming from Regal House in spring 2024. She serves as the executive editor for Alternating Current Press and *The Coil* magazine, and her work has appeared in numerous journals, including *Publishers Weekly*, *Los Angeles Review of Books*, and *The Nashville Review*. She's recently been a winner of the Feathered Quill Book Award, Pencraft Seasonal Book Award, Herb Tabak Choice Award, CIPA Evvy Book Award, and Readers' Favorite Book Award; a finalist for the Eric Hoffer Book Award, Chaucer Book Award, National Indie Excellence Award, Laramie Book Award, Da Vinci Eye Award, Clue Book Award, Richard Snyder Memorial Prize, Cowles Book Prize, American Writing Award, and Able Muse Book Award; a semifinalist for the Goethe Book Award and Willow Run Book Award; and longlisted for the Hillary Gravendyk Prize. This is her first collection of short stories, and it was the winner of the Shorts Award for Americana Fiction and a top-50 finalist in the Launch Pad Prose Competition. You can find her at leahangstman.com and on social media as @leahangstman.